And Midnight Never Come

Edited by
Hugh Lamb
and
Richard Lamb

KINGSBROOK PUBLISHING

Published by Kingsbrook Publishing

© Richard Lamb 2021

Story Selection © Richard Lamb

Story introductions © Hugh Lamb and © Richard Lamb

Introduction and Cover design © Richard Lamb

This book is entirely a work of fiction. The names, characters and incidents portrayed in it are the work of the author's imagination. Any resemblances to actual persons, living or dead, events or localities is entirely coincidental.

All rights reserved.

ISBN: 9798493862700

FOR MAGGIE

The driving force behind my every success and the most creative person I know.

CONTENTS

INTRODUCTION	Richard Lamb	1
MARIE ST. PIERRE	Hume Nisbet	4
ECCLES OLD TOWER	E. R. Suffling	10
MR. MORTIMER'S DIARY	Amyas Northcote	26
JUDGEMENT DEFERRED	Mrs. G. Linnaeus Banks	44
WAXWORKS	André De Lorde	80
THE VISION OF INVERSTRATHY CASTLE	F. Startin Pilleau	92
THE VISION OF INVERSTRATHY CASTLE SEQUEL	F. Startin Pilleau	113
THE FOLLOWER	Frederick Carruthers Cornell	129
IN THE INTERESTS OF SCIENCE	Anonymous	139
THE PAINTED COIN	Guy Thorne	149
THE CORNER HOUSE	Bernard Capes	165
THE HEADLESS LEPER	Frederick Cowles	184
OUR SCIENTIFIC OBSERVATIONS ON A GHOST	Grant Allen	191
MIRACLE IN SUBURBIA	Thomas Burke	213
EGO SPEAKS	J. H. Pearce	230
THE PHANTOM SHIP	William Hope Hodgson	237
A TWILIGHT EXPERIENCE	G. M. Robins	247
FATHER MARTIN'S TALE	R. H. Benson	258
THE BEAD NECKLACE	Alice Perrin	271
BEHIND THE WALL	Violet Jacob	285
AFTERWORD	Johnny Mains	296
ACKNOWLEDGEMENTS	Richard Lamb	299
ABOUT THE EDITORS		301

INTRODUCTION
by
RICHARD LAMB

When Hugh Lamb, my father, passed away in early 2019, he left behind an enduring legacy. The response to his passing, and the fond remembrances of those he had inspired, entertained and (he had always hoped) scared along the way were a soothing balm for my grief, but also fired my decision to republish some of his oldest, long-out-of-print anthologies.

My intention was to make some of those volumes, for so long only accessible as costly secondhand collectibles, available again to the wider audience. My father's desire had always been to share his passion with as many people as possible. This was why I avoided the limited-run, small press option, which was certainly open to me, and instead chose to self-publish through Kindle and print-on-demand. I wanted as many people to have the chance to enjoy these groundbreaking works as I could reach.

I republished *Victorian Tales of Terror* and *Terror by Gaslight*, each with some additional stories and contributions. Both were well received, for which I am most grateful. It seemed to me that this might be the right time to take a different direction.

Among the mountain of paperwork that my father left behind (he never owned a computer or dabbled with the digital world in any way) were folders stuffed with photocopied stories that he had never used. I set about cataloguing the stories, ascertaining the copyright status of each and determining if any of them had subsequently been used by other anthologists. I think it was during this process I realised that I actually enjoyed what I was doing.

What I also discovered in the midst of dad's archives were story lists for anthologies that never reached the publishing stage. I had no idea that had been the case and it was fascinating to see these plans for what might have been. *The Mayflower Book of Horror Stories* series is one that some may have heard about. Here were the story lists for all three volumes. An anthology entitled *Strange Stories*, later re-titled *Darkness Rising*, never saw the light of day. Nor, too, did *Terror by Night* and one collection which remained untitled.

Then there was *And Midnight Never Come*. The title struck me as much more poetic than my father's usual choices. He did love poetry, so it should have come as no surprise. This particular title was a quote from the poem *Doctor Faustus* by Christopher Marlow.

Now hast thou but one bare hour to live,
And then thou must be damn'd perpetually!
Stand still, you ever-moving spheres of heaven,
That time may cease, and midnight never come;

I had already decided I was going to publish a brand new anthology from the stories he left behind. Now here was my title.

My father's original story list for *And Midnight Never Come* went through a couple of alterations over the years. The lists were never dated so I cannot say when they were put together, or when they were amended. At some point, when dad realised the anthology wasn't getting

INTRODUCTION

picked up, the bulk of the stories found their way into some of his subsequent collections. In fact, the only two stories in this edition that were drawn from the original list are *The Bead Necklace* and *Ego Speaks*.

Most of the remaining contents of this book were taken from those folders of stories which had not yet found a home in a Hugh Lamb anthology, as well as six stories I chose myself, discovered during my researches.

I'm very proud of the new editions I produced in my father's name, and like to imagine that he would be thrilled about both their existence and his son's hand in their publication. *And Midnight Never Come* takes that pride a step further and gives me the opportunity to not only perpetuate my father's legacy, but build upon it.

As I said earlier, I have sincerely enjoyed the research, curating and writing involved in putting this anthology together. I can only hope that you, the reader, enjoys reading it as much as I enjoyed creating it, and that, in my selections, I truly captured the spirit of Hugh Lamb.

RICHARD LAMB
New York
2021

MARIE ST. PIERRE
by
HUME NISBET

If the introduction to his book of macabre tales is anything to go by, Hume Nisbet (1849-c. 1920) was a midnight worker: '(these stories were) thought out during hours of solitude when the bustling world was hushed in slumber, and solemn midnight granted to the mind the true conditions for the reception of the occult mysteries.' The results are certainly worth reading, as you'll see.

Hume Nisbet was born in Stirling, Scotland. He left home at the age of sixteen to spend the next seven years travelling around Australia. When he returned to Scotland, he got a job as art master in an Edinburgh college, and after eight years, went back to Australia, where he took up writing for a living after a brief spell as a publisher's agent.

During his frequent visits back to Britain, he took the time to put together and introduce The Haunted Station *(1894), from which comes* Marie St. Pierre. *In his introduction, Nisbet hinted strongly at the real-life origins of his literary phantoms. They were, he said, 'gleaned from reliable sources or personal experience.'*

Although one can be assured that Nisbet never personally experienced anything like the following tale, we can be grateful that his midnight scribbling brought to life so vivid an account of a lost soul's last, desperate measure.

* * *

> "Many a with'ring thought lies hid, not lost,
> In smiles that least befit who wear them most."
> —BYRON

"We were all assembled, a gay company—a very gay company—and I was the gayest of the gay. How giddy we can appear when the heart is ready to burst with misery! I sang to them alternately comic and sentimental ballads, played for them operatic selections, recited parts of some of my old stage pieces, until they wept with maudlin sympathy, or roared out with vulgar applause. They thought me so light-hearted, so coquettish, so happy. How they admired my beauty, followed with their greedy eyes each graceful motion, watched the ease with which I handled my fan, and envied my vivacity of spirits as I showed them my teeth and laughed! But how they would have shrunk back with horror could they have read the purpose stamped within my wretched and distracted mind!

"I sank back upon a couch with the book in my hand, studying it very carefully, yet taking time to glance up now and then with a placid smile at the poor puns of my brainless companion. Neither did I shudder when he inquired what was the title of the book I was poring so intently over, but replied carelessly as I handed it to him, 'De Quincy on Opium.' I laughed in answer to his remark that it was a singular study for a young lady, and turned lightly from him to it again, learning off by heart the deadly recipe—the proper amount of drops required for a girl of my fancied organism to sleep on for ever. I knew the consequences of an overdraught, therefore was all the more careful, for I did not wish to suffer too much pain, nor to disfigure my person in any way. I wished to look as fair and as interesting in that slumber as when awake, that they might all admire me as they had done before, that some might pity the shell who had no pity for Marie St. Pierre when pity would have done her good. I wished *him* to see me who had so falsely left me to suffer alone the bitters of a weak impulse, that he might also feel to the full the vain regret of a remorseful heart as he gazed upon the lovely morsel which his coldness had thrown from him. This would be my revenge for long nights of sleepless agony, and for this I spent every spare moment upon the pages, and every thought concentrated upon their contents, even as I played, and laughed, and sang.

"I was an actress, and ambitious; overmuch so, the managers thought, since they wished to humble my pride by offering to me a subordinate engagement; but they did not know my spirit when they attempted this: I was not to be brought down while the means of escape lay in my little bottle. The funds were ebbing low, with no means of replenishing except by stooping; yet I could afford to be cheerful when I knew that I should never require to stoop while I kept that little bottle. I loved a man, who had acted well when he could deceive a professional actress, but even his base desertion, my hidden shame, and breaking heart, could not affect my features while I was upheld by the proud consciousnesses that in my own hands lay my destiny; that in my desk, amongst his *billets doux* and perfumed love-tokens, reposed a little draught, like tho asp of Cleopatra among the roses, waiting but for my consent to waft me away from the memory of mortal woes.

"That night I made myself agreeable, and after a few hours of entertaining misery, my amused visitors departed to their respective and respectable homes, leaving me to myself. Graciously I returned their bows, pleasantly wished them all good-night and sweet repose; then, as the last disappeared, without a betraying look or tremor, took from the hand of my landlady the candle, and smilingly ascended to the solitudes of my chamber. The hall clock struck three as I locked my chamber-door, and laid the candle beside my desk on the dressing-table, while I sat down to gaze at the reflection of myself in the mirror. How deadly quiet the space around me seemed, yet how fearfully crammed it felt; it seemed as though ten thousand eyes were fixing themselves upon me to bear witness against the daring and impious purpose of my desperate will; as if the chamber were thronged with shadows who hung about me; as if arms were pressing upon me, and voices striving to shriek out their entreaties for me to pause and reconsider my mad intent. But I was resolved, and their efforts were idle. With a spiteful stamp, I sprang to my feet, and shook off the stupor of horror that was closing upon me, and taking from me my forced courage. While pressing my lips firmly to keep back a shriek, I began my last task upon earth. Opening my desk, I took from thence his letters. One by one I read them through again with a bounding heart and bitter scalding tears; I kissed them passionately; then, kneeling down, gathered them into a little heap on the hearthstone, and applying a light, watched them slowly consume to ashes, as my hopes had done before. These mute witnesses of my unwise love destroyed, I arose, and pouring some water into the basin, carefully bathed my eyes, so that the world might see no trace of the workings of the heart upon my countenance when it came to gaze upon it in the morning. Then, again sitting down to the desk, I commenced to pen a few last directions. I told them to spare the time of the coroner with his jury, for that my own hand had liberated my soul with the aid of laudanum but to bury the frail prison unbroken, as I had left it; thus, in my conceit, thinking on the looks that had ruined me. I gave no reason for my rash step, but finished the epistle by bidding all a kind farewell, bequeathing all that I did not require for grave purposes to the few friends I had left. This I sealed and left on my desk; then began leisurely to deck myself out for the tomb. I selected the white-satin robe in which he had first beheld me, dressed up my hair in his favourite fashion, and, seating myself upon the bed, arranged the folds of my costume most effectively; after which I reached over, and taking the phial from its perfumed nest, drew out the stopper, and with a silent prayer for pardon, but with a steady hand, I counted out the calculated drops into a wine-glass, and quaffed it quickly off. I had time to put back the phial and wine-glass, also to stretch myself upon the bed and think, before the poison began to operate. What were my thoughts during those silent moments I will not say; yet although stinging, I do not think they were so agonising as those which had racked my mind for weeks back.

"Then the air began to grow thicker and lighter methought. Although the candle was guttering and dying in its socket, silvery clouds rolled upwards from the floor to the ceiling, coining nearer to me, and waxing denser and brighter as they neared. I watched those vapours for some time with curiosity, not unmingled with fear, as I observed starry lights gleam through them and shift about; until, with a wild start, I beheld the cloudy columns burst asunder, and from their centre leap forth shining and dark forms, who surrounded me, and gazed upon me, the brighter ones with benevolent and pitying looks, and the darker ones with malignant leers. Then it flashed across my mind that I was looking on the spirits of the departed, and I felt that my time was drawing nigh. I tried to cry out, to push back the influence of those dark and loathsome phantoms, for it was them who seemed to come nearest me, as if they had the best claim upon my captive soul; but I could not keep them away, and only a low moan broke from my icy lips in place of the shriek that rent my bosom. Nearer they pressed, one upon the other, with ghastly faces, and glowing eyes peering upon me, and the weird fingers spreading out at me, until, in the midst of my awful terror and unexpressed abhorrence, I felt as if lifted up by demon talons and dashed down again into chaotic blackness."

ECCLES OLD TOWER
by
E. R. SUFFLING

Earnest Richard Suffling (1855-1911) had the rather unique distinction of being both a writer and a stained-glass artist, with a prolific body of work in both fields. He was the author of factual works on a number of subjects including church brasses, boating, Epitaphs, stained glass and the Norfolk Broads. He also published short fiction.

Suffling, the son of a London blind-maker, published his first book, The Land of the Broads, *in 1885 and his last,* English Church Brasses, *in 1910, one year before his death in the County Asylum (the reason for his internment remains unknown). In 1896 he published his only collection of short stories,* The Story Hunter, or, Tales of the Weird and Wild, *from which* Eccles Old Tower *is taken.*

Set in Suffling's beloved Norfolk, this is an unusual and rather romantic tale, haunting in its own way. Suffling is also kind enough to supply a glossary of Norfolk slang at the end for those scratching their heads at the language.

* * *

INTRODUCTION TO "ECCLES OLD TOWER."

You must know, gentle reader, that at Eccles, a village of about a score inhabitants, on the Norfolk coast, midway between Yarmouth and Cromer, stands an old church tower. It is quite upon the beach, so that at spring tides the 'send' of the waves comes round the base of the old flint tower, which must at some day, not far distant, fall with a mighty crash, a prey to the undermining and gnawing of the hungry sea, which in its insatiable encroachment annually devours hundreds of tons of the soft clay cliff, which at no point reaches a very formidable height.

North and south of Eccles the cliffs give place to sand dunes, or, as they are locally called, 'Marram banks,' which are kept in repair by a tax levied on all the villages between Norwich and the sea, a distance of nearly twenty miles. Norwich itself also contributes its quota, as if the sea once broke through the banks it would, by ditch, marsh, and river, run quite up to the ancient city, and submerge the portion which is contiguous to the river Wensum. The steeple at Eccles (or as it is called locally, and by the thousands of mariners who know it as a landmark, Eccles Old Tower) stands just above high-water mark, on the beautiful firm sands, for which the Norfolk coast is unsurpassed. It is of flintwork, the lower part being 'knapped,' or dressed, and the upper part of the natural flint. It is a circular tower with an octagonal upper chamber, but it is roofless, doorless, and windowless, excepting that the apertures, greatly decayed, still remain. The walls of the tower are unusually massive, and the whole structure rises to an altitude of nearly seventy feet.

The body of the church was pulled down about 1603, being then in such a bad state of repair that it was dangerous to passers-by; in fact, one wall was actually blown down in a gale, and the other razed to prevent an accident.

The foundations of the church still exist, but buried in the sand. It was a small church (the nave being only some sixty feet long), and as its remains are occasionally laid bare, the writer has had opportunities of measuring the various dimensions. Although these dimensions might be interesting to an ecclesiologist or or archaeologist, they would be wearisome to our readers, as they have nothing whatever to do with the story.

Round the huge fragments of the recumbent walls may be seen, after a visit from a heavy north-west gale, the foundations of the cottages which once formed the village. Cottage walls, out-houses, filled-up wells, fruit-tree roots, etc., are to be seen in all directions, and now and then, at rare intervals, a few coins and curiosities are picked up. When the ruins *are* laid bare, the place forms what might aptly be termed the Norfolk Pompeii.

It was while I was sketching the old tower, one autumn day, that I came upon a fisherman employed in breaking up some wreckage which had been washed ashore. The timber being full of old bolts, and consisting mainly of twisted, gnarled oak knees, was of no value save for firewood, otherwise it would have been in the hands of the coastguard. He was a very civil but reticent fellow, and I could not get a yarn out of him by any means without exerting my hypnotic power, which I did, obtaining, as a result, the following wild story.

ECCLES OLD TOWER

I am only a plain fisherman, with but little book learning; but I think I can muster up enough form o' speech to tell you one of the skeeriest tales you ever heard in all your born days.

It was the first week in January, 188—, that we had a dreadful gale from the north-west which came at the full moon; consequently the tides were high, and this here gale came with such a scouring force, that the soft cliffs melted away like a lump of butter in the glare o' the sun. The sand was swep' away right down to what you might term the foundations of the shore, and everything laid as bare as my forehead. I liken it to my forehead, which is kinder wrinkly, because there were great ruts and scars along the beach which had once been holls, decks, and lokes.

I and a mate o' mine walked along the beach next day, just to see if anything had been thrown ashore that would come in handy to a couple of poor chaps like ourselves; but little did we find, for some one had been pawkin' before us. Still, we got a useful length of two-inch rope and a couple of dantos, attached to a score fathom of decent net, so our walk paid for shoe-leather.

When we got to the third breakwater—for we live at Hasbro'—and peeped over, we were wholly stammed to see the old village of Eccles laid bare and plain like a map. There was the walls of the housen standin' up two foot and more in some places; and some of the door thresholds were still there, with the wood as good as ever. We could make out the shapes of the gardens, and could see where the fruit-trees had once stood, by the roots and tree-bolls that still remained.

In grubbing about with a pointed boat-streak, I roused out an old leathern bag with a golden guinea in it, and a piece of rusty iron tangled in the strap, which might have been a knife or somethin' of the sort in days gone by.

Afterwards we looked over the churchyard wall, and to our surprise found that many of the graves had been washed open; in fact, some of the coffins lay there nearly level with the ground, for you know we don't bury very deep in Norfolk, not more than four foot, and only one corpse in each hole. The coffins wor of a different shape to what they make 'em now-a-days, for they were long, like a seaman's chest, but broad at one end and narrow at the other, and the lid hinged on at one side.

Human bones were washing about in all directions, and a long line of them lay among the rubbish left at high watermark. We found one immense coffin near o the north wall of the church, which must have been seven foot long, if it was an inch. The lid was much decayed, and in some parts broken away; so we thought it no sin to prize the rest off, and see what was inside.

It was level full of sand, but when we scooped some of it out with our hands, we came upon the perfect skelington of a man, black with age, but nothing missing. It looked as if he might have been the giant Goliar that we read of in the Bible. He was no use to us, so we covered him up decent like, and as it was getting towards dark we took ourselves home agin.

Next day I borrowed old Garrod's dickey, and rode up to Stalham, and called on old Dr. Rix, for he was what some folks call a aquarian, or somethin' o' that sort, and showed him my guinea in the bag, and the old bit o' steel; and he gave me just what I asked him for 'em, and that was two-and-twenty shillings: he was pleased, and so was I, for it was just as much as I could earn in a fortnight. I stopped at his some time goldering about what I had seen at Eccles, and he up and told me, when I mentioned about the big skelington, that if I could bring it to him *intack*— that's not broken or any bits lost—he'd give me a five-pound note.

Lor, I wor soon home agen, I made the old dickey fly as if the Old 'un were arter us. Thinks I, this ought to be a single-handed job, and if I take a big poke and go alone, I shan't have any one to dole out halves to. So I got my spade and a lantern, a poke, and a fairish thumb-piece of bacon and bread, and everything else I wanted all ready, and then waited till near midnight, so that I knew the coast would be clear for the job.

It was a thick, starless night, with great grey snow-clouds rolling about overhead, and the wind from the north-east was a regular marrer-freezer, and I can't say I much cared for the work in hand; but, as the parson said when he went on a slide, "it's foolish to turn back," so on I went. The road was frozen right nubbly, and made me wobble about a bit, but by the time I got to the beach I was warm and comfortable, and got along more comfortable-like on the frozen sand, which was covered with snow in the hollows. The sand and foam from seaward was a bit unpleasant, but I didn't trouble much about that, for my thoughts were a mile ahead, with the skelington waiting for me at Eccles.

I had walked about half-a-mile along the beach, when down came the snow, wreathing and tearing about all mander of ways, and every now and then I got into the centre of a whirl that pulled me up short, and nearly took my breath away. This only lasted a few minutes, and then the squall cleared off as suddenly as it came on, and I got on much faster with my journey.

I passed the first and then the second breakwater, and by the light that the sea always gives, I was picking my way along very nicely, when, what should I see, but some one a-coming towards me along the beach. I had not lighted my lantern, as I only wanted that for my actual work, so it was possible the man approaching might not have caught sight of me, and as I did not want to be seen by any one at that time of night, especially by a coastguard, I dropped quietly on the sand in a hollow, in hopes that whoever it was might pass me by.

Down I went on my stummick, but kept my eyes on the man approaching, and found to my surprise that he was dressed in very light clothes; not a coastguard, I thought, at all events.

Closer he came, and then I began for some reason or other to dudder and tremble, but I can't tell why, perhaps it was the cold; anyway, there was nothing I could see in the stranger that should fright me; that is to say, not just then, when I felt the first symptoms.

But presently, when he came closer, I had some cause to shake, for what I saw was a man in a long white smock, which blew out in the wind behind him as he stalked along. The nearer he came the worse I felt, for he seemed to grow taller and taller every step he took.

Would he pass me?

Yes!

No!!

No, up he came, right straight to me, and I felt like fainting—or what I should fancy fainting was like, for I have never experienced it. When he came close, I could not have stood on my feet for the value of Norwich Castle; I was right terrified, although the man had not even spoke a word.

As I looked up he towered above me like a lugger's mast, and his great bare legs were right against me. I panted, for I could not speak, but presently, in a foreign sort of voice, the figure said—

"Hullo, my friendt, anything amiss?"

I looked at him again and my fear fled, for I immediately took him to be a shipwrecked mariner, cast ashore in his sleeping gear from some vessel.

My strength at once returned, and I stood upon my feet; but although five feet eight in my socks, and weighing fourteen stone in my oil-frock, I was only a baby by the side of my visitor, whose shoulder was more than level with the top of my head. This did not frighten me much, but when I looked at his eyes—Oh, lor! I thought I should have dropped on all fours again.

His eyes were red and glowing like the port-light of a ship, and when he spoke, the inside of his mouth seemed to reflect a fire, which must have been raging in his internal regions.

I felt real bad, but could not keep my eyes off that huge face, with its flaming eyes and mouth, and I vowed I would never come out, single-handed, skelington-hunting again—no, not for the whole R'yle Mint.

"Mine friendt," said the giant, "you are just de man I wandt der see; you haf a spade. You come mit me to Eccles?"

Would I? Could I say no?

I went.

We had but half-a-mile to walk, and that in a biting east wind, varied with still more piercing squalls of snow and sleet, and I trembled in every limb, while my heart rattled on like a donkey-engine getting in a chain cable — all bumps and thumps.

I looked at the marrams, and calculated what chance I should have if I tried leg-bail; but when I looked at the length of my companion, I gave it up as onpractical.

I was cold, although in what we call about here a 'muck swat,' but my new friend was all of a glow (especially about the mouth). He would have made a rare fiery speaker for the House of Commons; he would have frightened them that he couldn't convince by his speechifying.

His conversation was dreadful—I don't mean perfane or rude-like, but the things that man told me made my flesh creep on my bones. He wanted to make out to me that he had been buried three hundred years, just before the old church was pulled down!

I can swallow a pretty thick strand of a yarn, but this here fellow wanted me to swallow a whole cable, for he went on to tell me how, in 1584, he came over from Harlingen to Yarmouth, in a fishing-boat of which he was mate, and that while ashore he one day fell in with three or four fellows who were kinder interfering with a good-looking young girl. Being strong he went for the whole set of them, and got the girl away, but one of the gang struck him a blow with a heavy stick and broke his arm.

The girl's father came up and thanked the young Dutchman, and finding that his daughter's protector had broken a limb and could not work for a week or two, took him to a surgeon and had the limb set. He left him with the understanding that Dutchy would come and spend a week with them, when the doctor had finished with him. The old fellow was a farmer at Eccles, and being market-day, had as usual brought his daughter with him to Yarmouth.

Well, up to there was what the play actors would call Act One, and that was all very nice and proper, but just you listen, and you'll see how it will turn out.

By and by away goes the young Dutchman to Eccles, and of course he naturally fell in love with the mawther. But she wouldn't have him at no price. No, she thanked him, and tried all she could to make him comfortable, but—she already had a sweetheart.

This staggered Dutchy, but he had no idea of letting her go so easily, and as every one in the village was afraid of the giant, the girl's father ordered the banns to be put up, to make sure that his neighbour's son should not be frightened out of his rights.

Dutchy tried all he knew to get the girl to alter her mind for a whole week; and finding it in wain, he one morning disappeared.

That was what you might term Act Two. So far it had been all comedy, as the play-actors call it, but the last act was a violent and vicious one, as you shall hear.

The wedding-day came; the villagers flocked to the church; the ceremony took place; the bells rang out; and, according to our custom, the people fired their guns over the heads of the happy couple as they came out of the porch, on their way to the home of the bride's father.

All was perfect joy, but in another moment the joy was turned to horror, for as the young couple came from the north porch, and turned into the pathway leading round the foot of the old tower, a huge figure (it was Dutchy) sprang upon them, and like a flash of lightning struck them dead to the earth, before a hand could be raised to prevent it. The reeking knife he calmly wiped, and thrust into his waist-belt, and then stood glowering at the crowd, who kept at a very respectable distance from him. He told them of the hard-heartedness of the girl, and denounced her as she lay dead before him as an unfeeling creature, and bade them know that what he had done was his mode of revenge, or as he called it— Justice.

But where was the bride's father all this time?

Well, he had been busy, as you shall hear.

It is the custom of we Norfolkers to give what we call 'largesses' at marriages, comings of age, and such-like; and on this occasion the old man had pervided hisself with a little leather poke filled with small silver coins, to throw among the assembled crowd, and indeed he was occerpied in so doing when the death of his daughter took place. He knew it was no use going for Dutchy single-handed, so he just stepped behind the porch and loaded his gun with a handful of silver groats, and when it was done sprang out, just when the giant had finished his speech, and was turning to leave the place unmolested by the onlookers.

The old man shouted to him to stay or he would shoot; but, grasping the knife in his belt, the young fellow walked away, without taking any notice; whereupon the old man rushed after him, and aiming at his head, fired.

"Der oldt man did shoot mit der gun right tro mine neck, and I seize him, and gif him fon stap mit my knife, and den I vas dedt mineself," were the words of my uncanny companion.

Whether he killed the old man I cannot say, but he himself was killed, and all this three hundred years ago!

And this was the gentleman I was taking a walk with, much against my will, at night's-noon, as we say.

But then he went on with a lot more strange talk, about how he had a kind of holiday, or as we say frolic-time, 'lowanced out to him once every hundred years, on the anneversery of the day when all this piece of work took place; only he was not let loose, so to speak, till midnight, and then for only three hours.

Well, I'd heard some tough uns before, and didn't mind what I had heard; but them eyes!—when I looked up at his face they bowled me over altogether. He was no mortal, that I could take my davy on.

For a little Dutchy walked in silence, and I found *my* tongue and asked him if he didn't fare cold, seeing he only had a kind of shirt on!

He turned his eyes upon me, and then I saw I had made a mistake in asking such a question; fancy what a silly thing to ask a chap with a furnace in his innards. But he was not put out at my question, and volunteered a explanation, as the saying is.

He opened his mouth and asked me to look into it. Well, if I live to be as old as our neighbour Ives, and she is a hundred and three, I shall never forget the sight. He blazed internally like a dustpan of live coal, and the sight made my knees quiver, as if the heat of his breath had melted my marrer, or whatever it is holds a fellow right up. I've heard tell of men's hearts waxing faint, and I do believe that that night my bones were no better than wax, for hold my frame up straight I could not, however I tried, and I am not reckoned a coward when any job is on hand that wants a steady nerve and strong hand; and I've been out on the sea some rum wather too, but the sight down this fellow's throat done me entirely.

When he had shown me his furnace below, he went on to tell me that what I had seen was the sin burning within him, and it could only be quenched by the forgiveness of the girl he killed three hundred years ago.

Well, of course I could not say that that was all fudge, though I could not believe him, but the funny part of it was, that when we got to Eccles Old Tower there sat a young woman on the ruins of the porch in a kind of nightshirt, as if she was waiting for us. That of course showed me that there was some truth in what Dutchy had been telling me, and when I nodded to the young woman, she gave me a very pretty smile, and said she was glad to see me, and that now I had come matters might be set right, and they could obtain a little rest.

Then she chatted on and told me that she had for a long time forgiven Dutchy, knowing that he had that within him that must have burnt away all sin long ago, but that without a mortal witness she could not forgive him, as the sin had taken place on earth. She owned that it was her cruel conduct that had brought on the Dutchman's revenge, and now before me as witness she would forgive him, and seal the forgiveness with a kiss.

Lors me! when they kissed I thought the poor man would have been blowed to pieces, for he exploded intarnilly with a tremenjous report, and the flames shot out of his mouth, ears, and eyes like rockets, and went wizzing away in streaks right over the marrams, where they were soon swallowed up in the dark and thick air.

Now my legs did give way, and down I went with my back agen the church wall, and although I was spellbound, I could see and hear all that went on before me.

Dutchy, whose eyes and mouth no longer shone, snatched up my lantern, stooped over me, and took my brass box of matches and struck a light, then seizing the spade, he set to work, and very soon had the huge coffin out of the sand. But the strange thing about it was, that it was the very one I had come to rob, only now there were no bones in it, and it dawned upon my stupid brain that Dutchy and the skelington was one! Where he got his flesh and shirt from goodness only knows.

The young woman, who was very pretty and had long hair down her back, which blew out like a ship's pennant in the gale, helped the giant by holding the lantern, while he did the work.

The big coffin being placed above ground, away they went round to the other side of the church, where Dutchy set to work digging again, and after a little while cleared the second coffin, which I reckon belonged to the girl.

While this was going on I had raised myself on to my marrer-bones, and with my fingers hooked over the old church wall was taking a view of all their doings, and no doubt I was all eyes and mouth if any one could have seen me.

Presently the giant up-ended the big coffin and got it on his shoulder, and as he and the girl came round by the tower, she stopped and actually asked for another kiss. Such a request took my breath away, and to avoid the awful dullor which I expected would follow, put my fingers into my ears, but, would you believe me, it was as human a kiss as ever you saw, and not even a whiff of smoke appeared, let alone a tongue of flame, when their lips met.

He also carried the little coffin down to the water's edge, and then up he came, and dragged the big one down by the side of it, and there they lay, for all the world like two boats. Then back they came right to where I was, a-cowering by the flint wall, and says Dutchy—

"Tank you werry much for der lantern and der spade," and he held out his great hand as he added, "Farewell."

I was very loath, but I took it, and as true as I am alive, it felt damp and cold like the hand of a dead man, and sent a thrill along my backbone I shall never forget.

Then the young woman came forward and thanked me, and put forth *her* hand for me to shake, and I shook something very like a fish, but did not shudder quite so much, as I was a bit more used to it after the first shock, so to speak.

After that they walked down to their coffins and each got into the right one, and as I did not follow too close, Dutchy turned round and beckoned me to him, and with fear and trembling I obeyed, and tottered down to the water's edge.

"Now, mynheer," said he, "when you see der change kom, push der boads off."

I had no idea what he meant, but I shuddered out a kind of "Yes," and there they sat, till presently he cried out—

"Now den, push avay!"

As he spoke, I floated them off, and they appeared to melt partly away, and to change colour from the pinky tinge of life to the grey of death.

They floated: and by the sheen of the foam I beheld two skelingtons sitting in their coffins, scudding against wind and tide right out to sea, slashing through the great breakers as if they had no more weight or power than mists.

Dutchy's skelington arm was round where his companion's waist ought to have been, when I last saw them, as they burst through a big old roller that would have sunk a billyboy schooner.

Where they were bound for goodness only knows; neither do I care. All I know is, that I got home some time or other, for when I woke up the week after, they told me I was better, and that I had had brain fever.

When I got well, I went to Eccles to see if what I had got into my brainpan was all moonshine or no, but if you'll believe my word, the two coffins I had seen dug up by Dutchy were gone sure enough, which I take it proves my story to be ker-rect.

My nautical friend, on leaving my van, had not the remotest notion that he had told me a story, and as to my being able to send him to sleep, why he simply laughed at such a thing as an impossibility.

In his normal condition I tried in vain to draw him out to spin a yarn, but although he owned that he knew some "real rum 'uns," I could not prevail on him to tell me one. He merely sat and smoked, and did little more than carry on a disjointed monosyllabic conversation.

"Why will you not spin me a yarn, my friend?" I asked.

"Why, sir, you see," said he, "I ain't no scholard, and although I may *think* a great deal, I'm no sort o' hand at talking. I never could frame enough to tell anything in a kinder pretty way like some folks. No, sir, you don't ketch me opening my mouth to be papered [put in print] for gentlefolks to laugh and make game of me."

That being so, I had no alternative but to make him a victim, with the result chronicled above.

EXPLANATION OF NORFOLK WORDS.

1. holl, *a ditch.*
2. deek, *a hedge-bank.*
3. loke, *a lane.*
4. pawkin, *hunting for wreckage.*
5. danto, *a fishing-bitoy.*
6. stammed, *astonished.*
7. dickey, *a donkey.*
8. goldering, *chatting.*
9. poke, *a bag or sack.*
10. dole, *a share.*
11. mander, *manner.*
12. dudder, *to shiver.*
13. marrams, *grass-covered sand-hills.*
14. mawther, *a maid, a young girl.*
15. largesse, *a gift.*
16. dullor, *a distracting noise.*
17. frame, *to use big words.*

MR. MORTIMER'S DIARY
by
AMYAS NORTHCOTE

Amyas Northcote (1864-1923) has often been compared to M. R. James and yet never rose to the same prominence, probably because of his far more meager output. Certainly, it is not a wildly exaggerated comparison and the stories in his sole anthology, In Ghostly Company, *published just two years before his death in 1921, demonstrate the same sense of creeping dread and matter-of-fact menace.*

The son of a politician, Sir Stafford Northcote, young Amyas had a privileged upbringing, and was exposed to both theatre and literature by his father, who enjoyed a passion for both, including a fascination with ghost stories. Amyas attended Eton at the same time as M. R. James, although it is unknown if the two knew each other (one can speculate that even if they did not, they were subject to the same influences which subsequently found similar expression).

Mr. Mortimer's Diary, *taken from* In Ghostly Company, *is a wonderful example of why Northcote earned those prestigious comparisons, with its unemotional portrayal of human vanity and comeuppance, but it also exemplifies why Northcote deserves to be recognised in his own right as an accomplished writer of the macabre.*

* * *

The somewhat peculiar circumstances connected with the death of Mr. Roger Mortimer, an antiquary of no little reputation in his day, over twenty-five years ago, although a nine days' wonder at the time, have now been forgotten. Nay, the very name and fame of Mr. Mortimer himself have also passed into oblivion, save perhaps that his writings are still perused for the sake of curiosity by students of certain branches of antiquarian research.

As the last of Mr. Mortimer's relatives has recently died and there remains no one to whom the publications of portions of his diary can give pain, and as those latter portions, conveying as they do certain strong impressions of unusual happenings, possess a certain interest to psychical investigators, it has been decided by the gentleman into whose possession the diary has now come to lay the latter portion of it before the world, eliminating from it as a matter of course any portions which might yet cause embarrassment to anyone. Before touching upon the diary itself, it is necessary to recapitulate as briefly as possible the story of Mr. Mortimer and of his death.

Mr. Roger Mortimer was a gentleman born of well-to-do parents. He was an only child and was educated according to the usual practice of well-to-do folk; Eton and Oxford claimed him and at the latter seat of learning he became imbued with a passion for antiquarian research. After various essays, he finally settled down into specializing on Art in early Italy, and devoted himself to the study of Etruscan remains. He became gradually well known, first as a connoisseur and finally as a leading authority in this subject; he wrote several articles on it, one especially dealing with what he claimed to be a proof of certain close relationships between

Etruscan and Egyptian artistic works. This essay provoked a sharp controversy which, besides moving along the lines common to most battles between scientific experts, was marked by a regular attack on Mr. Mortimer by a man named Bradshaw, an assistant master at an obscure Yorkshire school. Mr. Bradshaw, in a letter to the *Times*, claimed to be the real discoverer of the objects on which Mr. Mortimer based his article and roundly asserted that Mr. Mortimer had stolen them from him, and had also purloined from him the genesis of the ideas which he was now presenting to the world as his own. Acting, as he said, under the advice of friends, Mr. Mortimer did not reply to the letter; a dignified silence, he maintained, was unquestionably the best answer to it. Mr. Bradshaw was apparently unable to substantiate his accusation, he was a poor, unknown man, Mr. Mortimer was wealthy and respected, and so the matter dropped. In private conversation Mr. Mortimer readily admitted that he had met Mr. Bradshaw accidentally when abroad, that the gentleman was, he believed, interested in antiquarian research, but that his sole connection with him had been to see that he was properly attended to during a serious attack of illness with which he had been seized during an expedition in the hills, whither he had gone unattended and where he was found lying ill in a miserable inn by Mr. Mortimer. The episode was gradually forgotten and Mr. Bradshaw was heard of no more.

In person, Mr. Mortimer was a tall, thin, dark and rather severe-looking personage. He was a well-informed man on many subjects besides his own speciality; and, while living a somewhat quiet life, he by no means despised society, more especially of the more serious type, and was frequently seen at various social gatherings. He was not a man of many friends, in fact, it would be rash to assert that anyone was admitted to close intimacy with him, but he was popular with a large circle, and discharged his social obligations in punctilious fashion. As already said, he was a well-to-do man and inheriting a comfortable fortune he did not dissipate it. But he was no miser, he spent freely on his hobby and was liberal enough to all those connected with him. His moral character appeared to be unimpeachable, his temper was equable; he would prefer to speak and act kindly rather than the reverse, and in a general way he may be summed up as a worthy member of the body politic, who whilst inspiring no particular affection equally inspired no dislike, save in the single and unexplained case of Mr. Bradshaw. He had been born of Roman Catholic parents and educated in that faith, but he had long abandoned the practice of any form of religion and was a convinced and almost militant upholder of the extreme materialistic school. Lastly it should be added that Mr. Mortimer possessed no near relatives, had never married, and, at the date of his death, aged fifty-six years, was apparently free from care and in perfect bodily health.

Mr. Mortimer had lived for a number of years in rooms in —— Street, kept by a couple of retired domestic servants. These rooms consisted of the first floor of a good-sized house and comprised a front room, used by Mr. Mortimer as his sitting-room and study, looking out on to the quiet and eminently respectable —— Street, and a back room of lesser size, which formed the bedroom. The two rooms were connected by a short, private lobby, out of which opened a small cubicle, which had been fitted up as a private bath-room. Of course, in addition to this private passage the two rooms both opened on to the public staircase. Mr. Mortimer had fitted up his apartments with a view to both taste and comfort; he spent much of his time at work on his researches in his sitting-room, which contained his private desk and papers and the walls of which were lined with book-shelves laden with many rare and precious volumes.

Objects of ancient and especially of Etruscan art were scattered about and several good water colours of Italian scenes decorated the spaces on the walls not occupied by bookshelves. The bedroom was more sparely furnished, but still every reasonable article of comfort was to be found therein. The remainder of the house was like the first floor, let as apartments for single gentlemen. At the time of the events which are now being recorded, the ground floor was under lease to a Mr. Andrew Scoones, an official in the Government service, the second floor, the one above Mr. Mortimer, was temporarily empty, while the landlord and his wife, persons of the name of White, and the little maidservant occupied the top floor.

Mr. Mortimer's life was one of great regularity. He was in the habit of being called precisely at eight in the morning by White, and then immediately repaired to his bathroom. In his absence White set out his clothes, and brought up to the bedroom a tray with the materials for Mr. Mortimer's rather slender breakfast, which he partook of in his bedroom. While he was thus breakfasting and completing his toilet, the sitting-room was tidied up and made ready for the day and thither he would repair to attend to his correspondence and to read his newspaper. If he were occupied in any special research or writing he would then devote himself for a time to that, otherwise he usually proceeded to his Club, the Megatherium, where he spent a large part of his waking hours. Here he lunched, if not engaged elsewhere for that meal, and then passed the afternoon in various ways, returning to his rooms at about seven, to array himself for the evening, which was passed either in some social function or at the Club. Normally he returned to his rooms shortly after eleven and proceeded forthwith to bed. This programme was maintained on Sundays and weekdays, winter and summer, varied only by an annual excursion from London, either on a round of visits or quietly to some watering-place. No life more calm or open can be imagined; there appeared to be no room in it for secrets and certainly if Mr. Mortimer possessed any they were closely guarded.

Such was the man, and such was the existence that was cut short by a mysterious tragedy on the night of July 16-17 in the year 18—. The story of this tragedy so far as it was revealed at the time now requires to be told.

The first sign of any unusual disturbance in Mr. Mortimer's regular form of life was noted by a waiter at the Megatherium—one George Robbins. This man was the regular attendant on the little table in the cosy corner of the dining-room at which Mr. Mortimer always sat. He appeared in the box at the Coroner's inquest and testified that on the evening of July 10th Mr. Mortimer was dining alone; he appeared to be out of spirits and ate but little. Opposite to his seat at the little table was another chair, but this was unoccupied and no place was set in front of it. Towards the end of dinner, Robbins was astonished to see Mr. Mortimer rise from his chair and move in what the witness described as, "a threatening kind of way," round the table towards the empty chair. Suddenly he stopped, leaned heavily against the table and appeared to be about to faint. Robbins came quickly to him and asked if he was ill. "Only a turn, Robbins," answered Mr. Mortimer. "Get me a glass of brandy." Robbins brought it, and found Mr. Mortimer already looking better: he drank the brandy and then said, "Take that chair away," pointing to the vacant one, "and never put it there again unless I have some one to dine with me."

Robbins obeyed and the incident was closed, but the man could not help observing that from this time on till the end Mr. Mortimer appeared always ill at ease and largely to have lost his appetite.

The next persons who were struck forcibly by a strange change in Mr. Mortimer were Professor Rich, the well-known historian, and a certain Belgian scientist, M. Émile V. The latter had left England at the time of the inquest and did not testify, but Professor Rich, who was, perhaps, the most intimate of all Mr. Mortimer's friends, stated that on the night of the 16th July Mr. Mortimer had dined with himself and M. Émile V. at the Megatherium. The Professor had been out of town for some days, and found himself pained to observe how ill and nervous Mr. Mortimer had become: he was in high but apparently forced spirits, drank more than was usual and kept announcing his intention of staying up all night.

"Few of us," he cried, "realise the beauty of dawn in the London streets. I shall stay here till the Club closes, and then I shall walk the streets till daylight comes. I'll have the police for company: perhaps you will hear of me as helping to catch a burglar. But I won't go home till morning." And he began to sing fragments of the well-known old song.

The Professor was deeply shocked and the Belgian gentleman astonished; fortunately they were alone in the small smoking-room, or Mr. Mortimer's conduct would have caused a scandal. Professor Rich began to expostulate with him, but with little success till Mr. Mortimer's glance fell upon the door. He suddenly became silent and very pale, then, turning to the other gentlemen, he muttered something unintelligible and walked straight out of the room. It was then about a quarter-past eleven and he must have returned direct to his rooms without even claiming his coat and hat. The Professor could not in the least account for this sudden departure; no one had entered the little smoking-room nor had the door been opened.

The last person to see Mr. Mortimer alive was Mr. Andrew Scoones who, it will be remembered, occupied the apartments beneath those of Mr. Mortimer. Mr. Scoones had resided in the house for some little time, but he had only a passing acquaintance with Mr. Mortimer, born of casual meetings on the stairs and similar accidental foregatherings. At this time, Mr. Scoones was busy with a literary article and as his day was absorbed by his official duties he was in the habit of working at night. For a long time he had been undisturbed by Mr. Mortimer, but for the past five or six days he had frequently heard that gentleman moving about his rooms at very late hours. He had not paid much attention to his neighbour's restlessness, however, until this night of July 16th, when he heard Mr. Mortimer enter his apartment at about half-past eleven and forthwith begin to move about uneasily. As he listened a curious sense of there being something very wrong began to pervade him; and gradually it began to become known to his subconscious mind that something serious was amiss in Mr. Mortimer's rooms. The impression grew stronger, and at last it overcame his natural shrinking from intruding on the privacy of an almost total stranger, and rising from his writing-table he proceeded upstairs. On reaching Mr. Mortimer's door he paused; inside he could hear Mr. Mortimer pacing to and fro and occasionally uttering an ejaculation, the nature of which he could not hear. Finally he knocked at the door. There was a brief pause, then it was flung wide open with such violence that it crashed back against the wall behind it and Mr. Mortimer appeared on the threshold. He was dressed in his evening clothes, and was very pale, but there were no signs of disorder either on his person or in the room, which was brilliantly illuminated. For a moment the two men looked at each other in silence, then Mr. Scoones, plucking up his courage, began:

"I beg your pardon, Mr. Mortimer, if I have disturbed you, but I fear you are ill."

"Ill," said the other, "what makes you think that?"

"I must renew my apology," answered Mr. Scoones, "but I heard you tramping so restlessly overhead, and it is so late, that I feared there must be something the matter and I came up to see if I could be of any assistance."

There was a longish pause, during which Mr. Scoones grew more and more embarrassed, then Mr. Mortimer slowly said:

"I thank you, Mr. Scoones, but I am not ill; I only trust I have not disturbed your rest and I promise you I will give you no cause for further complaint."

These words were uttered deliberately in a somewhat peculiar voice and Mr. Scoones, abusing himself for having placed himself in a foolish position, was about to say good night and turn away, when Mr. Mortimer suddenly burst out:

"Don't go, don't go, I am in trouble, grievous trouble."

He stopped abruptly and, turning round, stared into the brightly lighted, empty room behind him. To Mr. Scoones's imagination, it appeared as if he was confronting some foe, invisible and inaudible to others.

"I will gladly help you, Mr. Mortimer," said Mr. Scoones, "to the best of my ability, if you will give me an idea as to what I can do."

Mr. Mortimer turned towards him again. "If you would save my soul," he cried, "you will——"

As he spoke he staggered backwards one or two paces as if he were in the grip of a powerful enemy; he turned sharply again and stepping forward closed the door suddenly, swiftly and silently, and Mr. Scoones heard the key turned in the lock. He stood amazed. What had happened to Mr. Mortimer, and why had he closed the door so abruptly? He waited a moment; all was silence within, then bending towards the door, he called:

"Mr. Mortimer, Mr. Mortimer." There was no reply, and he tried the door: as he had supposed, it was locked. Again he called:

"Mr. Mortimer. Can I help you? What is the matter?"

The reply came instantly:

"There is nothing the matter. All is as it should be, but come again to-morrow."

The voice sounded choked and constrained; it differed in some fashion from Mr. Mortimer's. Again Mr. Scoones tried.

"I fear you are ill, Mr. Mortimer; for Heaven's sake open your door and let me in. I am sure you need help and comfort." Mr. Scoones hardly knew why he spoke the last two words, but as in a glass darkly he seemed to see a vision of a poor human soul fighting a lonely and a losing battle against the Powers of Darkness.

There was another short pause, then Mr. Mortimer's voice rang out clear and unmistakable on the horrified ears of his listener:

"In the name of the Devil, whose servant I am, cease to annoy me. To-morrow you shall know all."

Mr. Scoones, filled with horror and amazement, turned away and descended to his rooms, where he sat up awhile listening, but no further sounds were heard from Mr. Mortimer's floor; and at last, tired out, he retired to bed to be awakened next morning by White with the ghastly news of Mr. Mortimer's death.

As usual White proceeded to Mr. Mortimer's room at eight o'clock on the morning of July 17th. He knocked at the bedroom door, entered, and was surprised to find the bed empty and evidently unused, and to observe that all the lights in the room were fully turned on. Otherwise there was no sign of anything unusual except that the door into the little private lobby was open. Turning in that direction, White perceived that the light in the lobby was also burning, as well as that in the bathroom. He passed through into the sitting-room. Here at first all appeared to be in its usual condition, save that the room was brightly illuminated, but glancing towards the door White perceived Mr. Mortimer lying on the floor closely huddled up against it. He hurried over to him, and looking at him saw that his own hands were closely clenched about his throat and that he was dead. White endeavoured to raise him and to unclasp the gripping fingers, but found his clutch too firm to be relaxed. He at once rushed out to give the alarm, but even in his agitation noticed that the sitting-room door was locked, an unheard of thing, and that the key was on the inside. A doctor was summoned, and messengers to call the police and Dr. Bessford, Mr. Mortimer's usual medical attendant, were also despatched. By the time the latter arrived Mr. Mortimer's body had been raised from the floor and laid upon a sofa, but the doctor first summoned had not yet succeeded in removing the hands from the throat. In the presence of the police Dr. Bessford and his brother practitioner ultimately succeeded in releasing the deadly grip, and a hasty examination was made which disclosed the undoubted cause of death as self strangulation; the post-mortem later on showed that there was no bodily infirmity, nor any cause of death save this one alone. Both medical men testified to their amazement at so singular and so determined a form of suicide, and both, but especially Dr. Bessford, as well as White, commented on the peculiar look of abject terror on the dead face. There was no evidence found of any struggle or disturbance in the room, and Mr. Mortimer's clothing was quite in order.

The coroner's jury brought in a verdict of Suicide in the usual form; Mr. Mortimer's body was in due course buried; and the whole affair gradually passed into the limbo of forgetfulness.

Mr. Mortimer left no will or any instructions, and as his next of kin and heir, a distant sailor cousin, was then absent with his ship on the China station, Mr. Mortimer's solicitor took charge of his effects and affairs. The rooms in —— Street were given up, the furniture sold, and the books and manuscripts packed up and stored. On returning home, Lieutenant Mortimer did not trouble himself with unpacking the latter, and it is only since his death that they have again seen the light, and that the diary has become accessible.

It was apparently Mr. Mortimer's practice to keep a diary, but seemingly only spasmodically—at any rate, only fragments have been found. Unluckily there are no existing volumes of the date at which he was brought into touch with Mr. Bradshaw, so there is no clue to the real relations between the two men. The diary after a long interval had been recommenced about six months before Mr. Mortimer's death, but it is only of interest for the present purpose during the last eight days of his life. With this preamble the diary may now be quoted in full.

July 8th. "I was the subject to-day of a singular hallucination: I believe the spiritualist jargon describes it as clair-audience. I was in my rooms dressing to dine out with Lady L. when I distinctly heard the voice of James Bradshaw saying, 'The day of reckoning will come soon.' The impression was so strong that for a moment I supposed the man to have obtained admittance to my rooms, and to be speaking to me, but on looking round I perceived I was alone. There was no one in the sitting-room, and White, for whom I rang, assured me that he had admitted no one to see me. I am of the opinion that my subconscious memory has played me a trick and has recalled to my conscious self the last words that Bradshaw spoke as he flung himself out of the room at York, after refusing my offer of £1000. It is curious that this memory should have been revived after so many years, and even more curious that it should have been revived wrongly, for I am certain that the actual words Bradshaw used were, 'The day of reckoning will come some time.' However, it is useless to speculate on these tricks of the memory.

July 9th. "I have been feeling uneasy and depressed to-day. I cannot describe myself as ill, but I suppose I have been working too hard at my article for Robertson, and that the heat has helped to affect me; I will get away for a breath of sea air as soon as possible. It must be my physical condition acting on my mind, but I cannot get Bradshaw out of my head. I know that he considers that I did him a great wrong, but after all £1000 to a man of his means is certainly more valuable than a little notoriety or, as he would call it, fame. Besides, I greatly question if he, a totally unknown man, could ever have got his, shall I call it, discovery recognized by people of standing; it was far too revolutionary, and needed some one recognised as an authority to bring it forward. At the time of the York interview he failed to notice this point, any more than he would agree that, if I had not come to his help in Fialo and seen him through his illness, he would probably have died and his secret have died with him and been lost to the world. He is a most unreasonable fellow, and a mischief maker; I think I came well out of my encounter with him.

July 10th. "On picking up *Times* this morning, I noticed in the obituary column the death of James Bradshaw, assistant master at —— School in Yorkshire. He died on the eighth, so there goes Bradshaw into nothingness. For a moment I confess to a slight feeling of regret for the man, but it passed quickly; he was an enemy of mine, though an impotent one, and it is better that he should have gone. While I fail to see how he could have done me harm while alive, yet it is certain he can do me none now that he is dead.

"A most extraordinary and rather perturbing hallucination occurred this evening. I was dining alone at my usual table at the Club, and had nearly finished dinner, when, looking up, I saw James Bradshaw sitting in the chair directly opposite to my seat. He was plainly discernible as he sat quite motionless gazing at me with a diabolical grin and, save that he looked several years older, he was exactly as when I last saw him at York. I looked at him for a minute, then impelled by a sudden emotion and forgetful of the *Times* notice I rose from my chair, and moved round towards him. He did not stir until I was close upon him, and then—he simply was not there. I leaned against the table feeling sick and faint and when the waiter came to my side I sent for some brandy. This revived me, but I have told the man never to leave an empty chair opposite me again. The vision was so clear, and the appearance of the figure so menacing that I feel unnerved. I know it is hallucination, imagination, nonsense; and yet——

July 11th. "My mind must be seriously affected. I slept badly last night, and woke unrefreshed; I have had dreams but I cannot recall them, but all this is nothing to the trouble that has begun to pursue me in my waking hours. James Bradshaw is here in my rooms, he follows me to my Club, he goes with me wherever I go, whether alone or with others. I cannot see him, but I know that he is here, and I constantly hear his voice. He taunts me with what happened at Fialo years ago, something that none but he and I know, he threatens me, he laughs at me. I know that it must be hallucination, but it is horribly vivid. I know that Bradshaw's body is rotting in the earth, and his spirit dissolved into nothingness, what is it then that tortures me in his form? I have been so maddened that I have answered him back, or is it answering myself back? I do not know; I can only cling to the belief that it is some bodily derangement. Dr. Bessford returns from his holiday to-morrow, and I will seek help from him. I can go to no stranger. It is now past one o'clock in the morning, and I have been walking to and fro, and wrestling with James Bradshaw for hours. I must rest, I must rest, but sleep, oh, my dreams will murder sleep!

July 12th. "After a hideous night, I went early to see Dr. Bessford. He tells me after careful examination that physically he can find nothing wrong with me, but that mentally I appear to be over stimulated. I must rest. What farcical nonsense! While he was actually saying the words, Bradshaw was whispering in my ear: 'Your soul is given to me.' What shall I do? What can I do? Bessford has given me a sleeping draught; I will try and see if this will not give me at least one night of immunity from my persecutor.

July 13th. "How have I lived through the night, how can I live through the day, how can I continue to exist? Last night, I took my sleeping draught and forthwith my body was steeped in sleep, but my spirit, released from its earthly casing, became the sport of the powers of evil. For what seemed ages I fled through vast, grey, misty spaces, hounded ever by James Bradshaw. Wildly I endeavoured to hide, for I knew whither he was driving me. At last he seized me and dragged me onwards and now I know there is a Hell, for I have seen it, mine own eyes have seen it; for an instant, for an eternity, James Bradshaw swung me suspended over the Pit, and then with a yell of laughter he freed me, and I woke. I woke in the pale light of early morning to see Bradshaw's form by my bed-side. I stared at the figure, which stood distinct in the early light, motionless, but with threatening arm upraised, and then I heard its voice, clear but sounding as if from far, far away: 'In four days you shall be mine for ever.' It vanished, and I have lived through another day, too crushed and hopeless to think.

July 14th. "Last night I passed free of disturbance, and I have felt less sensible of the hideous presence. Perhaps I can yet escape; perhaps there is yet mercy for me. For have I been so evil a man that I deserve such a doom as Bradshaw threatens? I know I have my faults, I know I have done things that cause me shame, but is there no repentance? Is there really a God of mercy to appeal to? Surely there must be, surely that Hell, which I have myself seen, is not the doom of all mankind. What shall I do? I will make amends to any I have wronged in the past; I will try and lead a better life in the future. First, I will write openly and fully and make public the whole truth of my dealings with James Bradshaw, and if he has a family I will seek them out, and make what reparation is possible and humble myself before them. Then there is that affair of Campion; he at any rate is alive, and I can straighten out matters there; and there is Ellen; she, poor, loving soul shall have justice. But I must have time to do these things, although I will not delay in commencing them; for I must not die till my tasks are all accomplished. To begin with I must sleep; Bessford's draught gave me an experience I dare not repeat, so I will get a small bottle of opium—that will give me sound sleep.

July 15th. "The opium worked well enough and I slept soundly, but I woke in an agony of fear with the voice of Bradshaw resounding through my room: 'You have two days left.' I sprang out of bed and called out something, I cannot say what, some prayer, some appeal. My answer was a mocking laugh dying away in the distance. I shall go mad. I must have time to repent in, I cannot, I will not, I dare not die yet. But how can I help myself? I have forgotten how to pray. I have denied and forsaken my God for so long that now He has forsaken me. Can no one help me? Yes, there is Father Bertram to whom my dear dead mother used to go in trouble. Can he and will he help me? I can but try.

"The powers of Hell have prevailed, I am a lost soul with none but myself to help me. In accordance with my resolve I set forth to visit Father Bertram, and was fortunate enough to find him at home. He greeted me civilly but coldly—no wonder, renegade that I am. But when I began to try and tell my story my tongue was tied, I *could* not tell my tale, for incessantly James Bradshaw was whispering in my ear, whispering words of blasphemy and despair. I stammered out some inanities and fled the house. Bradshaw walking by me laughing gleefully.

July 16th. "I woke once more from a drugged sleep to hear the voice of doom proclaiming: 'To-morrow I will claim you.' But he *shall* not do so, I will not die, I dare God or Devil to take my life till I have accomplished my purpose. Let me think calmly; I am under a spell now, a spell which tells me I must die to-morrow. Let me break that spell; let me but survive over to-morrow, and the power of evil will be defeated. I have but to preserve my will power for one day, and I am safe. I will seek outside help, the help of man, it is the night I dread. Well, I will keep in the company of my kind all night, they will preserve me from self-destruction. I will remain at the Club as late as possible, dining with Rich and that Belgian friend of his, as he has asked me to do, then I will go out into the streets and find some friendly constable, who will let me be his companion through the night watches: but nothing shall induce me to spend the night in my rooms. In the morning I shall be safe.

The day so far has been quiet and undisturbed, if I can get through the night as I propose, I feel I shall have conquered in the fight. Alone I shall have done it: God has deserted me, the Devil assails me, but I defy them both; I will not die to-night."

These are the closing words of the diary. It will be remembered that the unfortunate man returned from the Club to his apartments at about half-past eleven that evening.

JUDGEMENT DEFERRED
by
MRS. G. LINNAEUS BANKS

In her introduction to Through the Night *(1882), Isabella Banks remarked on the strange anomaly 'that the era of hard science and scoffing unbelief should have given so many mystic and ghost stories to our literature'. And she was right, of course; the hard-nosed Victorian age gave birth to a host of spectral tales. Mrs Linnaeus Banks was merely echoing the bewilderment of so many authors who found an avid market for their collections of ghost stories.*

Mrs Banks' Through the Night, *subtitled* 'Tales of Shades and Shadows', *was based on her own experiences and contact with others who had, as she put it, been 'visited by apparitions'. Isabella Banks, however, came from a most unfanciful background. Born in Manchester in 1821, she was the grand-daughter of James Varley, discoverer of the use of chloride of lime. At the age of twenty-five she married the poet and journalist George Linnaeus Banks, and it seems he must have encouraged her to write. Her first book appeared in 1865 and she went on to publish over twenty more. as well as* Through the Night, *Mrs Banks wrote two other books of short stories -* The Watchmaker's Daughter *(1882) and* Sybilla *(1884) - which are almost perfectly representative of Victorian literature as it passed through its moral preaching stage.*

A keen antiquarian, Isabella Banks amassed an

extensive collection of shells and fossils, and garnered many odd tales for use in her stories. The bulk of her fiction seems to have appeared after her husband's death in 1881; she published at least two books the next year, and she continued writing until her death in 1897.

The following tale, taken from Through the Night, *is a sprawling reminder that the past will always catch up with you eventually. It is also a story which, given the technological advances since its publication in 1882, would be impossible to render convincingly these days.*

* * *

CHAPTER I

ON BOARD THE BEGUM

A trading vessel—the Alcestis, from Bahia to Liverpool—found the Begum drifting helplessly as a log in the billows. Yet she was a stout ship, well rigged, and seemingly in good condition. When the look-out sighted her, Captain Somers changed the course of the Alcestis to come within hail of the apparently disabled craft. But only the scream of the curlew answered the loud "Ship, ahoy!" though the cry was thrice repented.

Under the conviction that something was wrong with the silent vessel, he still bore down upon her. As they neared, his glass told him that the boats were gone from her davits, and that the man at the helm was the only visible creature on deck.

"Ship, ahoy!" again pierced the stillness. A handkerchief fluttered for an instant above the helmsman's head, and a faint echo seemed to come across the water.

A boat was lowered from the Alcestis. As the men

pulled steadily towards the mysterious stranger, Captain Somers, who was himself in charge, saw that the figure-head was a woman, and next read her name, 'The Begum.'

Cries of horror burst from the lips of the boarders at the sight before them. Captain, mates, and a couple of seamen lay gashed and dead upon the deck, where pools and rivulets of blood lay black and festering; and, sad as anything to see, a fine hound stretched in their midst, killed, no doubt, in the defence of his master.

The man at the wheel—by his garb a passenger and a gentleman—was the only living thing aboard, and he had fainted as Captain Somers stepped upon the deck, apparently from exhaustion caused by wounds.

The sun was broiling bot, and the stench from the exposed bodies was pestilential.

Tho first care of Captain Somers, after the restoration of the survivor was to commit the slain reverently to the deep and next to make such disposition of his own crew as would best enable him to the Begum in tow, and so preserve the sound teak-built ship and cargo for her owners.

Some hours elapsed before the rescued man was able to throw any light on what was a manifest tragedy. When he did relate the story it was with shuddering horror and many pauses, yet with strange and almost studied precision.

"My name is Stanhope—Alfred Stanhope. I went to India with my parents when a mere child. They have been dead I several years. I was summoned from India to take possession of a fortune, inherited and bequeathed to me by a relative: and after winding up my affairs in the Presidency, I embarked on the Begum with my private secretary, Oliver Craven. The Begum, Captain Manners, was bound from Madras to London, with a cargo of rice, silk, sugar, and spices. There was also specie on board, for consignment to English bankers. Myself and secretary were the only passengers. There was a sufficient crew to work the ship with ease, had Captain Manners been so minded.

"We had baffling winds at the Cape, and our voyage was protracted—not, however, to any alarming extent; yet Captain Manners harassed his seamen with fatiguing duties, which I, a landsman, regarded as excessive. I may be in error, having no knowledge of seamanship. On the plea that provisions ran low, the men were put on short rations, and the allowance of grog was diminished. I am not prepared to say it was not a necessary precaution, but the consequences were terrible!

"A spirit of discontent prevailed. We had called at Madeira for fresh fruits and water. One or two of the men sought leave to go ashore. It was denied, and denied harshly. I ventured to remonstrate with the Captain; was told to mind my own business; he was the master of his ship, and would do as he chose.

"One glorious morning, about a week ago—I have lost my count of days, but it was the 4th of August—I sat writing in my cabin, Selim, my dog coiled on the rug at the open doorway. There was a trampling of feet overhead. He gave a low growl, sprang to his feet and rushed on deck, the first to hear the mutterings of the storm and the plashing of the red rain.

"The slumbering mutiny had broken out. I reached the deck unarmed, to find sailors and officers in fierce conflict, and my secretary, in the very midst, endeavouring in vain to quell the strife. Poor Oliver paid the penalty for his rashness. My faithful hound, rushing forward to defend him, fell a sacrifice at the outset. Before I could seize a cutlass, or strike a blow in self-defence, I felt the sharp sting of a bullet through my arm, and almost simultaneously a blow from a marlinspike stunned me.

"I must have lain senseless an hour or more. I recovered to find myself stiff and sore, in a pool of blood; amidst silence profound and terrible.

"It was some time before I attained full consciousness of my awful situation. The Begum had been abandoned by her mutinous crew, and I had been left for dead— among the dead.

"I managed to creep to my cabin and obtain a draught of brandy. Fortunately, the bullet was embedded in the muscles of my left arm, and I contrived to extract it with my penknife. Doubtless, I did it clumsily; but I did it, and, moreover, plaistered and bound the wound."

"Had I not better examine it?" asked the surgeon of the Alcestis, rising, and coming forward.

"It is not necessary, sir," answered Mr. Stanhope, waving him back somewhat stiffly; "the wound is healing."

The surgeon coughed slightly, as he retired disconcerted, and Mr. Stanhope resumed:

"I discovered that the ship had been plundered, my cabin ransacked, money and valuables carried off. They had victualled their boats well. I could find no provisions beyond a few biscuits and a little water."

"I thought rice and sugar were part of the cargo?" suggested Captain Somers.

"Yes; but I was too weak and unskilled to procure them."

"Humph! They would be in the hold, and neither East India sugar bags nor rice bags are made of cast iron!"

There was a world of contempt for a land-lubber's imbecility in the captain's tone.

"The ship tossed and drifted at the will of the wind. My situation was horrible. If I went on deck the open eyes of the dead men seemed to follow me. If I went below I could signal no passing vessel. On the second day I resolved to throw the bodies overboard. I shudder as I think of the result." (He did shudder, indeed.) "Round the corpse of Oliver Craven, my secretary, who deserved a better fate, I wrapped a piece of canvas, and as well as I was able, having one arm disabled, dragged it to the side and pitched it over. There was a downward plunge, and then——"

"Some brandy for Mr. Stanhope, he is fainting."

Mt Stanhope rallied, again waving back the officious surgeon, and continued:

"The canvas had slipped, and Craven's head and shoulders rose and fell with every wave that lapped the vessel's side, and life seemed to look out of the wave-washed eyes, from which salt tears ran down the white cheeks. It was an awful sight, yet it fascinated me. If I turned away, I was certain to look back, and as certain to see Craven's pale face and glassy eyes before me."

Mr. Stanhope drew his hands across his own as if to shut on out the sight.

"Two days more, and a couple of friendly sharks rid me of the horrid spectacle. But not of that on deck, and I had neither strength of body nor will left to cast another corpse into the sea. Even poor Selim had to lie where he fell.

"In all that time no vessel hailed us or hove to. I saw sails in the distance, but what signal I could make was unheeded. I felt abandoned even of Heaven, and gave myself up as lost. Whither the sepulchral ship was drifting—into what solitary sea, I knew not.

"The sleepless nights spent below were haunted by visions of the scene on deck. Prayer seemed frozen on my lips, and morning found me at my post at the helm, with reality before me and my own certain fate in contemplation. The very sharks appeared to multiply and grow more ravenous as they followed steadily in our wake!

"When yon found me, Captain Somers, I was on the verge of madness. My debt of gratitude to you will never be cancelled."

The statement made on their arrival in port to magistrates and shipowners by Mr. Stanhope, though precisely the same in all points of fact, was still more concise. He had recovered somewhat his composure, and told his tale with quiet gravity, and with none of the nervous tremor which had marked and broken his first narrative.

Yet he must have suffered greatly, his hair and unshorn beard being white as foam when he was picked up, though gave his age as twenty-eight, and in answer to surprised inquiry said that on the morning of that fourth of August his hair had been dark brown—a statement borne out by the reddish light in his cavernous eyes. He looked much older; but no doubt an Indian sun, as well as his terrible experience, were accountable for that.

He was apparently a man who had his feelings well under control, yet no effort could hide his perturbation and reluctance to revisit the Begum for the purpose of collecting his own papers and property; as also the luggage of his unfortunate secretary, of which he offered to take charge for transmission to the friends of the murdered man.

Of everything in the shape of money or jewellery, cabins and bodies had alike been despoiled; how Mr. Stanhope's watch had escaped them was a marvel. The owners of the Begum were prompt in their offers of cash for immediate use, but Mr. Stanhope had with him letters of credit, which had escaped confiscation, and which were duly honoured.

The story found its way into the newspapers of the time, 182—; and had he been so minded, Alfred Stanhope would have been pushed into notoriety. But this seemed repugnant to his feelings. He said, curtly—

"I decline to be made the hero of a tragedy." And again: "My own business requires my presence elsewhere."

Those who would have fêted and lionized him were disappointed, and whilst one half pronounced him sensitive, the remainder voted him haughty and imperious.

His stay in Liverpool ended with the official inquiry. That terminated, Mr. Stanhope sent on his luggage by carrier, and ensconced himself in a corner of the Royal Mail coach for transmission to London. It was a glorious day in September, but be shivered, though he was wrapped in a long, straight, fur-lined cloak which reached to his heels, and in which he shut himself up as in a sentry-box. The very sealskin cap on his head had flaps to cover his ears, and had there been another to cover his mouth, he could not have been more silent and self-contained.

A chirrupy little man on the opposite seat made sundry attempts to draw him into conversation, but failing, turned his attention to more sociable fellow-passengers. Not even when they stopped to change horses or alighted for refreshment was he more accessible. He ate and drank of the best, and paid freely, but his taciturnity increased, if possible, as they neared London. For a man about to take possession of an estate, his cogitations seemed to be of the gloomiest. It might be his past experience led him to fear legal thorns before the full-blown rose could be plucked, or, it might be, a feminine rose as thorny.

If so, he troubled himself in the one case unnecessarily. His credentials were indisputable. Recent investigation had already established his identity, and Messrs. Falconer and Robb, of Verulam Buildings, solicitors under the will, both remarked, "Mr. Stanhope's resemblance to his late uncle," so no impediments were thrown in his way; and he took possession with as little delay as the law permitted, confirming Messrs. F. and R. in their position as solicitors to the Stanhope estate.

Alfred Stanhope was by no means a poor man when he left Madras. His uncle's will had superadded money in the bank, money in the funds, and house property in town, to the old entailed mansion in Warwickshire, with its well-wooded and extensive grounds.

"I understand you have not visited Stanhope Court since you were quite a child," said Mr. Falconer to the new owner; as their travelling carriage passed through the lodge gates, and swept under a long avenue of limes, from which the leaves were beginning to fall.

"Not since I was five years old. My father and uncle quarrelled at the time, and afterwards held aloof. They were only reconciled when my father was about to sail for India some four years later."

"Your memories of the place will consequently be very dim." observed the lawyer.

"Very." I remember only an irregular building, large rooms, and gloomy passages, with a gallery of grim pictures, of which I was half afraid. But I have not to be told that its foundation was laid in Tudor times, and its latest addition was when George the Third was King. I have memories, too, of a kennel of yelping hounds and a stud of hunters," continued Mr. Stanhope, half questioningly.

"Your memory docs not deceive you," said Mr. Falconer. "The late Mr. Stanhope was an inveterate fox-hunter, and you will find stables and kennels much as he left them."

"Shall I? Then I shall make a clean sweep of the whole lot. Send them to auction before the week is out!" was the abrupt and somewhat acrimonious retort.

"Indeed! Then you are not a sportsman?" interrogated rather than asserted Mr. Falconer, with uplifted eyebrows.

"Not an English sportsman, certainly. He who has hunted the antelope, with the cheetah for his hound, and the tiger, with an elephant for a steed, will not care to ride pell-mell over hedges and ditches to witness the worrying of a fox!" And Mr. Stanhope's lip curled unmistakably.

"You speak of the hunting-field with all the force of familiarity, until really, Mr. Stanhope, I can hardly realize that you left England so young," observed the solicitor, in some astonishment.

He was put down by the Anglo-Indian's haughty sarcasm—

"Men who read, sir, need not travel the world for information on such topics."

"True, true!" assented his interlocutor, with the mental rider—"Hang his impertinence! He is as haughty as if he were the Great Mogul."

The haughtiness subsided into sufficient condescension, when stepping from the carriage he entered the wide hall, hung round with sportsmen's trophies, and, passing between a double file of servants; acknowledged their cheer of welcome, and the salutation of butler and housekeeper with almost the first smile Mr. Falconer had seen upon his face.

CHAPTER II

AT STANHOPE COURT

"Hush! The place strikes chilly as a vault!" muttered Mr. Stanhope, as the cheering subsided. Then aloud to the curtseying housekeeper (a buxom dame), he said, "I trust yon have large fires, Mrs. Hudson. I have never been warm since I set foot in England," and he visibly shivered under his fur-lined cloak, though there was an ample fire burning in the hall at the time.

"Yes, sir, in all the rooms. Mr. Falconer gave particular instructions, after our dear old master's funeral (how you do shiver, sir!) that the place should be kept well aired, and I trust you will find everything satisfactory."

"As satisfactory as English skies and heavy English masonry will permit, I daresay."

"Do you think the conjunction of an Indian bungalow and an English sky would be more satisfactory, Mr. Stanhope?" put in Mr. Falconer, with a sort of dry chuckle.

"It would be lighter, and brighter, and scarcely colder, sir." answered Mr. Stanhope, in a tone which 'put down' the little, wiry, bright-eyed solicitor for the second time that day.

The housekeeper came to his relief. "Your chambers have been prepared, gentlemen, and dinner will be served in an hour—unless, Mr. Stanhope, you would prefer to go over the house at once."

Mr. Stanhope deferred the necessary tour of inspection to the morrow, and both gentlemen were shown to their rooms to refresh after their journey.

There were cheerful fires in bedrooms and dressing-rooms; and as the flames danced and flickered, they were reflected in well-polished furniture of dark mahogany, and swing-glasses in oval frames. But windows and tall four-poster bedsteads were draped with dark velvet hangings, loaded with silk lace and deep bullion fringe; and doubtless to the man reared from boyhood amongst the lightsome fittings of bamboo and gauze, their heaviness was oppressive. He had declined the assistance of a servant, and now, instead of dressing, paced the room with his hand at his throat, panting for breath, and muttering in gasps, "What is the matter with me? The very air of the place might be tainted; it seems to stifle me. I can hardly breathe. But I must overcome it, if I would enjoy the good the gods have sent me."

The faint baying of a hound from the distant kennels smote his ear. He turned ghastly white, even to the lips.

"My God! What was that?" He sank into an arm-chair before the fire in absolute faintness. "What a fool I am!" he murmured. "It is one of those infernal fox-hounds. I'll have none of their yelping about the old court."

He had thrown his cloak aside and sat there, a white-headed, white-browed man, with a dark skin, a massive forehead, a long, but not straight, nose; a straight upper lip, a close mouth, broad jaws, full rounded chin, and deep-sunk, red-brown eyes, that seemed to pierce the very fire to question it, so keen and searching were they. Yet, at times, they were furtive and stealthy as those of a panther; at others restless and timorous as a fawn's. Indeed, the entire face was one of many meanings, many expressions, and though Indian life, and the fearful tragedy aboard the Begum, had blanched his locks and lined his young face prematurely, there was no questions he was a handsome man of fair proportions, on whom reserve and hauteur sat not ill.

He was still asking its secrets of the fire, when the second dinner bell rang. He started up, drew his hand across his brow, and flung his open palm outward, as if he threw something from him.

"I will brighten the dull place before I bring *her* here," was the burden of his thoughts, as he hurried his toilette.

A respectful servant was in waiting to conduct his new master to the dining-room. This was a long, lofty, dark-panelled apartment, with well-worn carpet, and three windows, across which ruby curtains hung in folds as massive as the antique chairs and tables. Between each window was a mirror reflecting the lights from its own candelabra, and the flames from the sputtering wood fire on the open hearth opposite, and—that which was the most conspicuous thing in the room—a full-length picture of a stalwart man, in a scarlet hunting coat, buckskin breeches, and top-boots. His one hand rested on the neck of a bay mare, a hunting cap and whip were in the other, and by his side stood a long-nosed, tawny fox-hound.

As the picture caught Mr. Stanhope's eye he gave a perceptible start, and for an instant held his breath; but only for an instant. Coming forward, he apologized to Mr. Falconer for being a few minutes beyond time, and then turned to survey the painting more fully.

"My late uncle's portrait, I presume," said he.

"Yes," responded Mr. Falconer, "and, but for his sixty years and florid complexion, a marvellous likeness of yourself. Your grey hair assists the resemblance. It is astonishing how family features are transmitted from generation to generation."

Judkins, the old butler, with the freedom of long service, here struck in: "If I may be so bold, I would say as Mr. Stanhope here is more like to our old squire than to his own father; at least as I remember him before he went to Indy, three an' twenty year ago."

"Ah, that would be when my father and uncle parted in anger, never to meet again. Judkins, what wine have you there?"

The subject thus waived was not resumed. The picture had, however, a strange fascination for the new owner of Stanhope Court. Whenever he lifted his head his eyes sought it furtively, but with a look in which pain and pleasure mingled.

When the meal was over and the servants dismissed, the twain drew nearer to the fire, wine-glasses were filled, cigars lighted, and in the midst of the fumes they talked of many matters, mostly connected with the estate and the late fox-hunter's will.

"And you have no idea what was my uncle's motive for leaving Oliver Craven so substantial a legacy as two hundred a pounds a year?"

"Not the slightest. Mr. Robb drew up the will, but received no instructions which gave a clue either to his reasons, or to the young man's connections or antecedents. He was simply described as 'Oliver Craven, sometime secretary to my late brother Alfred, in Madras, and now secretary to my nephew Alfred.' Our late client, though a jovial, social being amongst his fellow-sportsmen, was close and reserved in all personal and private matters. Have you no suspicion?"

"None. Craven came to India, bringing with him a whelp from the same litter as that in the picture"—pointing upwards with his cigar—"and a letter to my father, urging, as a special favour to himself, that he would push the fortunes of his protegé—a namesake, whose parents had been friends of his own. This was seven years ago. The young man said he had no recollection of his father, and that he was then in mourning for his mother. He served us with faithfulness and intelligence, and I lament, deeply lament, that he should have been so tragically cut off from the enjoyment of my late uncle's well-meant bequest."

"Of course, the money reverts to you in consequence of his death?" said the lawyer.

"I do not intend to touch it. I gather from letters and a miniature I found amongst Craven's luggage that he had been long engaged to a young girl in his own rank. I shall seek her out, and make the annuity over to her."

"My dear Mr. Stanhope, this is, indeed, noble. I——"

"It is justice, sir, not nobility," interrupted Mr. Stanhope, rising. "I will leave you to your wine, Mr. Falconer. I am unused to your mode of travelling, and must plead fatigue as my excuse for retiring early."

Mr. Falconer heard him address a servant in the hall.

"What dogs sleep on the premises—within the house, I mean?"

"Well, sir, there's Snap, the bull-terrier, an' Grip, the mastiff, an'——"

"Turn them all out before you go to bed, and see that no dog crosses the threshold again, as you value your place."

"Strange!" murmured the lawyer. "Fancy a nephew of old Noll Stanhope with an antipathy to *canis*. The old sportsman would have disinherited him could he have foreknown it."

"Strange!" echoed the chorus in the servants' hall. "Turn them animals out! Why, its enoof to make t' old master turn in his coffin!"

They might not have thought it so strange could they have seen through their closed eyelids and chamber-doors the stranger sight of their new master, in slippered feet and dressing-gown, in the dead of the night, wandering about the deserted rooms below, and holding his light to the portraits in the picture gallery as if to print them on his memory!

The formal tour of inspection took place the next morning, the housekeeper and butler acting as guides. They, no less than Mr. Falconer, were surprised at the tenacity of Alfred Stanhope's memory.

"He was such a little thing when he ran about the place last, and his nurse frightened him with that grim picture in the black frame."

They were in the picture gallery at the time.

It *is* a grim picture. I can scarcely look upon it without a shudder even now," said he, in answer to the housekeeper's remark.

"No doubt recent events have given it force," observed Mr. Falconer. "The fierce, murderous eyes of Cain and the imploring ghastliness of the stricken Abel must be like realities to you."

"Like realities, indeed!" echoed Mr. Stanhope, in an undertone, as he turned away with a face scarcely less ghastly than that of the painted Abel.

There was a second portrait of his uncle, with the inevitable canine pet, close to the doorway; and by its side one of Alfred Stanhope's father, both taken in their prime. But be merely paused to note the resemblance between the brothers ere he stepped across the corridor (lighted at one end by a wide mullioned window, emblazoned with the Stanhope arms), and into the library.

Here he drew a deep breath; and sat down, as if to look around.

The door by which he and his attendants had entered lay behind him in the extreme corner of the wall at his right hand. On the same side was the fire-place, originally open, but which had been closed in beneath the massive carved shelfless chimney-piece with glistening Dutch tiles, and fitted with a modern grate—that is, modern a century ago. The heat of the bright fire in the sweeping semi-circular grate shone on the polished tiles, and radiating, glowed afresh on the brass fender and equipments, and on the margin of polished oak-floor left bare by the square Turkey carpet. An immense mullioned window confronted the fireplace, and through the ermine and gules of its stained escutcheon the morning sun fell in ruddy patches upon the solid centre table. A ponderous escritoire held possession of the wall at his back, and before him stood open the chief door of the apartment, covered with crimson baize, spangled with brass nails, and through its two-foot vista he saw its duplicate closed. An army of old books, in good but dingy uniforms, were ranged in rank and file on shelves, which left no inch of spare wall uncovered. New books there were apparently none, and the place had the aspect of hasty furbishing up; yet, as Alfred Stanhope surveyed it from his high-backed arm-chair, a smile of satisfaction swept over his weary-looking countenance. He rose.

"Mrs. Hudson, I will thank you to have another table brought in, and let tiffin—I mean luncheon—be served here. In future; unless I have more than one guest, I shall take my meals in this library."

"Very well, sir, your wishes will be attended to," said the housekeeper, as her master left the library, with Mr. Falconer in his wake; but turning to see her own amazement reflected in the butler's rubicund face, she clasped her uplifted hands with the exclamation, "Laws, Mr. Judkins, how tastes do differ to be sure! When did old master ever put foot in the library, I wonder?"

"Well, Mrs. Hudson," replied the butler, sententiously, "what's one man's meat's another man's poison. Old master liked dawgs, and hated books; the now master hates dawgs, and maybe likes books. It's all one to me, if he don't put a padlock on the cellar door, and turn all the old servants adrift."

Alfred Stanhope did not turn his uncle's household adrift. But he made a clean sweep of kennels and stables. Hounds and hunting-stud went under the hammer, and all superfluous trainers, grooms, and stable-boys were dismissed with pensions or gratuities.

An open hand will atone for a close mouth and many eccentricities; and so, on the whole, Alfred Stanhope grew in favour with his dependents, though he preferred the companionship of books to that of fox-hunting squires, and sat shivering, over the library fire, instead of warming his blood with a brisk canter in the crisp autumnal air, and started like a woman at the report of a gun or the bark of a dog.

CHAPTER III

OLD PAPERS

There were no railways to whisk people hither and thither, without notice or preparation, at the date of this narrative. Letters and messages did not fly on wings of steam and lightning. People and business went on in an easy jog-trot fashion, and no one then thought the world too slow or felt themselves the worse. Then newspapers were too dear, and too few, to find their way daily to every breakfast table; and their news was not always of the newest.

Thus it happened that when Mary Lloyd, schoolmistress, of Lupus Street, Pimlico, picked up a fragment of newspaper which had done duty as wrappage to a pupil's luncheon, and read thereon a report of the 'inquiry into the mutiny and abandonment of the Begum,' the inquest was over, and the survivor of the massacre quietly established at Stanhope Court.

Poor girl! It was well for her that it was Saturday, and that her scholars had separated for the week; well that she was alone when the direful paragraph met her eye, and felled her as with a blow from an unseen hand!

Her little maid-of-all-work, dish-washing in the regions below, heard the scream and fall, and rushed to her assistance, wiping her hands on her coarse apron as she ran.

Their lodgers were out, and the small domestic was at her wits' end, but she had sense left to raise the head of her young mistress from the uncarpeted floor, using work bags for pillows, while she ran for water to sprinkle her with.

As Mary revived, the tender-hearted maid replaced the side combs which had fallen from the dark-brown ringlets, and looked ruefully at the tall Spanish back-comb which lay shivered on the floor. But she never doubted the truth of the explanation that the fall arose from sudden dizziness caused by over-fatigue.

Two music pupils, coming an hour later, found her stretched on a sofa with her hair disarranged, "looking white and awful," and went home with their lessons deferred through their teacher's illness.

"Oliver Craven killed! Oliver dead! Her Oliver—her good, true Oliver, for whose sake she had kept single all these years; to whom she should have been married this very month! Could she ever bear to look again on the wedding-dress he had sent her, which was even then being made up? Oh, that she had listened to his pleading seven years back, and kept him in England—her husband, her own, her Oliver! Yet how *could* she marry whilst her poor paralyzed mother claimed her care? How burden him with such a charge? How stand in the way of his advancement?"

So ran Mary Lloyd's conflicting thoughts as she lay on that chintz-covered sofa in her semi-scholastic back parlour in Lupus Street, with one hand over her tearless eyes and burning brow, holding together the head that seemed just as ready to break, in its desolation.

And she *was* desolate.

At the death of her father she inherited little besides a good education, a loving heart, strict integrity, a resolute will, and the charge of a paralyzed mother. He had insured his life for three hundred pounds, and with that and their tolerable stock of furniture, Mary Lloyd, with no relatives to assist or oppose, before she was eighteen took the house in Pimlico, let a portion to lodgers, and converted the remainder into a 'School for Young Ladies.' Had she waited twenty years she might have dubbed it an 'Establishment.'

It was during the settlement of her father's affairs that she met with Oliver Craven, clerk to a solicitor in Lincoln's Inn Fields. He was struck at once by the fearless energy of the young girl, and her untiring affection for her helpless mother. Of her beauty I think he only discerned that hers was the the beauty of goodness; yet she stood above the common height, her limbs well-proportioned, her head erect on a somewhat full throat, her brow was broad and reflective, and if her nose was not classical, and her upper lip was somewhat stiff, the lines of mouth and chin were tender in their curves, and she had the very mildest of clear grey eyes.

The concern he had evinced for her friendless position, the desire he had shown to serve her, created an interest in Mary Lloyd's breast for Oliver Craven, and love was not far behind. He was her sole confidant, her sole counsellor in the many trials which beset her progress, and when be announced Oliver Stanhope's offer to send him to India under good auspices, a very earthquake seemed to rend them asunder and shatter the temple of her hopes.

But when her lover proposed to remain in England at the risk of his patron's displeasure her negation was final.

"I will wait for you, dear Oliver," she said, "any number of years, but I will not destroy your prospects nor can I burden you with the care of my mother, and so a double duty compels me to say 'Go.' "

And now that he was no more, for the first time she questioned the basis of her decision. It was she who had sent him to India; she who had been the cause of his death!

All that day and the next her mind was racked with torturing agony. With Monday came her pupils and her duties, and in their obligatory performance the strain relaxed little by little. the violence of grief and self-accusation subsided; but the wound in her heart was unskinned, the void unfilled, and "Oliver! Oliver!" seemed written in red on every lesson-book, or slate, or copy she touched.

She substituted black crape and bombazine for the delicate Indian silk in the dressmaker's hands, and "the loss of a friend" was the answer to all inquiries.

A week later, a letter with a black seal, from Messrs. Falconer and Robb, made her formally acquainted with that which she already knew, and with the further fact that Alfred Stanhope, Esq., made over to her his right of succession to a legacy of two hundred pounds per annum, bequeathed by the late Oliver Stanhope to his young protegé, Oliver Craven, knowing her to have been his secretary's affianced wife.

Her wound bled afresh, and now she wept. Had Oliver but lived, how happy might they have been with such an assured income! Then she doubted her right to accept it, and after some correspondence, the solicitors, at the instigation of their client assured her that she had no alternative—the deeds were already executed. If that was a fiction she was not lawyer enough to know it.

Her grateful letter of thanks was duly forwarded to Mr. Stanhope; but much as she wished to thank him in person, no interview had as yet taken place.

Yet such a meeting could not be far off, since, in a fit of very unusual confidence, he had told Mr. Falconer that be had been so much attracted by the miniature amongst Oliver Craven's papers, and the good sense of Miss Lloyd's letters, that he purposed making her acquaintance as soon as the first tumult of her grief had subsided. And Mr. Falconer having but n low opinion of woman's constancy, duly confided to Mr. Robb that he thought Stanhope Court would not be long without a mistress.

The last swallow had departed on his African tour, with the nightingale close in his wake; the green woodpecker laughed his loudest as old October gripped the trees with firm hands, and shook to the ground their crimson foliage; and along with the rustling leaves down went the hard dinner of nuthatch from his claw, to be pounced upon by the merry squirrel gambolling at the roots of the oak, and stowed away for leisurely digestion.

The month was dying in a flood of gold and purple splendour when its last sunset glories fell on the escutcheoned window of Stanhope Court library, and flecked with black spots and great crimson patches the papers spread on the oak table, and the warmly-clad figure bending over them.

Alfred Stanhope raised his head, and, as his eye rested on the exaggerated escutcheon tinging his papers, he cast himself back in his chair with a sigh of utter weariness; and, looking upwards at the window, murmured sadly: "Always the same; always those great red quarterings falling athwart my hands, staining my books and papers as if with great blotches of blood. It affects my sight; and but that all the crazy antiquaries in the country would cry out upon me, I would remove it. And then the motto mocks me with its 'A Deo et Rege!' Well, well, 'familiarity breeds contempt.' I shall grow indifferent in time."

The old escritoire was open, and he was apparently going over its contents to destroy or conserve at his pleasure. The paper before him went with a toss into the waste basket, as he laid his left hand on a packet of letters, yellow with age, and tied round with a faded ribbon. They were addressed to 'Oliver Stanhope, Esq.,' in a cramped female hand, but no dated post-mark gave a clue to their antiquity or order, so he took up one haphazard.

He had taken it up listlessly enough, and paused with it half unfolded in his hand to ring his bell to have the fire replenished; but whatever he found therein—when the footman came to learn his pleasure—he sat with the square discoloured sheet held tightly in both tremulous hands, poring over it with eager eyes, too absorbed to note the entrance of the man or heed his twice-repeated query. But glancing prematurely at the signature, he started to his feet with an exclamation so sudden and vehement, that the servant went back to his fellows and said, with much commiseration, that "Master must have had a sunstroke or something in India, for he sure never could be right in his head. What with his fancies that dogs were growling when there was never even a ghost of a dog within the park palings, an' his shivering over the fire, an' starting and bouncing only to frighten honest folks, he never could be right in his upper story."

The man had jumped to a false conclusion; his master had as clear a head as any in the shire; but he had made a discovery such as would make any man leap to his feet and cry out, if he had a spark of feeling in him.

It was the story of a woman's weakness and man's depravity he read in those letters—the story of a silly girl caught in the toils of a dashing blade, allured from home, her scruples silenced by a clandestine marriage, afterwards repudiated as informal when satiety or jealousy needed a pretext to cast her off, and brand her child with illegitimacy.

The dashing blade had been Alfred Stanhope's sporting bachelor uncle; the disowned woman had signed herself—*Margaret Craven.*

CHAPTER IV

MARY LLOYD

November was but three days old when a knock, which made Mary Lloyd's heart beat, came to the door of the 'Ladies' Seminary' in Lupus Street. It was Thursday, and her holiday afternoon, on which she gave only music-lessons. The last of her music pupils had gone home, the square piano was closed, and she sat down in her dead mother's rocking-chair by the fire in utter desolation—desolation of heart and home; a void not to be filled by her pupils' love or the respect of their friends.

The face, paler and thinner than of old, was not improved in tone by her black dress; but what she lost in colour she gained in gravity and repose.

The little maid handed in a black-edged card, and before Mary could well decipher the inscription in the waning light, the visitor had followed his pasteboard into the dim room.

The man was so muffled in a long fur-collared cloak and a cashmere shawl worn over throat and mouth, as if to guard both from damp, that all she could discern besides was a mass of white hair, dark skin, and a pair of searching eyes that seemed to look her through.

"Candles," she whispered to the maid, as she rose to receive the stranger.

The girl retired, closing the door behind her.

There was a momentary hesitation, caused apparently by the gentleman's reluctance to speak before the servant, during which Mary Lloyd contrived to spell out the card in the firelight. A smile of pleased surprise crossed her face.

"Mr. Stanhope," she said, advancing, "this is, indeed, an honour I did not expect. How pleased I am at this opportunity to express my——"

He stopped her with a deprecatory wave of his hand.

"The honour, Miss Lloyd, is mine."

What was there in the motion, or the tones, which came thick through the muffler to make her start?

The maid brought two mould candles in tall brass candlesticks, and placed them on the table.

"Will you not remove your wraps, sir; the room is warm?"

"After the heats of India, I find all rooms cold."

The door again closed. The girl's heavy step was heard to go downstairs. He loosened but did not remove his shawl.

"You wrote to me, Miss Lloyd, for a miniature and some letters of yours found amongst the effects of my late secretary?"

There was a huskiness as of deep emotion in his voice as he added: "I have brought them with me."

Mary could scarcely trust herself to speak.

"Thank you, sir; you are very kind," was all that issued from her quivering lips.

"But"—he laid a packet on the table—"pardon me, I am most reluctant to surrender them. I have looked at your semblance until the image is painted on my brain and heart. I would not wrong the memory of your lover; yet time——"

She rose, with an indignant protest on her lips.

"Mr. Stan——"

The next syllable was inaudible. The lips parted; but she stood motionless and rigid, unable to utter a word.

He had unclasped his cloak to get at the packet, and the shawl had fallen aside.

As she confronted him with eager, open eyes, and gasped, "*Oliver!*" he, too, started to his feet, and caught her fainting figure ere she fell.

She had made her discovery prematurely.

If kisses, showered on lip and brow and check, could vivify a swooning woman, surely his might have brought her back to consciousness; but she lay white and helpless in his arms so long he was fain to place her on the chintz-covered sofa and look around for some restorative. A common bottle of smelling salts stood on the mantelshelf, telling its tale of frequent need. Its application ere long brought back the colour to her checks, a faint sigh stirred the curl that had fallen across her face; her eyes opened, to rest on the grey-haired man kneeling by her side with anxiety, love, and dread striving for mastery in his countenance.

As the soft light came back to her eyes, he drew her head once more to his shoulder, and placing his hand on her mouth lest she should scream, whispered:

"For God's sake, Mary, darling, command yourself; it is Oliver, your own Oliver, who bids you be calm and cautious, as you love him."

She had thrown one arm around his neck, and was sobbing as if her heart would break, saying, in broken gasps between her sobs:

"They told me—you were—killed—I—I—I—Mr. Stanhope—he—I—do *not*—understand—they—the lawyers—he—oh, Oliver! Is it indeed you?"

"Yes, darling, yes—your own love come back for his sweet wife. You will be my wife, Mary, will you not? You will let nothing part us, will you?"

Kisses did duty for punctuation as he spoke, and Mary, in bewilderment and bliss, could only kiss him back in answer. The sea had given up its dead to her, and she in fullness of joy and gratitude was dumb.

In his face love and joy seemed dashed with a shadow of distrust—some haunting presentiment of evil appeared to contract his thoughtful brow as if with pain.

The maid in the kitchen waited impatiently a summons for the tea-tray. They sat, oblivious of common things, side by side on the sofa; she with her head on his throbbing breast lulled in a delicious calm; he, with his arm gripped round her waist, as if some powerful foe were about to wrest her from him.

The treacherous calm was soon broken.

"Mary," he whispered, as if the nodding mandarins on the mantelshelf were listening, "Mary, I have a strange tale to tell you, but first I want your solemn promise—your oath—to be my wife in the face of everything and anything."

"You have my promise, dear. You know my *love*; if that cannot suffice, what oath could bind me, Oliver?" She looked up proudly as she spoke.

"Hush, darling, not so loud! You must not call me Oliver, I am Alfred—Alfred Stanhope now."

"Alf—what? I do not understand."

"Do not look so strangely, Mary! I have a confession to make. Nay, darling, do not shrink from me. What I have done I have done for your sake. Nay, listen! It is not so bad, after all.

"Mary, my love, I need not tell the dreadful story of the mutiny; you know it. But, dearest, Mr. Stanhope was the one killed. I, your Oliver, was wounded and left for dead. As I dressed my own wounds with lint from his medicine chest, it flashed across my mind that he had not a relative to take his estate; that no one in England had seen him from a boy, and that if they had I bore a strong likeness to him. By his death I was deprived of an appointment, and if ever I got home could only wed you to poverty. Mary—Mary, darling, the temptation was strong! I resolved to personate him—to be Alfred Stanhope to all the world but you. I knew all the intricacies of their affairs from my own mother; knew all the family traditions; I could not fail. I threw his corpse overboard, and then——"

"Then, Oliver Craven, after sufferings that should have taught the falsity of your policy, you took false oaths, before God and man, to magistrates and lawyers; and thought that *I*, the child of a Christian clergyman, would be an accomplice in your fraud. Better the deepest poverty than such dishonour."

She had gradually loosened herself from his clasp, and now stood before him erect, with indignation and shame burning in her calm eyes. She seemed transformed, and he sank cowed before her.

"Mary, Mary, forgive and pity me! If I erred, it was for you. I would make you a mistress of Stanhope Court, close the sad volume of your drudgery here, and fill your life with all that luxury or love could give."

"Had you come back to me an honest man, without a shilling in the world, I would have been proud of you, and love would have dignified drudgery. But now——" She crushed her face up in her hands in anguish unsupportable.

In vain he tried to move her. At length: "Mary, said he, in lower tones, "I am not the impostor you think. I made a discovery three days back which staggered me and nearly drove me mad. Had I not proclaimed myself Alfred Stanhope, I might yet have claimed the estate in my own right. *Oliver Stanhope was my father."*

"Your father?"

"My father, dear one. Whether his marriage with my mother was legal or a vile cheat I have yet to ferret out and prove to clear her fame. But I *shall* do it some day, I *know!"*

He would have taken her in his arms again, but she held aloof and begged him to depart. He was abject in his entreaties. Then fear lest she should denounce his fraud took hold of him—the quiet woman so like a pythoness with scorn.

But he mistook her.

"Go, sir. No eloquence of yours can move me from my sense of duty. You have done me a wrong in opening my eyes this day. Dead, and buried in the everlasting sea, I mourned and worshipped you; living, the master of Stanhope Court, I can only strive to forget you. You have dropped your identity; I shall not recall it. Your secret is safe with me."

Hearing the outer door bang, the maid came upstairs to find Mary Lloyd on the hearthrug senseless, and the fire out.

She called loudly to the lodgers, and with their help the prostrate schoolmistress was carried to her bed.

Haggard, careworn, wretched, Oliver Craven—Mr. Stanhope—went back to his ancient mansion to envy the very lodge-keeper who opened the gates, his smiling wife and chubby children: went back to cower and shiver over his library fire, to hear the yelping of imaginary hounds, and fancy uncle, father, and cousin lurked behind him in the Shadowy corners of the room; to feel all the agonies of remorse deepened by failure; to feel his life bleak and barren henceforth. Himself a dry twig, having neither root, nor sap, nor leaves, fit only for the burning; scorned, contemned, despised by her for whom he had perilled his own soul.

During all that week he ate little; drink much he dared not, lest he should babble and betray himself. Then, to fly from his very self, he mounted a blood mare he had retained, and dashed helter-skelter over the park, leaving his groom far in the distance, and coming home hours afterwards with his horse in a lather to dine in solitary state.

He wrote a guarded letter to Mary Lloyd, signing only

'Stanhope;' and again a second, but no answer came. Her silence struck him with a greater chill than her indignation. He posted up to town. In spite of the weather, which tried him severely, he began to take long walks, into the circuit of which Lupus Street was sure to come every half-hour.

There was something unnatural in the silence of Miss Lloyd's house for a school. No string of little misses issued forth at noon with bags and slates; no little faces peeped surreptitiously over the wire-blind; there was no echo of music-practice heard in the quiet street.

A light in an upper window at night—a doctor's gig calling morning and evening—filled his soul with agony and apprehension. The doctor's groom, thinking no wrong to take a fee like his master, let out that a young lady was "lyin' ill of brain fever; an' not like to get better."

Truly Mr. Stanhope's punishment had begun. What would he not have given for the right to penetrate to the sick room, and minister to the poor creature he had himself stricken down?

He introduced himself to the doctor, and then introduced a noted physician; laid Covent Garden Market under contribution, and sent in anonymously jellies and chickens sufficient to supply a household of invalids.

Youth and a sound constitution triumphed. In January, Mary Lloyd re-collected her scattered flock, and having aged years in these two past months, set herself resolutely to work as an antidote to care.

And now she wrote to Mr. Stanhope to reject emphatically the use of Oliver Craven's annuity.

It was in vain he urged that he owed her reparation, even if she persisted in rejecting him, and that Oliver Craven's money belonged of right to her. She returned for answer, "I can be silent without a bribe;" accompanied by the deed-of-gift torn in pieces.

"Firm as granite—and as silent, I know—is the rock on which I have wrecked my hopes," said he who to the world and to us is henceforth Alfred Stanhope. "But I will prove to her that I have legal right to bear my father's name, and to sit in his ancestral home; and I will make my name known and respected beyond a posse of fox-hunting squires."

CHAPTER V

AT THE BAR

All that year a demon of unrest seemed to possess Stanhope; he returned at last the calls of such county people as were not inveterate sportsmen. The Court was surrendered to upholsterers, as Mrs. Hudson rejoiced in preparations for the reception of guests to enliven the gloomy mansion. Women angled for the interesting man with the prematurely grey hair, burning eyes, aristocratic bearing, and fine estate; yet there was not a member of the Warwickshire Hunt but grieved over the degenerate scion of a race whose stud and pack had been the boast of the shire for centuries.

He visited, and was visited. He overlooked his estate himself, went and came, searching the registers of all the out-of-the-way churches in and about Doncaster, where Margaret Craven had met Sir Oliver Stanhope at the races; and he found time also to resume his law studies, and the examination and docketing of old papers.

Yet the shadow never lifted from his brow, and warmth never seemed to penetrate his chilly frame. To Mr. Falconer he had explained that he had been premature in addressing Miss Lloyd, who was not cast in the common mould; and that she had rejected alike his suit and settlement as insults. So true—and yet so false in everything!

So it got bruited abroad that Alfred Stanhope's gloom and eccentricities grew out of a love disappointment; and even his own servants accepted the story, his valet having somewhat to say of a miniature worn round his master's neck, and kissed and gazed at in supposed privacy.

And so the months went on to the anniversary of the day when Oliver Craven and Alfred Stanhope changed places. The glorious sun poured in through the library window, and, as usual, the red quarterings stained floor and table as if with pools of blood; at least, so the nervously-sensitive man deemed. But he had made the discovery of *fact* which closed his eyes to fancies.

An old, worn register of the marriage of Oliver Stanhope and Margaret Craven, spinster, performed in the parlour of the Clifford Arms, Skipton, by John Knowles, Clerk in Holy Orders, and witnessed by Martha and James Cragg (the innkeeper and his wife). The letters were imperative demands for money by the said John Knowles, in consideration of his having falsely denied his priesthood to the young wife some two years earlier, at the bidding of the said Oliver, which demands were attended with threats of recantation unless further bribed to hold his peace.

At the precise moment when Alfred Stanhope was thanking God for one load taken from his heart, Mrs. Hudson ran to the butler in his pantry, white and trembling.

"Oh! Mr. Judkins, I declare I've just seen Oliver Stanhope and his dog walk from the picture gallery, and cross the corridor to the library door!"

"Nonsense, Mrs. Hudson! You're dreaming."

"I tell you I saw him; people don't dream in broad daylight. I mean him when he was young. He looked as if

he had walked out of a picture frame. I declare I trem—
— Hark! What's that!"

The ferocious barking of a dog was heard from the library; servants, mindful of their master's interdict, rushed thither to remove the intruder. Opening the first door, sounds of scuffling were heard to mingle with the bark; a groan, a fall, and—stillness.

They found their master extended in a fit on the floor, the red lights from the window staining his face and bands, which still grasped the precious certificate.

His neckcloth was loosened; water was dashed over him; still he did not revive. A groom, with some knowledge of veterinary matters, drew a lancet from his pocket, and bared his arm for blood-letting, exposing a terrible scar. There was another on the throat.

As he plunged in his lancet he said, "Them's oncommon like dog-bites, them be. No wonder th' squire hates 'em mortally."

The bleeding doubtless saved life, and the groom pocketed his reward; but Alfred Stanhope left the Court shortly afterwards, and seldom returned to it—never in the autumn.

He took a house in Cavendish-square, and chambers in the Temple, and after the necessary study and formulas emerged a full-blown barrister, to the surprise of all his circle. He had turned to active work to shut out troublesome thought.

To Mary Lloyd he sent duplicate copies of all documents which attested his birth, and implored her, seeing indeed he was a Stanhope, to receive him once again. What tears, what anguish it cost her to deny him, how she wavered, he never knew; he only read her brief, "I cannot," and crushed the letter up in a paroxysm of mute agony.

Had he needed briefs they would have been as rare as

the dodo; he was rich and fashionable, and they came to him in shoals. Perchance after the first start his sound early-acquired legal knowledge, his acumen, and terse, trenchant eloquence might, in a measure, account for this. He rose rapidly, passing older and less influential men on the road, until his fiftieth year saw him appointed to a vacant judgeship. Envy and congratulations followed him to the bench.

Ah, little knew his foes or his flatterers of his haunted life, of the fits which grasped, and shook, and worried him, when August suns were bright and fierce! Little knew they of the miniature and marriage certificate worn together close to that man's heart. In the twenty years which had elapsed since he took possession of Stanhope Court, society had discussed and forgotten many romances more recent than this, and match-making matrons had given him up as impracticable for very many years.

His appointment was yet new, when in the Autumn Assizes he sat on the bench, for the first time, in a large seaport town within his circuit.

Amongst the names on the charge-sheet Judge Stanhope noted these of James Smith and Owen Nicholson, accused of piracy, mutiny, and murder on the high seas. There were a number of counts in the indictment, some of which dated back more than twenty years. A mate, who had turned informer, was the chief evidence against them.

The judge was observed to flush frequently during this trial, and to make several efforts to taste the water in a glass before him, yet to put it down ere it reached his lips.

The piracy was the more recent offence. The prisoners, with others not in custody, had taken forcible possession of a barque, to which they were attached as able-bodied seamen, had put the captain and officers ashore in the Antilles, and, hoisting the black flag, had committed outrages enough to hang them three times over.

It is with James Smith our story lies. Under the *alias* of John Jackson, he had formed an item in the crew of the Begum. He was now indicted for that, with others not in custody, he had, on the 4th of August, 182—, in the spirit and act or mutiny, murdered, or connived at the murder, of Captain Manners and certain other officers of the said Begum, together with one Oliver Craven, a passenger.

The prisoner pleaded "Not guilty;" but the evidence of the informer was too strong to be shaken. The jury, without leaving their box, declared the man guilty on all the counts. At this stage the judge, who was evidently ill, appeared scarcely able to proceed with the case.

As he put to each prisoner in turn the question whether he had anything to say in arrest of judgment, the court was electrified by the change which came alike over the prisoner at the bar and the judge on the bench.

"Ay, my lord, I have this to say, that I am *not guilty* of the murder of Oliver Craven, and that *you, Oliver Craven,* sitting there alive, to judge other men, know it! And I accuse *you*, my lord, in spite of wig and gown, of the murder of your master, Alfred Stanhope, as was our passenger on the Begum!"

His words rushed like a torrent of lava through the breathless stillness of the court; and the very officials, who pressed forward to check him, themselves fell back at the wave of his brown hand, and his impetuous speech.

"Ay, ay, my lord," he cried, "for all so grand as you sit there, I know *you* and you know *me*. Didn't I see you steal up the companion-ladder and shoot Mr. Stanhope down with his own pistol? And when your master's dog sprang upon you, and would have worried you, didn't I shoot the brave beast through the head to save the life of the sneaking cur as wasn't worth it? And if we left you aboard to take your chance, what better did you deserve? Who made the men discontented first? You, Oliver Craven! I call God to witness I tell no lie!"

The officials rushed forward to stop him, but at this juncture a low growl was heard in the court. All eyes were turned to the bench, towards which the prisoner pointed with an excited gesture, and a quick—"See! See!"

The impalpable form of a man, who might have been Judge Stanhope's younger brother, stood by his side, fitting a halter round his neck; and there, too, a tawny foxhound crouched, in act to spring.

Horror fell upon the court.

The face of the judge purpled, foam issued from his mouth and flecked his scarlet robes, and from his black and gaping lips came a sound more like a bark than aught human.

He fell forward, snapping at those who would have supported him.

The court was adjourned; the sentence of the prisoners deferred.

But the judge was carried from the court to die in his robing-room—according to doctors—of hydrophobia, the virus of which must have been for all those twenty years lurking in his veins.

Can we say that judgment had been deferred in his case? If so, it had been pronounced at last—and executed!

In a will made many years before, he had left Stanhope Court and all which it contained to Mary Lloyd. But the quiet maiden lady refused to administer, and the place—with its evil reputation of being haunted—passed to strangers.

WAXWORKS
by
ANDRÉ DE LORDE

Here is a story with a very interesting history. In 1914 a French silent horror movie called Figures de cire *was released, then re-released in 1918 as* L'Homme aux figures de cire. *In English it was known as* The Man with Wax Faces. *The movie was based on a short story by Grand Guignol playwright André de Latour, comte de Lorde (1869–1942). De Lorde, in turn, had adapted the story from a stage play he had written with Georges Montignac, the play being performed at the Grand Guignol, Paris, in 1912.*

The short story appeared in Charles Birkin's anthology Terrors: A Collection of Uneasy Tales *in 1933 (part of his* Creeps *series), credited, correctly, to André de Lorde. It then resurfaced in Peter Haining's* Gaston Leroux Bedside Companion *(1980), credited, incorrectly, to Gaston Leroux (author of* The Phantom of the Opera*) under the title* The Waxwork Museum. *As a result, Leroux has sometimes been credited as the creative force behind the movies* Mystery of the Wax Museum *(1933), and* House of Wax *(1953). However, both were based on a story by Charles S. Belden.*

There are a few opinions about how the story became so bafflingly misattributed, but by far the kindest is a simple confusion with chapter IX of Leroux's novel La double vie de Théophraste Longuet, *entitled* Le masque de cire (The Wax Mask).

Incidentally, the film, believed to have been lost, was recently discovered in 2007, and restored by French production company Lobster Films.

Waxworks *is widely considered to be one of the first pieces of fiction to feature a waxwork museum, and it is presented here, under the correct billing, as it appeared in Birkin's 1933 anthology.*

* * *

One winter's evening four young men were dining in a fashionable French Restaurant on one of the boulevards. The room was brilliantly lit with great silver lamps, the reflection from which caught the women's jewels making them flash like fire. The Hungarian Band played soft, sentimental waltzes.

It was that time of the day which lends itself to romance. The storm outside accentuated the warmth and comfort of the room. Man is an egoist, and it is only when he pauses to compare his mode of living with that of those who are less fortunate than himself that he fully appreciates his luck. Whilst the quartette sat over their wine their thoughts strayed to the slums where, at that moment, 'down and outs,' soaked through to the skin and buffeted by the wind, would be dragging in the streets seeking in vain for shelter. Being extremely young they revelled in this conversation, conjuring up vivid pictures and sparing no detail.

The eldest of the four was a good-looking fair-haired boy named Pierre de Lienne. "It is an ideal night to plan a crime," he remarked laughingly, tilting his chair and blowing smoke-rings towards the ceiling.

"When authors invent a murder story they never fail to

call the elements to their aid. For example," he continued, "imagine the stage in a theatre with sinister scenery. It is wet and stormy, and one of the unfortunate men, of whom we have been talking, enters. In a crevice of the wall one can see the murderer hiding, a knife gleaming in his hand! Imagine the tension in the audience! The effect is instantaneous."

He broke off, pointing to one of his companions. "Why, look at Jacques, he's scared already!" he exclaimed.

"Yes, you are quite right," replied the boy, who had been listening with rapt attention. "I hate these gruesome stories. Can't we talk about something else?" he asked, pouring out some wine.

They all laughed.

"I have always been nervous," said Jacques. "As a small child I was terrified of going upstairs alone after dark, but my people made me do it. I used to scream and yell, clinging to the banisters and refusing to move. This fear was due to the fantastic stories I had heard from my nurse about blood-curdling inns on the side of lonely roads, where they roasted strangers in the oven; of highwaymen who, in plundering, forced their victims to undergo the most frightful tortures; of nightly apparitions; women clothed in white; corpses awoken from eternal sleep and ghosts fettered with chains. She wrecked my nerves, the stupid woman. Of course, I am braver now, though I still look under my bed before going to sleep!"

"But the very fact that you have the courage to look shows that you aren't really frightened," said his neighbour, Louis Monnier. "What would you do if you found a man hidden there?"

"Oh! well," replied Jacques, "I suppose I realize that my fears are purely imaginative. It is a case of laying the ghost."

"Fear comes from within," said Pierre. "It is unaccountable and cannot be explained. Often there seems no cause for it, and with many it is a nervous illness. The man who is healthy in mind and body knows no fear, but with highly-strung people it is an incurable malady."

"Here, steady," interrupted Jacques. "I am as healthy in body and mind as you are."

"A moment ago you said you had disordered nerves."

"I don't agree with what you have been saying, Pierre," said Edmond Souturier, who had not hitherto taken part in the discussion. "Men are brave," he continued, "when as soldiers they face death on the battlefield and as sailors fight against storm and shipwreck. Just as are the doctors who during an epidemic expose themselves to infection every moment of the day, and the missionaries who are in continual danger of being murdered by savages. We all appreciate the great courage shown by these men, don't we? But I am convinced there is not one of these who could swear that he has never been afraid. Fear is bred by certain mysterious influences and before vague dangers, which often fail to materialize. It comes from outside, and that is why it comes, above all, during the night, which changes familiar objects, giving them uncanny appearances. No one is proof against this sort of fear."

"Indeed," cried Pierre. "In spite of what you say, I swear that I would keep calm, however spooky my surroundings!"

"Very well, then. Are you willing to take on a bet?" asked Edmond.

"Yes, rather."

"Then I suggest that we take you to the Boulevard de La Chapelle, or better still to somewhere near Pierre-Lachaise. We will leave you there for the night, and in the morning will expect you to tell us quite frankly if you have been afraid."

"That won't do," said Pierre, smiling. "I shall meet with material danger there in the form of apaches, and I don't relish being stabbed to prove to you that I am fearless!"

"All right then," replied Edmond Souturier. "What about a night in the cemetery itself among the tombstones? You might see some of the ghosts which terrorized Jacques' infancy!"

"Surely that is locked up at night?"

"We can bribe the gatekeeper."

"I daresay, but it's no joke getting thoroughly wet through and finishing up with an attack of pneumonia!"

"I thought as much; you are trying to get out of it!"

"Not at all, but find something more to my taste. Let me see, what can I suggest? A horrible place, but where I can keep dry."

"A night shelter?"

"No thank you. They swarm with vermin."

"A public-house in the Faubert district?"

"There again there is the danger of being knifed!"

"A den—or a low dance-hall?"

'Good Lord no! None of these will fill me with the fear of the unknown."

"I have it!" cried Jacques. "The waxwork museum!"

"I didn't know there was one. Where is it?" questioned Edmond.

"What! Do you mean to tell me that you haven't seen it at the Montmartre Fair? It is the most horrible place you can possibly imagine! All the celebrated crimes are represented there, and there are also reproductions of executions, drinking and opium dens and the dregs of society, all fashioned in a yellowish wax which makes you feel quite sick. I visited it in broad daylight, but soon hurried out!"

"Where is it now?"

"Still at Montmartre. Only it has moved from Boulevard Rochechouart to Saint Pierre."

"Are you positive?"

"Yes. I went that way yesterday, and it was still there."

"Does that suit you?" asked Edmond.

"Yes, it sounds just the thing. It will only be a question of tipping the manager."

They settled their bill and were surprised to find that it was ten-thirty. No one had noticed the time during the absorbing discussion.

While waiting for a taxi Jacques drew Pierre aside, saying, "Are you in dead earnest?"

"Why, of course," replied Pierre.

"I wish you wouldn't go," pleaded Jacques. "I have a queer feeling something terrible will happen to you!"

"Don't be an old woman, Jacques!"

"By the way," said Edmond, joining them. "How much will you bet me?"

"Is twenty-five louis enough?" said Pierre.

"Done," replied Edmond. "The conditions are that you will spend the whole night in the waxwork museum, and to-morrow you will tell us quite truthfully whether you were frightened or not."

"I promise to do exactly as you say," said Pierre, laughing as usual.

They started off. It was not raining so much, and the wind had subsided a little, but when at last they arrived at their destination it was utterly deserted. The awful weather which had kept the sight-seers at home had driven the proprietor to take shelter in a wine shop, where they eventually found him.

Edmond proceeded to explain the object of their visit, but at first the showman refused to show any interest, evidently suspecting burglary. However, the sight of a small wad of notes overruled his objections, and he agreed reluctantly to take Pierre to the museum.

The others went with him as far as the entrance, where they wished him good night.

Jacques and Louis hailed a cab and set off homewards, whilst Edmond remarked that he was going to finish up the night by dancing in Monmartre.

Pierre followed the showman, who, with a lantern in his hand, opened the door and pushed aside a curtain. He led the way down some rickety steps through the boards of which the rain had oosed, making them dangerously slippery. He raised the lantern so that Pierre could see the surroundings.

A livid glare revealed the reproduction of the late Gouffé. Pierre restrained a desire to laugh as he gazed at the figure of the poor wretched man, half suspended in the air with his tongue hanging out of his mouth; whilst the hangman, his veins swollen with the effort, pulled the rope.

The man walked slowly, stopping frequently to flash his light on some fresh horror. Once scene carried out exactly the picture which Pierre had evoked in the restaurant. A deserted street in a distant quarter—a winter's night—the murderer hiding in a dark corner and pouncing out on the unfortunate wayfarer.

The obscure artist who had modelled all these heads must have been gifted with a very highly developed sense of horror. He had given to the murderer a particularly sinister and brutal expression, and to the murdered the most repulsive contortion of features that can be betrayed by death which has come in some terrible manner. Pierre was highly amused and, in order to please the man complimented him on the models.

Next there came a row of grimacing heads belonging to ten or so celebrated people who had been guillotined. They were resting on blue velvet stands and leaning forward a little exposing the severed section. Lined up as on parade and fashioned in dirty coloured wax with decayed, tobacco-stained teeth showing through long, drooping whiskers, they hardly made a pleasant picture.

At the end of this mournful row stood a guillotine under which was stretched the decapitated body of a man. The knife was a dull crimson and his head lay in the basket. This was followed by a series of tableaux representative of the man's life from his early days to the events leading to the gallows!

"We can't go any further," said the man, "so I will leave you the lantern. I can find my way back in the dark."

But Pierre, anxious to win his bet, refused the loan of the light.

The showman departed and he was left alone. Somewhere in the surrounding blackness a clock struck midnight. It had stopped raining, but the wind, although quieter, moaned and whistled, inflating the canvas walls, which enhanced the unwholesome atmosphere.

He lit a match and found a chair; buttoning his overcoat about his neck he sat down with the intention of going to sleep. His thoughts wandered to his friends, who were by now snug between their blankets, and he shivered a little. How the dreary hours until dawn were going to drag!

He got up and lighting a cigarette began to stroll up and down; from time to time stopping in front of a glass case where the red glow from the cigarette end revealed the pale faces of his weird companions, but somehow he no longer found them amusing. They irritated him, and tired of walking he went back to his chair and sat down again; something pressed against him, and feeling in his pocket he found the small loaded revolver, which he always carried at night. This he transferred to his overcoat pocket and shut his eyes.

He had dozed for some fifteen or twenty minutes when he was awoken with a start by a violent gust of wind. What was that moving? It sounded like footsteps. He strained his ears and, lighting a match, peered round the museum. For a few seconds the malignant evil faces leered at him. "Oh! My God, what hideous things!" he exclaimed, and began to feel desperately depressed.

Unable to sit still he wandered about again, and in his confusion jostled against something cold and hard. Putting out his hand to steady himself he realized with repugnance that he had touched the knife of the guillotine! Swaying a little he lit another match, the faint beam of light betrayed the figure of a man who seemed to be towering above him holding a knife in his hand! The match flickered out and darkness once more enveloped him. He lit another: now he was in front of the grinning heads! The moan of the wind reminded him of the sighing of lost souls.

"Pull yourself together," he cried aloud "It is ridiculous to be frightened. Fancy letting the cold get the better of you!" As he spoke a rat raced across the floor, uttering little sharp cries. It scrambled on to the boards which supported the wax figures, and disappeared.

The clock chimed. Pierre listened intently, convinced that he heard the noise of footsteps, it sounded as though someone were pacing the museum. It was utterly dark. The wind swelled the canvas.

He found himself picturing his gruesome roommates,

and their frightful faces took feverish possession of his brain. He no longer wondered if he was afraid. He knew that fear was gaining on him! An unreasonable and foolish fear which he was determined to conquer. He struck a third match and held it up, forcing himself to look round. He closed his eyes instantly, all the livid faces seemed to have become alive and were fixing him with a glassy stare; they were repellent and contorted.

A cold sweat gathered on his forehead. He swivelled round, surely something had touched him? This was horrible—more than he could bear—he must get out. Fearfully he stumbled towards the little staircase, but to his dismay found that the door was locked. He tried shaking it, but it was sufficiently strong to make it impossible for him to break it open. He realized with frightful sureness that he was a prisoner until morning. Staggering back to the museum he lit another match, but the sight was more than he could stand, and he hastily blew it out, throwing it on the floor.

It was raining a little again and the wind was still moaning. Suddenly a shrill whistle rent the air, echoing round the room; it repeated itself twice, then still, unbroken silence reigned. A ghastly, intense silence, which seemed heavy and menacing, full of the unknown. He dared not stir, and horrible visions of the assassinated Gouffé floated across his mind. He was haunted by the swollen, lolling tongue, and the guillotine looking calmly down on the decapitated body.

Now he was sure someone was lurking outside the museum. He tried speaking aloud to reassure himself, but the sound of his tremulous voice only served to make the atmosphere worse, and the words stuck in his throat, so that he was forced to relapse into silence.

A fresh terror overcame him. He was certain all the wax figures were moving towards him, crowding round to stifle him. It was airless, and he put out his hands to push them away. His teeth chattered, and he was rooted to the spot.

A chuckle rang through the museum. It came from the direction of the line of horrid heads! His heart pounding like a sledge hammer he turned swiftly, expecting an onslaught from the unseen enemy, and clutched convulsively at his revolver.

There was complete silence again for a few seconds, until suddenly the chuckle was repeated.

His strength gave way. The fear of being smothered by the figures had increased; they must be getting very close now. The minutes seemed like eternity. He tried to reason with himself, arguing that he was unnerved by the awful dark silence, and that he had imagined he heard the noise. He breathed more easily, but only for a few moments, for now, again, the mocking chuckle echoed. This time he realized that it had been no trick of his imagination. That last laugh had been near him. He must find out where it came from.

Taking his courage in both hands he lighted one of his matches and looked. He saw 'it' at once above the row of guillotined heads. It was another head grimacing like the rest! Haggard and pale with a wagging tongue! Good God! This decapitated head was beginning to move! It was alive! He could bear it no longer, and drawing out his revolver, fired.

A little blood spurted from the forehead as the head fell upon the others!

Pierre, grasping his revolver, fell fainting on the floor.

Early next morning the showman, arriving to release Pierre, tripped over a body which was stretched across the ground. He recoiled, horror-struck, seeing a bullet wound in the forehead. He tried to lift the body, but soon realized it was futile, for the man was stone dead!

Aware that he could do nothing he looked round, and noticed that the canvas which covered the flimsy structure of the museum had a large tear in it just above the row of guillotined heads, and that a little blood had reddened them!

He leant through the rent and called out. No one answered. He ran quickly to the door and unlocked it. Lying in a crumpled heap on the floor was the young man he had shut up in the museum the night before.

He hurried in and tried to raise Pierre, but before he had time to dodge aside the boy had hurled himself at him and was trying to strangle him. His brain had been turned! Hearing the man's cries people came to his aid, and they managed, with some difficulty, to overpower the madman.

The inquest revealed the name of the dead man to be Edmond Souturier. It was he who, in the middle of the night, tried to frighten his friend for a joke in the hope that he would win his bet. He had passed his head through the canvas covering, leering and chuckling, but he also was turned into a wax figure!

THE VISION OF INVERSTRATHY CASTLE
by
F. STARTIN PILLEAU

F. Startin Pilleau was the pen name of a multi-talented man called Frederick Startin Pilleau. It would certainly seem, from the scant biographical information available, that Pilleau was a master of many disciplines.

Born in 1852, Pilleau was an Associate of the Royal Institute of British Architects, a librettist who collaborated on many operas (including with fellow fiction writer S. Baring-Gould), and a member of the British Chess Club. It is with the latter that Pilleau seems to be most associated, with the publication of his book The Dynamic Chess Notation: Whereby Any Possible Move in a Game of Chess Can be Accurately Described by the Use of Two Letters Only *(1890). This impressively titled book detailed a telegraphic chess code, devised by Pilleau.*

When he wasn't engaged in his Architectural business with partner Frank Ernst Thicke, or writing for operas with George John Learmont Drysdale, or devising new methods for conveying chess moves, Pilleau was writing short fiction for The Strand Magazine. The Vision of Inverstrathy Castle, *published in the magazine in 1894, ended by inviting the readers to offer their opinions on how the story should continue. By all accounts they did just that and, the following year, Pilleau published a sequel resolving the story. Both are included here.*

* * *

I am, as I think all who know me will readily admit, a peaceful man, and not one given to poking his nose into other people's business. I do not take any pride to myself for this, but at once admit that other people's affairs do not interest me, for, no matter how spicy a scandal may be, unless it be directly connected with sport of some kind or other, I turn a deaf ear to it. All mysteries and secrets I abominate, except secrets of the turf, and few even of these have sufficient hold on my memory to last over a good night's rest. Why, then, I ask, should I, of all people in the world, be the unwilling recipient of one of the strangest and most horrible mysteries it has ever been the lot of man to conceive?

True, I share the burden of the secret with one other man, my old friend Tom Farquharson; and it is, I fully admit, a considerable comfort to feel that he bears, equally with myself, the responsibility of the silence we have hitherto maintained respecting the extraordinary occurrence that I am about to relate, for, in consequence of what happened last week, we have, after considerable discussion, determined to lay the facts of the case before the public, taking care, of course, to suppress the real names of the people concerned.

Without further preamble, then, I will at once set forth, in as few and simple words as possible, the strange events to which I have referred.

It was on the 11th August last year that I travelled up to Scotland, in fulfilment of a long-standing engagement, to shoot grouse at Farquharson's ancestral place in Sutherlandshire; and when I add that I had been travelling, almost without stopping, ever since I left the Austrian Tyrol, in order to arrive at Tom's in time for the 12th, you will readily believe me when I say, upon my weary journey at last ending, I arrived at Inverstrathy Castle more dead than alive.

It was shortly after 8 o'clock p.m. when I got there, and the house party had just sat down to dinner; Tom, however, came out to greet me, and urged me to hurry up and join them as soon as possible. But I pleaded that I was dead-beat, and much too done-up to put in an appearance that night, so he considerately gave way to my solicitations; then, promising to send me up something to eat to my own room, he hurried back to his guests.

Inverstrathy Castle is a fine specimen of one of those grand old Scottish strongholds one reads of in Sir Walter Scott's novels, and, tired as I was, I greatly admired the magnificent collection of armour and trophies of antique weapons, grouped round the fine old hall, and up the sides of the broad, black oak staircase, the balusters and newels of which were carved with a boldness one seldom comes across in modern times.

My accommodation, I found, consisted of two rooms: a large, but rather gloomy, bedroom, hung from floor to ceiling with rare old tapestry and furnished throughout with old oak, the ancient four-post bedstead, carved with quaint designs, being almost hidden in a deep recess; and a dressing-room opening out of it, in which, I was glad to see, a modern bath had been fitted up, of which I determined to immediately avail myself.

Having done so, and donned an old, and consequently comfortable, shooting suit, I sat down to a tempting repast, which one of the footmen had spread while I was enjoying my tub.

Since I have made up my mind to take the public into

my confidence, I will not keep back anything, however unimportant it may seem, and I therefore at once confess that I partook freely of that cosy meal, and made short work of the bottle of Heidsieck the man had been thoughtful enough to provide. Then, having lighted a cigar, I drew a comfortable chair up to the fire and proceeded to finish a racy novel I had purchased on my journey.

Let me recapitulate: I was tired out by my journey; I had had a comfortable warm bath; I had eaten a substantial meal and swallowed a bottle of champagne; and I had then sat down in a luxurious chair in front of a cheerful fire. Is it remarkable that I fell asleep? I think not; I believe ninety-nine men out of a hundred would have done the same. Anyhow, I fully admit, I did fall asleep and that my sleep was long, and sound, and undisturbed by dreams, as an honest, tired man's sleep should be.

How long I slept I cannot say, but suddenly I awoke with a start, in consequence, as I thought, of somebody bringing a dazzling light into the room, and before I could collect my scattered senses, the tapestry at the further end of the room was pushed aside and a lovely girl, in evening costume, with a most beautiful but terror-stricken face, rushed frantically in and fell on her knees on the hearth-rug just in front of me: and as she fell, I noticed that a curious, antique jewel, shaped like a heart pierced by an arrow, becoming unfastened, slipped, without her knowing it, from off her neck to the floor.

Startled by her sudden and unaccountable appearance, I was on the point of rising to her assistance, when, to my further astonishment, from precisely the same spot as before, the tapestry was again pushed aside, and a tall, handsome man ran into the room with a drawn dagger in his hand, which, before I had time to interfere, to my unspeakable horror, he plunged to the hilt into the heart of the poor girl.

With a yell of dismay I sprang from my chair to seize him by the throat, when, just as I got to him, to my amazement both he and his victim suddenly and mysteriously disappeared; nor could I discover the slightest trace of the tragedy I had seen take place before my very eyes. Long I stood, completely bewildered and dumfounded, and then, persuading myself I must have been dreaming, I undressed and went to bed.

Next morning, the remembrance of what had taken place the previous night returned to me in full force, and the first thing I did was to carefully examine that part of the room from which both the actors of the tragedy had appeared; but, though I found no difficulty in pushing aside the tapestry, I could not discover any trace of a door. I, however, found, somewhat to my surprise, that the wall was wainscoted to the height of about 7ft., not only at that end, but forming a high dado all round the room. I imagine therefore that Farquharson, or one of his predecessors, finding the room too dark and gloomy with so much black oak, hung the tapestry round the walls to brighten it up a bit.

While dressing, I debated with myself whether or not I should tell Farquharson what I had seen, but came to the conclusion that neither he nor anyone else would for a moment believe it could be anything more than a bad dream, engendered by my overeating myself. Indeed, I was myself very much of the same opinion, and so dismissed the matter from my mind. Once, however, during the afternoon, when Farquharson and I happened to be alone together, I remarked how greatly I admired Inverstrathy Castle, and then casually inquired whether, by any chance, it were haunted.

"Haunted!" he replied, "why, of course it is. Who ever

THE VISION OF INVERSTRATHY CASTLE

heard of an old Scotch castle that wasn't?" But upon my pressing him further to tell me the history connected with it. he confessed he was unable to do so, and admitted that neither he, nor anyone else so far as he knew, had ever seen or heard anything of a supernatural nature. Here the conversation dropped as we resumed the business of the day.

We were a merry party that night at dinner, and it was close upon ten when, at last, Tom suggested we should join the ladies in the drawing-room; but as I had by no means recovered from the fatigue of my journey, which had been, moreover, aggravated by my disturbed night and the long day on the moors, I once more got him to excuse me, went straight to bed, and in a quarter of an hour, or less, was sound asleep.

I was undisturbed for a couple of hours or so, when, again, I suddenly woke up with a strange feeling of terror, which was by no means diminished by finding the room brilliantly illuminated by some unseen light. I sat up, wondering where on earth the light could come from, when the tapestry at the further end of the room was again pushed aside, and, again, the self-same young lady rushed into the room, and fell on her hands and knees on the hearthrug; again I noticed the jewel she wore slip from her neck to the floor; and again the tall, handsome villain followed her, and once more plunged the cruel dagger into her heart; and then, as my heart stood still with horror and fright, the light was suddenly extinguished, and all was utter darkness.

At first, I freely admit, I was much too terrified to move, but at length I screwed up sufficient courage to fumble for the matches on the table by my bedside, and, after one or two failures, at last succeeded in lighting a candle; but, though I got up and carefully examined every nook and corner of the room, all was exactly as I had left it when I went to bed, nor could I find anything to account for the strange light I had seen. Once more I critically examined the panelling behind the tapestry, at the spot from whence I had seen the figures issue, but could discover nothing. With a trembling hand, I then turned up the large Persian hearth-rug, and there, at the very spot I had seen that ghastly murder committed, I fancied I could detect a slight difference of colour in the floor; but as it was of oak, polished by centuries of rubbing, and almost as black as ebony, I could not be certain, in the inadequate light, if such were really the case or not, and I therefore determined to return to bed and examine it more carefully in the morning.

It was some time before I again got to sleep, which, under the circumstances, I think was scarcely surprising; nor is it to be wondered at that, when at last I did do so, I slept so heavily that it was an hour later than the time I had intended to rise when I again woke up. Jumping out of bed, I dressed as rapidly as I could, and then descended at once to the breakfast-room, forgetting, in my hurry, to pursue my investigations of the night before. Judge, then, of my amazement when the first person I saw, on entering the breakfast-room, was the young lady of my vision! I could not possibly be mistaken, for her beautiful face had indelibly photographed itself on my mind; besides, too, there, hanging on her neck, was the identical jewel I had noticed on the unfortunate girl I had twice seen murdered.

Of course I carefully scrutinized the rest of the company, fully expecting to discover, in one or other of them, the villain of the tragedy; but no one there in the least resembled him, and though many others entered the room afterwards, he was not among them. I came to the conclusion then that either he was not staying in the house, or else had already breakfasted and gone out.

After breakfast I took an early opportunity of telling

Farquharson I wished to speak to him privately, and he at once led me to his own sanctum. I immediately asked him who the young lady was, and, after hearing my description, he informed me she was a Miss Craig, a distant cousin of his own.

"And I tell you what it is, my boy," he added, "if you're touched in that quarter you couldn't possibly do better, for not only does she come from a good old stock—in fact, her great-grandmother married my great-grandfather—but she is an heiress in her own right, for, though of course Inverstrathy Castle descended through heirs male to your humble servant, she is the sole survivor of the Craigs of Craigcrathie, a place second to none in Scotland, about forty miles from here in Ross-shire."

I hastily disabused his mind of any such intent on my behalf, and then briefly related to him all I had seen the two previous nights.

Of course, as I fully expected, he pooh-poohed, at first, the whole story; but I pointed out that it was very strange I should have immediately recognised Miss Craig, a lady I had never seen in my life before.

He admitted that was peculiar, to say the least of it, but, after a moment or two, added:—

"I tell you how it was, old fellow. You arrived here dead-beat, and evidently, while you were going to your room, you caught sight of Miss Craig—without, at the time, particularly noticing the fact. Nevertheless, her exceptional beauty made such an impression on your susceptible heart, that you dreamt about her. And now I come to think of it," he added, "I remember her being late on that occasion, for I recollect her coming into the dining-room just after I returned from seeing you."

"That may be," I replied; "but how is it I had the same dream, if dream it were, two nights running? Besides, too,

I never saw Miss Craig at all yesterday, and surely I should have been much more likely to dream of one of the other ladies who were at dinner?"

"Perhaps so, but one can never account for dreams. You did not see Dora yesterday, because she kept her room the whole day with a violent attack of neuralgia. But if the coincidence of your recognising in her the victim of your tragedy tells in one way, surely the absence of your villain tells equally strongly in the other?"

"Well, perhaps you are right. At all events that is the rational, common-sense view to take of the matter; all the same, I wish you would make an opportunity to carefully examine my room with me."

"Why, certainly. Let's go at once."

We were crossing the hall to do so, when Miss Craig called out:—

"Oh, Tom, you're just the very man I want. Mrs. Fergusson is anxious to see the family ancestors, so do come with us and act cicerone, for I always jumble up the old people together, and Mrs. Morgan is so dreadfully prosy."

"Right you are," said Tom; "come along, Bob, you had better come too."

I was only too glad of the opportunity, for I am a bit of a connoisseur as regards pictures, and had often heard Tom expatiate on the treasures of his gallery, especially the Gainsboroughs and Sir Joshuas.

It is not necessary to go through all the gems of that magnificent collection; suffice it to say, they more than came up to my expectations, when, while I was lost in admiration of a splendid portrait of a Sir Donald Campbell, by Vandyke, I heard Tom call to Miss Craig, from quite the end of the gallery:—

"Come here, Dora, for a moment, and pay your dutiful

respects to our mutual ancestress, the Lady Betty Colquhoun. I don't wish to natter you, my dear, but, methinks, I can trace a distinct likeness between you; allowing, of course, for the deterioration of the species."

"Deterioration yourself, sir," she laughingly replied. "I am sure it is much more marked in the male than in the female line. Is it not, Mrs. Fergusson?"

Roused from my reverie, I joined the group, and found them looking at the full length portrait of a young lady dressed in the fashion of the sixteenth century. That the portrait was a speaking likeness of Miss Craig there could not be two opinions; but what immediately struck me was, that the Lady Betty Colquhoun wore around her neck the identical jewel which Miss Craig was then wearing, and which I had also seen on the neck of the lady of my vision. Although I instantly spotted it I might have easily overlooked it, as it was partially hidden beneath a lace collar the lady was wearing, but the jewel had made such an impression on my mind that I recognised it in a moment, nor could I refrain from calling the fact to the attention of the others; upon which Miss Craig said:—

"Why, what sharp eyes you must have! I have gazed at Lady Betty hundreds of times, and yet never noticed it before. Evidently this is the identical jewel, for it is an heirloom in the family."

"Indeed!" I said, "and is there any legend connected with it?"

"Oh, dear, yes!" she replied. "It is supposed that no harm can ever come to the owner so long as she is wearing it, and so, as I am very superstitious, I always keep it round my neck, even when I go to bed."

I then asked whether there were any particular history connected with Lady Betty, but both Tom and Miss Craig declared that, so far as they knew, there was not, but that, if there were, Mrs. Morgan would be sure to know it, as she was far better up in the traditions of the family than either of them; Miss Craig adding:—

"You had better be careful to get the right side of Mrs. Morgan, if you want her to divulge state secrets, as she is a difficult woman to humour, and not always willing to impart the information she undoubtedly possesses."

Shortly after, we separated to pursue the ordinary avocations affected by people staying in a country house; but I, still thinking of Miss Craig, Lady Betty Colquhoun, and the antique jewel, sought out Mrs. Morgan, and, after a little judicious flattery and Machiavelian diplomacy, for which I have ever been noted, turned our conversation to the picture gallery.

Long were the anecdotes she told me of pretty well every member of the family except the one I wished to hear about, till at last I had to ask her the direct question, whether there were any story or legend connected with the Lady Betty Colquhoun.

At first she was very reticent and tried to put me off, but when she found I pertinaciously returned to the subject, she admitted that her mother had once told her a strange tale with regard to that lady, but whether there were any truth in it or not she could not say. After a little more diplomatic handling, I at length got the story out of her, which, divested of her circumlocutions and embellishments, was shortly this:—

In the latter part of the sixteenth century the then Lord of Inverstrathy—one Ronald Farquharson—married the Lady Betty Colquhoun, although it was whispered she had already given her affections to the Laird of Carosphairn. Be that as it may, Ronald Farquharson seems to have had a highly jealous, passionate disposition, and they had been married but a few months, when it became a matter of common notoriety that scarcely a day passed without some desperate quarrel between them. Matters, however, were kept within the bounds of respectability for three years, during which time the Laird of Carosphairn seems to have been abroad; but upon his return, the relations between the Lord and Lady of Inverstrathy became still more strained. Although, some nine or ten months afterwards, a son and heir was born (whom their friends hoped might prove a bond between them, and be the means of a reconciliation), matters grew worse instead of better, and Ronald Farquharson was, more than once, overheard making the most disgraceful insinuations to the unfortunate Lady Betty.

At that time the castle was considerably smaller in extent than at present, the whole of the east wing, and part of the west, having been added in the early part of the seventeenth century, and Ronald and Lady Farquharson, it seems, occupied the identical room I was sleeping in.

One night, after the servants had gone to bed, the nurse, who was sitting up with the child on account of some infantine complaint, overheard her master and mistress having a more than usually serious altercation, and had just made up her mind to inquire what was the matter, when the noise quieted down, and she heard their voices no more. Next morning, however, her mistress had disappeared, and it was rumoured that, driven desperate by her husband's brutality, she had fled in the night to the Laird of Carosphairn, with whom she had eloped; at any rate, neither she nor the laird were ever heard of afterwards, and it was supposed that, endeavouring to cross to the Orkneys in a fishing smack, they had been wrecked during a terrible gale that was raging all that night.

I asked her whether the gallery contained any portrait

of Ronald Farquharson as well as Lady Betty, but she informed me that, though undoubtedly there had been one, as the records proved, it had, unfortunately, perished, along with several others, during a fire which destroyed a large portion of the castle in 1639, soon after which the whole place had been renovated and enlarged by Angus Farquharson, the grandson of Ronald; the central portion, in which were the old state rooms, only being left untouched.

This was all I could get out of Mrs. Morgan, except that, when I cross-questioned her on the subject of the castle being haunted, she reluctantly admitted to having heard some idle tale of a lady, in a white evening costume, being seen about the place at midnight, but had never seen anything of the apparition herself.

Armed with this further information, I sought out Farquharson, and we, there and then, made a thorough examination of my room, but though we found an undoubted stain of something or other on the floor, under the hearth-rug, that was all the success we had, and Farquharson was more than ever convinced that my vision was nothing but a bad nightmare.

"I'll tell you what it is, old chap," he said. "If you like, I'll come and sit up with you here to-night, and see if this precious vision of yours recurs."

"Done with you," I cried, and we then joined the ladies in the hall for afternoon tea. That night, after the ladies had retired to their rooms and we had played a few games of pool, Farquharson reminded us we were to make an early start the next morning to shoot over the outlying moors, and we all at once turned in, Farquharson going with me to my room, as agreed; then, producing a couple of packs of cards, he said:—

"Look here, my boy, as this is likely to prove a long job—for I don't suppose you'll be satisfied till two or three o'clock, unless anything happens in the meantime, which I'm quite sure won't be the case—we had better have a little *écarté*; so fill up your glass" (he had taken care to send the necessary materials to my room), "and cut for deal."

"All right," I replied. "A sovereign a game, as usual, I suppose?" and we at once commenced.

Now, both Farquharson and I, without being gamblers, were keen card-players, this being by no means the first time we had sat down to a bout of *écarté*. We had played a dozen games or so, the luck so far proving fairly even, and had become so absorbed in our occupation that the real reason for our sitting up together had quite vanished from our minds, when, in the midst of one of the most exciting hands of the evening (the score was three all, I'd turned up the nine of clubs and Farquharson was playing 'on authority,' little knowing that I held king, knave, eight of trumps, as well as the king and another spade), just as I was about to say "I hold the king," preparatory to marking it and then trump the king of hearts, which he had already led, the light in the room suddenly increased to quite three times its previous brilliancy!

We both started round just in time to see the tapestry once again pushed aside, and the beautiful girl, so like Miss Craig, yet also so like the Lady Betty, rush forward, with terrified face, and fall on her knees on the hearth-rug. Once more the antique jewel slipped from off her neck to the floor; once more the evil-looking scoundrel followed her into the room; once more he raised the naked dagger in his hand; and then, for the third time, I witnessed that horrible murder, without being able to stir a step to interfere. In a quarter of a minute or less it was all over, and the light had resumed its normal brilliancy; then Tom, shaking off his apathy, rushed forward to where the deed had been committed, calling to me to bring the lamp.

He hastily turned up the rug, exposing the same stain we had seen in the afternoon; but whether it was only our imagination or not I cannot say—it certainly appeared to us to be much fresher and redder than before.

"Well! What do you say to my vision now?" I asked. "Do you still persist in maintaining it was only a dream?"

"Don't be an ass," Tom replied. "Of course I believe in it. How can I doubt the evidence of my own senses? I am, however, determined to trace the mystery to its source. Depend upon it, the Lady Betty never eloped at all, and that the whole story was a foul slander, concocted by her brute of a husband, who had murdered her in a fit of passion. Come, let us once more examine the panelling behind the tapestry."

This we did, but for a long time without any success, when, in stooping to hold the lamp in a more favourable position for Tom to examine the skirting, I placed my left hand against one of the stiles of the wainscoting to steady myself; and, as I leant against it, I fancied I felt a slight current of air issuing between the stile and panel. I called Tom's attention to it, and he struck a match and held it to the spot, when there could be no doubt there was a distinct draught of air blowing the flame away from the woodwork.

This was enough for Tom. "Wait here," he said, "till I get a few tools." And off he went, returning a few minutes later with a centre-bit, crowbar, a couple of chisels, and a screw-driver. This last he managed to insinuate into the small crack we had discovered, and endeavoured to force away the panel from the upright. At first he could make no impression on it, but after he had worked it up and down a bit, he must have accidentally touched a spring, for the whole panel suddenly swung away from him, nearly precipitating him head long through the opening it had disclosed. We found then that the panel had formed a secret door, opening directly on a flight of steep, stone steps, built in the thickness of the wall, up which a cold, damp air was blowing, drawn up, no doubt, by the heat of my room.

Excited by the success of our efforts, we at once determined to push our investigations further, so, snatching up the crowbar, Tom stooped through the doorway and began to cautiously descend the steps, while I followed after, lighting the way with the lamp. After descending thirty-three steps we reached the bottom, and found a passage stretching away in front of us. We followed this for 50ft. or 60ft., and then, to our disappointment, came to a dead stop; for either the passage itself had come to its natural ending, or else it had been purposely walled up.

After a careful examination, we came to the conclusion the latter was the case, for although it had been built to look as much as possible like the side walls, we found there were no through stones in either angle, both being straight joints; and, upon holding the lamp well up, we could see that in one place there was a space of a couple of inches or so between the top stone and the ceiling.

Tom hastily ran back with the lamp, leaving me in the dark, a situation I did not altogether relish. However, he soon returned with a chair, mounting which, he worked away with his crowbar until he dislodged a large stone, which fell with a startling thud on the floor. After the first few stones were removed the rest was easy, and, between us, we had soon made an opening sufficiently large to scramble through, when we found ourselves in a small chamber about 8ft. square, evidently an old dungeon.

At first we thought it was empty, but upon Tom poking his crowbar into a heap of rubbish which lay in one of the corners, a portion of it fell away, exposing, to our horror, the hand and part of the fore-arm of a skeleton. We quickly set to work to remove the rubbish heap, and soon lay bare the entire skeleton, which, from its size, we concluded was that of a woman, and close to it, on the floor, we further discovered the hilt and a portion of the blade of what was evidently a dagger, the rest of the blade having been eaten away by rust. Solemnly we looked at one another, and then, without a word, made the best of our way back to my bedroom.

After we were once more safely in my room and had each mixed a stiff glass of whisky-and-water, Tom said:—

"You see, it is just as I thought. I haven't a doubt in my mind but that my worthy ancestor, Ronald Farquharson, murdered his unfortunate wife, whose skeleton we have just discovered; that he hid her in yonder dungeon, and himself walled up the passage to prevent his crime from being found out; and then set abroad the shameful story of her having eloped with the Laird of Carosphairn, to account for her absence. It is a terrible business; but, thank goodness, it can't have anything to do with poor Dora."

"And yet," I said, "the lady of the vision was undoubtedly like Miss Craig."

"Not more like her than the Lady Betty," he quickly returned."

"Perhaps not. Did you notice the face of the villain who murdered her?"

"No; from the position in which I was sitting, I could not see his face at all, but only his back; I am, however, perfectly convinced it must have been Ronald Farquharson. Don't you agree with me?"

"No, I certainly do not!"

"Good heavens! Why?"

"For a very obvious reason. Both the girl who was murdered and the ruffian who butchered her *were in modern evening costume!*"

"Great Scot!" exclaimed Tom, "so they were! How do you interpret that?"

"I cannot say. I don't know what to think. The whole thing is perfectly inexplicable to me."

"But if the vision were not that of Ronald Farquharson murdering the Lady Betty, what was it?"

"Ah, indeed, what was it?"

"Besides, too: how can you account for our finding the secret stairway opening from exactly the spot from whence they came? And, still more, the significant fact of our discovery of the skeleton and dagger in the walled-up dungeon?"

"I tell you I can account for nothing."

"Well! What's to be done?"

"Nothing, I suppose. I don't see what good we can do by spreading the tale abroad. I think it is a clear case where 'masterly inactivity' should be the order of the day. Let us keep the secret to ourselves, at all events for the present, and watch what happens."

We discussed it some time longer in all its bearings, and then, Tom agreeing with me, we fastened up the secret door and separated.

Next day Miss Craig left, and though Tom again sat up with me that night, nothing happened to disturb our *écarté*, and the day following I had myself to leave, having received an important telegram calling me back to London.

Nearly a whole year passed without anything occurring to remind me of my strange experience at Inverstrathy Castle. I had seen Tom frequently in the interval, and he had told me that, though he had more than once slept in the room I had occupied there, he had never again seen the vision. Again the 12th of August was approaching, when I was to join his party as before, when, one day, he called upon me to explain that, scarlet fever having unfortunately broken out in Inverstrathy Castle, he was compelled to put everyone off. That afternoon, I was walking down Regent Street, thinking how I could best re-arrange my plans, when, as I was crossing the Circus towards the Criterion, a gentleman overtook and passed me, and, as he did so, his walking-stick accidentally knocked against my arm. He turned round, politely apologized, and then hurried down Waterloo Place; but, slight as the glimpse was which I got of his face, I immediately recognised him as the villain of my vision.

At first I was so staggered I stood stock still, and was nearly run over by a passing cab; then, recovering my senses, I hastened after him, keeping him in sight till he turned up Pall Mall and went into the Megatherium Club, of which I am also a member. Entering after him, I saw him go into the smoking room, and then I inquired of the hall-porter who he was. He informed me he was Sir Philip Clipstone, and that he had only recently returned from India. I immediately jumped into a hansom and drove to Tom's town house at Albert Gate, and, directly we were alone, I said:—

"Tom, I've just seen the villain of our vision!"

"Nonsense! I thought that he had died a natural death."

"So I hoped, but this afternoon I undoubtedly met the identical man we saw murdering Miss Craig at Inverstrathy Castle."

"I wish you wouldn't persist in saying it was Dora. I'm more than ever convinced that it was a vision of Ronald Farquharson murdering the Lady Betty, and not Miss Craig at all."

"Possibly—though I don't think so myself. Anyhow, I saw the murderer, no matter who his victim was."

"Are you sure you weren't mistaken, or misled by some strong resemblance?"

"No; I tell you he was the very man. I could not possibly be mistaken. Remember, I saw the scoundrel three times, and his villainous face left far too great an impression on my memory ever to be effaced; and I tell you I saw him to-day while I was crossing Piccadilly Circus, and recognised him in a moment, although his face was naturally without that diabolical expression I saw on it at Inverstrathy Castle."

"What did you do?"

"Followed him, of course, and tracked him to the Megatherium Club, where I ascertained who he is."

"And who is he?"

"Sir Philip Clipstone."

"Good God! You don't say so?" said Tom, starting to his feet. "Why, although Dora never even heard of him till about two months ago, I received a letter from her barely an hour since, announcing their engagement! What's to be done?"

"What's to be done? Aye, there's the rub! Ought we, or ought we not, to inform Miss Craig, or Sir Philip, or both, of what we saw at Inverstrathy Castle?"

Long we argued the point; one of us, no matter which, thinking we certainly ought; the other equally convinced that we ought not. Neither could persuade the other to adopt his view of the case. Each was perfectly certain he only was right, and words grew high between us, even threatening to jeopardize the warm friendship that has existed since our school-days.

At last a happy thought struck Tom, that, changing of course the names of the parties concerned, and the *locale* of the tragedy, we should lay the simple facts of the case before the public, inviting expressions of opinion on this knotty point, from any who feel competent to give one.

I eagerly agreed to this suggestion, and I can therefore only request, gentle reader, that, after having carefully weighed the pros and cons, you will communicate your valuable opinion to the editor. But do not delay too long, for I hear Sir Philip, as is only natural, is pressing Miss Craig to name the happy (?) day. Should she or should she not, before doing so, be informed of the possible consequences of such an act? And if they do marry, will their conjugal life end in the horrible tragedy both Tom Farquharson and I saw enacted in my bedroom at Inverstrathy Castle?

THE VISION OF INVERSTRATHY CASTLE - SEQUEL
by
F. STARTIN PILLEAU

The extraordinary number of letters sent to the Editor, in response to the invitation given at the end of my story entitled 'The Vision of Inverstrathy Castle,' which appeared in the Christmas Number of THE STRAND MAGAZINE for 1894, must be my apology for intruding myself once more before the readers of that world-renowned periodical. Those who read that story will remember that my old friend, Tom Farquharson, and I were diametrically opposed as to the expediency of informing either, or both, of two young people (who, at that time, were engaged to be married) of a vision we had seen concerning them; and that we determined, after much discussion, to lay the facts of the case before the public, inviting such as felt competent to do so to give us their advice upon the matter.

I now take this opportunity of tendering my thanks to those who so promptly responded to my appeal, and who will, I think, take an interest in hearing the *dénouement* of the story. But, for the information of those who did not read the first story, at the Editor's request, I will begin with a brief summary of what took place.

I, while a guest at Inverstrathy Castle, occupied a haunted room. In the night the room was suddenly lit up;

a young girl, terror-stricken, rushed into the room, closely followed by a man, who killed her. The vision was repeated the following night. I was much surprised to find staying in the house a young lady named Miss Craig, who was exactly like the girl of my vision, and who also bore the same strong resemblance to a portrait of a Lady Betty Colquhoun, an ancestor of Tom Farquharson. There was a story attached to the place that, about the end of the sixteenth century, one Ronald Farquharson married a Lady Betty Colquhoun; but after three years of torture from her husband, the lady was said to have eloped with an old lover. I explained the whole matter to my host, who watched with me that night, when the vision again appeared. We pulled some of the wainscoting away and discovered a secret passage, at the end of which, in a dungeon, was a skeleton of a woman. Farquharson believed that his ancestor must have murdered his wife, hidden the body himself, and set going the story of the elopement. We were greatly perplexed for a solution to the mystery, as both the actors in the visionary tragedy were in modern evening costume. A year later, I met the villain of my vision in London. I told Farquharson of this, who informed me that Sir Philip Clipstone, the villain, and Miss Craig, the victim in the tragedy, were engaged to be married. We were very much troubled as to whether it was our duty to inform the engaged couple of what had taken place, or not; and this was the point which we determined to lay before the public.

The story, however, did not appear in print until it was too late for me to profit by the advice so freely offered by my readers. In the meantime, many important events happened, which it is now my purpose to relate. Firstly, poor Farquharson, having returned too soon to Inverstrathy Castle, caught the fever and died (after but ten days' illness), thus leaving to me the sole responsibility of either telling Sir Philip Clipstone and Dora Craig what we had seen, or keeping silence and letting events take their own course.

Secondly, almost immediately after poor Tom's death, both Duncan Farquharson and his younger brother Charles, first cousins of Tom's (the former of whom had succeeded to the Inverstrathy estates), were drowned while coming hack from Madeira (where they had been yachting) to take possession of the property.

Thirdly, Sir Philip Clipstone and Dora Craig, in happy ignorance of what might be in store for them, and not knowing the importance of delay, or the excellent advice about to be tendered them by the public, calmly took the matter into their own hands and were quietly married on the 2nd of October, just about the time of the wreck of the Albatross, poor Duncan Farquharson's yacht.

Fourthly, in consequence of this last tragedy (the wreck, not the marriage) Sir Philip succeeded to Inverstrathy Castle and property.

It was one of the society papers which informed me, much to my surprise, of this last event; for I had not, until then, any idea Sir Philip was related to poor Tom. It seems, however, he was a second cousin, and took the name of Clipstone in consequence of inheriting an estate, in the West of England, provided he added the testator's name to his own, so that his full style and title was Sir Philip Farquharson Clipstone, Bart., and is, now that he has succeeded to lnverstrathy, Sir Philip Clipstone Farquharson, Bart.

It was with a feeling little short of dismay that I heard of this rapid development of Dora's destiny, and every day I half expected to hear of some terrible *dénouement*, but this was not the case; on the contrary, for the first few months the young couple seemed to be even more devotedly attached to each other then young married folk usually are. And whenever I met them in society, which was pretty often, even my suspicious glances could not detect the slightest appearance of duplicity in the lover-like behaviour of Sir Philip to his charming bride.

At first, it was only at the houses of mutual friends that I had an opportunity of observing them, for, although Lady Farquharson immediately recognised me on the first occasion of our meeting after her marriage, and at once introduced me to her husband, the acquaintance, for a time, went no further. Indeed, it was not till after the Oxford and Cambridge Boat-race that it rapidly ripened into a warm friendship. It happened, on that occasion, to be one of those unusually beautiful spring days which, now and again, visit our desolate shores, giving promise of better things to come, a promise, alas! but rarely fulfilled, and we were a merry party on Lord Coverdale's steam launch.

It was the first time I had seen Lady Farquharson without her husband, and I gathered, from what she was telling Lady Coverdale, that Sir Philip had been summoned away, on urgent business, just as they were leaving home.

No need to describe the event of the day, which, in fact, proved to be a mere procession; suffice it to say that, after the boats had passed, and the usual number of steamers and other craft were pressing in their wake, a clumsily-steered launch bumped against our quarter. The shock was not great, but more than sufficient to cause Lady Farquharson, who was standing near me, to lose her balance and fall into the water. Quick as thought, I jumped in after her, and easily managed to support her till a friendly boat took us on board.

It was a simple act, and one which anyone else would have done in the same circumstances, though, from the exaggerated thanks which Sir Philip showered upon me when I took Lady Farquharson home, you would have thought I had done something unusually heroic.

Fortunately, neither of us took the slightest harm from our immersion, for, as I have said, it was a glorious, sunshiny day. Had it been otherwise, it might have proved a more serious matter, at all events for Lady Farquharson, who, at that time, was in somewhat delicate health.

From that time my friendship with the Farquharsons rapidly progressed, and scarcely a day passed without my spending an hour or two in their society. Occupying, as I soon did, the post of confidential friend to the family, I had every opportunity for observing the relations between husband and wife. At first, I had not the slightest doubt as to the genuineness of Sir Philip's adoration of Lady Farquharson, and it was not till some time afterwards that I first began to suspect that there might be a slight 'rift within the lute.'

It is difficult to explain why my suspicions were aroused at all, so impalpable were the symptoms; but I had not lost any of the impressions of that horrible vision at Inverstrathy Castle, and my perceptions were in an abnormal condition of tension, so that I seemed to intuitively understand, rather than actually observe, that all was not quite right between them. They were both still delighted to see me whenever I put in an appearance, but on more than one occasion I could not help feeling that they looked upon my advent as a relief; that my appearance, in fact, had probably been the means of putting to an end a somewhat heated argument between them. Two or three times, too, I felt quite convinced that Sir Philip was on the point of taking me into his confidence. but some slight interruption on each occasion, unfortunately, prevented his doing so.

At length, in June, they left London for Scotland,

having pressed me to join them in August for the shooting, and, though my heart bounded when the invitation was given (for what might I not witness in that gloomy old castle?), I determined nothing should prevent my going, and endeavouring, if possible, to avert the awful tragedy I felt convinced would otherwise take place.

In the early part of July I received a hurried letter from Sir Philip announcing, with much pride, the birth of a son and heir, and stating that, though the youngster had made his appearance somewhat sooner than was expected, both mother and child were doing well.

So far, so good. I was delighted at the news, and could only hope the boy would be a tie between his parents. Another week had barely passed, when I got a second letter from Sir Philip saying that Lady Farquharson was not going on quite so satisfactorily, but that he fully hoped and believed she would be all right again long before the 11th of August, when I was expected. "In fact," he added, "I wish it were possible for you to come here sooner, for there is a matter, about which I do not like to write, but which I should much like to talk over with you. However, I fear, from what you said, that that is not possible, but pray do not delay your visit a day longer than you can help, and please do not refer, in any way, to what I have said, when next you write."

These words set me thinking, and my thoughts were not pleasant. What was it he wished to discuss with me, but did not like to put into writing? And why was not Lady Farquharson to know anything about it?

Twice more I heard from Sir Philip, and, though each time his accounts of Lady Farquharson's health were more than satisfactory, there was a depression about the letters which seemed to me very ominous.

At last the 11th of August arrived, and I once again

found myself in Sutherlandshire; but, as I had been visiting friends only some twenty miles off, I managed to reach Inverstrathy Castle in time for afternoon tea.

Both Sir Philip and Lady Farquharson gave me the heartiest of welcomes, but I was at once struck and grieved to see a marked and most distressing restraint in their behaviour. Though their bearing towards each other was precisely what one would expect, it wanted but a very superficial observer to detect the lines of worry and care, which were only too apparent, on the countenance of each.

I had no opportunity of getting a word alone with Sir Philip, though I could see he was most anxious to do so, and tea was barely over when, in all the glory of infant pomp and state, the future 'Sir Philip' was ushered into our presence.

It would be difficult to say which of the two, Sir Philip or Lady Farquharson, was the more idiotically devoted to the child, and it did my bachelor heart good to see the extraordinary change his presence made in both my host and hostess. All signs of worry or care seemed to be at once wiped out from their faces, and they out-vied each other in their protestations of love and devotion. Nay, more (somewhat, I confess, to my surprise), neither seemed in the least jealous of the other, but alternately hugged and kissed the little chap, as they called each other's attention to his marvellous intelligence—which, by-the-bye, I could not myself detect—in a manner which only young married people, with their first six-weeks-old infant, could possibly appreciate. When, however, the 'phenomenon' was once more claimed by his nurse, I was concerned to see the same worried, anxious look gradually overcast their faces. Lady Farquharson, however, seemed to do her best to shake the depressing influence off, and laughed and chatted in a manner that would have been most cheering, had it not been so obviously forced. At length she rose, and suggested I might, perhaps, like to go to my room, adding, with a smile: "I think you already know your way there, as I understand from Mrs. Morgan, who is still here, that it is the same one you occupied when staying here with poor Tom."

I confess to feeling considerably appalled at the idea of again occupying that haunted chamber; but, not seeing how I could get out of it without making a fuss, I determined to make the best of it.

The moment Lady Farquharson left, Sir Philip eagerly asked me to accompany him to his study; but, as we were going there, one of the footmen informed him that the steward wished to see him immediately about some matter of importance. He, therefore (very reluctantly I could see), said we must defer our chat till after dinner, and I at once went to my room to dress.

How well I knew it! There was the self-same antique four-poster, the same Persian hearth-rug in front of the fireplace, under which lay the blood-stain, or what Tom and I believed was a blood-stain; and the same rare old tapestry hanging round the gloomy walls. Of course I went at once to the farther corner to see if the secret door had been tampered with. I had no difficulty in finding it, for it opened of its own volition when I drew away the tapestry in front of it. Probably Tom had broken the spring when he forced it open on that memorable occasion, and had not been able, or had not troubled, to repair it, trusting to the heavy tapestry to conceal it.

I could not resist peering through the opening and down the stone steps, but refrained from descending them, turning back into the room with a shudder, as I recalled to mind the walled-up dungeon below, and its hidden skeleton.

My first impulse was to move a heavy oak press, which stood close by, in front of the secret opening; but, finding it heavier than I calculated, I desisted. Thank God I did so, and that I took no further means to fasten up the door!

It was a dreary, though sumptuous, repast that we sat down to, and I could see that both my host and hostess were struggling painfully to appear at their ease. I did my best to keep the conversation alive, but failed dismally, except when I spoke of the 'phenomenon'; then, indeed, both my entertainers opened their lips, and I had no cause to complain of their silence. But one cannot, or at least a bachelor cannot, converse for ever on infantine matters, and the conversation soon lapsed.

At length the weary dinner came to an end, and Lady Farquharson left the room, presumably for the nursery. We filled up our glasses, and I prepared to listen to what I knew Sir Philip was so anxious to tell me, when, before he had barely commenced, Lady Farquharson hurriedly came in and said, with tears in her eyes:—

"Oh, Philip! I'm sure there's something dreadful the matter with baby!"

"Good God! you don't say so?" said Sir Philip, starting up and turning ashy pale. "Excuse me for a moment, there's a good fellow, while I go and see," and both the fond parents hurried from the room, leaving me, once more, in ignorance as to what it was Sir Philip was so anxious to impart to me.

No doubt I am a cold-blooded, heartless bachelor, but I could not refrain from chuckling at the absurdity of Sir Philip's and Lady Farquharson's behaviour. The little beggar had been lively enough a couple of hours before, and it seemed to me highly improbable there could be anything serious the matter with him. It was half an hour before Sir Philip returned, and he then informed me he had already sent off an express for Dr. McDonald, who lived some five miles off. He was in a most terrible state of anxiety, and walked up and down the room in a nervous, agitated manner, which was most distressing to witness. Thinking to distract his attention, I suggested it was a good opportunity for him to tell me what he was so anxious I should hear, but he answered:—

"Not now; I couldn't do it. I'm absolutely distracted with anxiety. My dear fellow, you don't know what an awful life Dora and I have led the last three months, and now, just when little Phil seemed sent on purpose to comfort us, for aught I know, he may be dying."

"But what does the nurse say?" I inquired. "She seems a sensible sort of woman, and, I suppose, has had experience in these matters."

"She's an old fool," he irritably replied, "and the sooner she goes the better."

"But what does she say?" I persisted.

"Why, she says there's nothing at all the matter! As though his mother and I couldn't see for ourselves that he's terribly ill."

"What are his symptoms?"

"Oh, I don't know anything about his symptoms, but, anyhow, he's pretty bad; and, if anything were to happen to him, God knows how it will all end!"

Fortunately, Dr. McDonald soon arrived, and Sir Philip at once conducted him upstairs. It turned out, as I fully expected, the wildest of scares, the doctor assuring me that there was absolutely nothing whatever the matter with the kid, except the very slightest amount of indigestion. It was ludicrous beyond description, yet pathetic, too, to st.: poor Sir Philip's face brighten, as, after the severest cross-examination of the unfortunate doctor, he was forced to believe the child was not *in extremis*.

We spent a much pleasanter evening than I at all anticipated in the smoking-room (for Lady Farquharson only appeared to say good-night, and returned at once to her beloved offspring's cot), and I found Dr. McDonald, whom Sir Philip had insisted on putting up for the night, a most amusing companion. Long and racy were the yarns we regaled each other with, Sir Philip spending his time mostly in going backwards and forwards to the nursery, and it was pretty late before we turned in. When at last we did so, I had not the slightest intention of going to bed, as I expected little rest in that haunted room, but determined to sit up all night and see what would happen, when, upon casually looking out of the window, I was considerably surprised to see Lady Farquharson hurrying across the lawn. Astonished that she should be out so late, I watched to see what would follow, when, to my still further astonishment, she returned clinging to Sir Philip's arm, apparently endeavouring to persuade him to return to the house with her. Seemingly he would not do so, and although they were too far off for me to hear their conversation, I could distinctly recognise Sir Philip's voice raised in angry altercation.

What was the meaning of it all? Was he intoxicated? Was that the horrible mystery which darkened both their lives and caused that anxious look of worry I had seen on both their faces? Yet, no, this could scarcely be the case, for Sir Philip clearly wished to take me into his confidence, and I knew too much of human nature to suppose he would confess his domestic happiness had been wrecked by his own vice.

Puzzled as to what could possibly be the solution of the mystery, I turned from the window and sat down by the fire. After a time I must have fallen asleep, but my rest in that fateful room was ever destined to be brief, and I could not have slept more than a couple of hours at most, when again I wakened up with a horrible feeling of terror.

This time no vivid, unnatural light was the cause of my awakening, but the most awful, ear-piercing shriek, and, as I started up, once again I saw the tapestry at the farther end of the room drawn aside; once again the lady of my vision, so like Lady Farquharson, rushed into the room and fell upon her knees on the hearth-rug; once again the antique jewel slipped from off her neck to the floor; and, once again, that bloodthirsty villain, so terribly like Sir Philip, raised his dagger to plunge it into her heart.

With one bound I sprang at his throat, and this time the vision vanished not from my eyes. This time my hand clasped human flesh, instead of empty air, and I desperately strove to wrest the dagger from his murderous hand. Fierce was the struggle between us; frantically I endeavoured to choke back his breath with my right hand as I grasped his wrist, as firmly as I could, with my left. Backwards and forwards we swayed in deadly silence, till at length, tripping over the prostrate form of Lady Farquharson, we both fell heavily to the ground, he, alas, uppermost! I knew now it could only be a question of a few moments, for in falling I had lost my hold on his wrist; but I desperately clung to him with both hands and knees, twisting and turning to avoid the fatal thrust. At length the decisive moment came, when, kneeling on my chest, the infuriated ruffian raised the dagger to plunge it into my breast. I even saw the light from the fire flash upon the blade as he waved it round his head, and then, just as it was descending, to my unspeakable relief and amazement, the door burst open and Sir Philip himself, followed by Dr. McDonald, rushed into the room, and, at the very last moment, freed me from my antagonist.

So soon as I had sufficiently recovered, Sir Philip

gave me an explanation of the terrible mystery, which was shortly as follows:—

It appears that Sir Philip had a twin brother, who, delicate from his birth, had spent the greater part of his life travelling. While crossing the Libyan Desert, in the early spring of that year, he had received a severe sunstroke, which, in consequence of his not being able for some time to get proper treatment, and acting upon an already feeble constitution, had left his mind permanently affected, so that, when he at last reached England, he was quite incapable of taking care of himself. It seems it was his unexpected arrival which had prevented Sir Philip accompanying Lady Farquharson to the Oxford and Cambridge Boat-race.

At first the experts hoped that, with proper attention and absolute quiet, he might, to a greater or less extent, recover; and it was in accordance with that advice that Sir Philip had taken him to Inverstrathy.

It was naturally a great blow to Sir Philip, who was devoted to his brother, and to Lady Farquharson, and they sedulously kept the matter a profound secret, though Sir Philip suggested that I, being such an intimate friend, should be told. Lady Farquharson, however, at first, was strongly against it, and, in deference to her wishes, he abstained from doing so. The change from London to Inverstrathy, so far from proving beneficial, seems to have had an entirely opposite effect upon the invalid, and it became necessary to isolate him entirely from the rest of the household. Sir Philip had, therefore, set apart for his use a suite of apartments on the ground floor (marked X on accompanying plan of Inverstrathy Castle), which were in communication with the identical dungeon-like chamber Tom Farquharson and I had broken into, and which Tom seems to have denuded of its uncanny contents, for I heard nothing of any skeleton having been found there. This chamber is at the bottom of the Watch, or Eagle Tower, at the north-east angle of the castle, and Sir Philip caused a doorway to be made in the outer wall, so that the invalid could get exercise in the old bowling-green, which is quite secluded from the rest of the grounds.

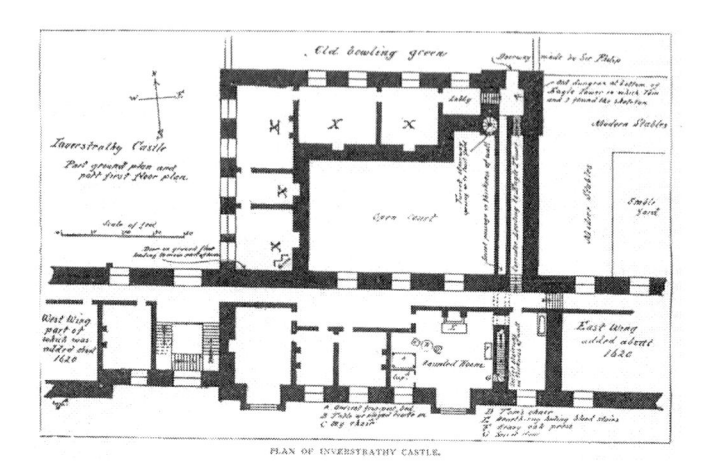

PLAN OF INVERSTRATHY CASTLE.

Although these precautions were deemed advisable by Sir Philip and Dr. McDonald (who was in close attendance on the invalid), it was not for a moment supposed that there was any fear of a homicidal tendency developing on the part of the unfortunate patient, though, on the evening of little Phil's birth, Lady Farquharson had been considerably alarmed by his flourishing a knife in her face. He had, however, immediately quieted down upon Sir Philip's interference, though ever since he seems to have taken a violent antipathy to his sister-in-law, who, in consequence, rarely ventured into his society.

In consequence of the scare of little Phil's supposed illness, the usual surveillance over the patient had been somewhat relaxed, and Lady Farquharson, happening to look out of the nursery window, noticed him walking about the garden. Not wishing to alarm her husband, she went out and coaxed him back to the house, and some hours later, fearing he might have again effected his escape, she went to his rooms to see if all were right. Shading the lamp she carried so as not to disturb him, should he be asleep, she passed softly through the door leading to his apartments, and was much alarmed at not finding him in any of his rooms. She at once turned back to tell Sir Philip, when, as she reached the last room, which communicated with the rest of the house, to her horror he sprang out from behind a screen, where he had been hiding, with a naked dagger in his hand, and intercepted her escape.

Scarcely knowing what she did, Lady Farquharson dashed back through the other rooms, pulling the doors to behind her, and thus gaining a few yards' start from her infuriated pursuer, whom she heard close behind, upsetting various pieces of furniture in his desperate eagerness to overtake her. At last she reached the old dungeon, but, to her dismay, found the door, leading to the old bowling-green, locked. Not knowing what to do, in her despair she threw herself against the only other door she saw, and which she believed led to the turret staircase. Fortunately it was not very firmly secured and gave way, and she at once fled along the secret passage which Tom and I had previously discovered.

By this time the madman was fast overtaking her, and, by the time she had mounted the thirty-three steps, was but a yard or two behind her. Had the secret door leading into my room been fastened, or had I persevered in dragging the heavy oak press in front of the opening, nothing on earth could have saved the poor woman from her doom; as it was, as the reader already knows, I was enabled to rescue her, though I very nearly lost my own life in doing so. Luckily Sir Philip, who had been paying another anxious visit to the nursery, and had ruthlessly called up Dr. McDonald, on account of some fancied change for the worse in the child's condition, heard the scuffle in my room, and they both came to see what was the matter, in the very nick of time to free me from my insane antagonist. Thus, happily, ended my terrible experiences of the haunted chamber at Inverstrathy Castle, but whether the horrible vision which Tom and I saw was the premonition of coming events, I leave others to determine; suffice it to say that, although I have spent many a night since at Inverstrathy, and have always, at my own request, occupied the haunted room, my rest has never again been disturbed; nor should I say, judging from my own personal observation, are the relations between Sir Philip and Lady Farquharson ever likely to be other than that of a most devoted couple. I may add that Sir Philip's unfortunate brother was at once removed to a private asylum; but I fear, from what I hear, there is small chance of his recovery.

THE FOLLOWER
by
FREDERICK CARRUTHERS CORNELL

Frederick Carruthers Cornell OBE (1867–1921) was first and foremost a soldier, whose military career spanned the Boer War and the First World War and earned him the Order of the British Empire. He was also a geologist, prospector and, of course, author.

Cornell studied music and languages before moving to South Africa in 1902 and serving in the South African Native Labour Corps. He also served as an editor of The Cape Register.

His body of work included The Glamour of Prospecting: Wanderings of a South African Prospector in Search of Copper, Gold, Emeralds, and Diamonds *(1920), and a collection of short stories entitled* A Rip Van Winkle of the Kalahari and Other Tales of South West Africa *(1915).*

This short tale highlights his love of prospecting, but perhaps also his healthy respect for pursuing those aims in an honest fashion. Or else...

* * *

In a desolate and lonely spot near the wide expanse of mud-flats which form the mouth of the Orange River there stands the roofless ruins of an old farmhouse. It's stone walls of huge thickness, and the high stone kraal with huge iron hinges only remaining where once swung a formidable door, speak eloquently of the time where this remote part of Klein Namaqualand, in common with the islands and lower reaches of the Orange River, was infested with bands of Hottentot outlaws and robbers, and when the daring white man who had ventured among them kept his scant flocks and herds under lock and key, and guarded them with a strong hand.

To the south, towards Port Nolloth, stretches seventy-odd miles of desolate, waterless sand-scrub; eastward lie vast expanses of similarly dreary, featureless, undulating scrub, beyond which rise the mysterious mountains of the Richtersveld and hundreds of miles of uninhabited country; westward is the wide lonely ocean; and to the north, across the Orange River, lie the dreaded sand dunes of German South-West Africa.

It was in the direction of the dunes, gleaming silver-white in the clear moonlight, that the eyes of the three white men—prospectors—who had foregathered in this lonely spot were turned as they sat, finishing their evening meal, beside a bright fire that lit up the broken and roofless walls. They had met after months of lonely wanderings. Sidney and Ransford amongst the mountains of the Richterveld, Jason from long arduous expeditions along the Great Fish River and amongst the trackless sands across the river. The talk had been of the dunes; of men lost and dying of thirst a few miles from camp; of terrific storms that lifted the sand in huge masses, and whirled it across the land, overwhelming all it encountered; of whole dunes that were shifted by the wind, leaving gruesome things disclosed in the hollows where once they had stood; of diamonds, danger and death.

"Yes!" said Jason, "there's many a man been lost

since the diamond rush first started; gone away from camp and never turned up again—died of thirst most of them, of course, though I daresay the Bushmen accounted for some. Sometimes the sand has overwhelmed them and buried their bodies forever. Sometimes after a big storm it gives up its dead as the sea does. I've seen some queer things there myself. Once near Easter Cliffs, after a terrific storm had shifted all the dunes, I came across the bodies of a dozen white men, all together and mummified and wonderfully preserved. God knows how they died and how long they'd been there!

"But the weirdest thing that ever happened to me up there was when Carfax disappeared. You remember Carfax? A tall, bony powerful chap he was, quite dour, and with a strong vein of superstition in him. Anyhow, he was a good prospector and a reliable man, and when the rush for the northern fields took place about two years ago he was one of a party of four of us who had been landed with a few kegs of water and bare necessities on the waterless coast opposite Hollams Bird Island. Here we searched in vain for diamonds, the dunes being exceptionally difficult and the wind came up every afternoon converting the whole country into a whirling chaos that it was impossible to see in, or work in—next to impossible to exist in.

"On the third evening, after an exceptionally strong gale had nearly choked, blinded, and overwhelmed us, Carfax did not turn up in camp, and though we searched all the following day we found no trace of him—not a vestige; for one of the worst things about the dunes is that when the wind is blowing the spoor is filled up almost immediately with drifting sand; though peculiarly enough a day or two later the spoor will show again, when the light sand again has been blown out. He had only a small water-bottle with him, the heat was like Hades itself, and we all thought he was dead.

"But on the second night of his absence—I shall never forget it—the wind had gone down completely, and the long stretches of white dunes lay clear and bright in the white moonlight. The other fellows lay asleep on the sand, exhausted, for we had had a terrible day, but I couldn't sleep—I never can in bright moonlight. And after tossing around for some time I got up to get a drink. Poor Carfax was still in my mind, and I stood thinking of him and gazing out in the direction in which he had gone, straining my eyes in the forlorn hope of seeing something moving; but the dead silver-white was unbroken by a single speck.

"I stood thus for some time, and was turning once more towards the others when a faint movement in the vague distance caught my eye. Yes! Something or someone was crossing the ridge of a big dune in my direction! A jackal maybe? No, it was too big for that; the faint form was certainly that of a man—or were there two? I didn't wait longer, but, running back and grabbing a water-bottle, I started off at a run towards who ever it was.

"Moonlight is puzzling sometimes, and I could scarcely make out if there was one figure or two; one seemed to follow the other at a little distance. But as I got nearer I could see it was Carfax—alone. 'Carfax! Carfax!' I called out, 'thank God you're alive—we'd given you up!' He made no answer, but came on slowly and falteringly, turning repeatedly as though to gaze behind. Now I saw that he was in the last stage of exhaustion; his face was drawn and ghastly, and his cracked and swollen lips were moving rapidly in broken, incoherent words; his sufferings had plainly driven him out of his mind. He snatched at the water-bottle and drained it at a draught; then clutching me by the arm, he pointed across the dunes.

" 'There! There! See! He follows me always, since I found the diamonds! Look! Look!'

"As he pointed, his face ghastly with fear, and I too looked back, to see I knew not what. Was he followed? And by whom? I had thought at first there had been one following; but no, there was nothing to be seen. Who could be following him in this desolate place? But still he clutched my arm, and gibbered, and pointed back, and now my eyes were playing tricks again; surely there was a shadow! No, there was nothing there—no human being at any rate. Possibly it had been a jackal. So soothing him as best I could, I helped the poor demented fellow back to camp, he with many a backward look of fear, and I myself with an uncanny feeling that we were being followed.

"Well he was delirious for days; and when the cutter came back to pick us up and take us to another spot father up the coast he was too ill to be moved, so we rigged up a bit of a tent and I was left to nurse him till the boat returned again. It was a weird experience, alone in that desolate spot with a madman for company; for though he quietened down after the others had gone he still had the hallucination of being followed and watched; and especially in the night, when I wanted to sleep, he would seize me by the arm and point through the tent door to the bright moonlight outside, 'There! There!' he would mutter, 'don't you see him? Look at his square-toed boots and brass buckles. See how his ghastly dead eyes glare! Keep him away from me—they are mine!' And in my overstrung, nervous state I could have sworn on one or two occasions that I, too, saw such a figure.

"He gradually got calmer and more himself, and then he told me a strange tale of what had happened to him in the dunes.

"He had been overtaken by a sandstorm many miles from the camp, and had struggled on till absolutely exhausted, not daring to lie down to rest lest the fast whirling sand should overwhelm him; and when late at night the wind had fallen he was hopelessly and utterly lost, and had thrown himself down in a sheltered spot deep hollowed out by the wind between two gigantic dunes, and had at once fallen into a deep sleep of exhaustion.

"Then he had dreamed—a startling and vivid dream that had seemed half reality. He saw three men come down over the big dune to close beside where he lay—rough-looking men in a costume of long ago, with cocked hats, broad breeches, and buckled shoes; and the moonlight shone on the brass hilts of their cutlasses and pistols. They took no notice of him, but, stooping, began to pick up the bright diamonds that Carfax now saw covered the sand before them. Soon the bag was full and a quarrel arose; for he saw two of the men draw their swords and fight fiercely, whilst the other, a tall hawk-faced man, stood by and watched, holding the bag. At length one fell, pierced through by the other's broad blade; and as the victor stood over him the hawk-faced man cut him down from behind, and stood laughing horribly and holding the bag of diamonds before their dying eyes. And as he laughed one of them, with a last effort, drew a pistol from his belt and shot him dead.

"At the report the scene vanished, and Carfax awoke with a start. The dream had been so vivid that the pistol shot seemed still to be ringing in his ears, and he sprang to his feet, scarcely knowing what he should see. The air was clear of dust now, and the moon shone brightly; and by its light he saw a few paces from him a prostrate form partly covered with sand. He bent over it; it was the body of a man, a man dressed in a strange old-world costume—a dead man, dead hundreds of years, and mummified and wonderfully preserved by the sands that had covered him deep through the centuries, until the big gale of yesterday had lifted the heavy pall. Huddled nearby lay two other indistinct forms; and Carfax, his dream still vividly before him, knew well what they were.

"Yes! There, too, lay the leather bag at his feet! And trembling with excitement he knelt and plunged his hands into it, and drew out a handful of big, dully gleaming diamonds. And as he gazed at the treasure his hand was clutched in an icy grasp, and turning in terror he found the horrible eyes of the dead man glaring close into his own.

"With a scream of horror he wrenched away his wrist, and still clutching the stones, fled madly across the dunes, pursued by the fearful figure of the long-dead man. Stumbling, falling, on and on he fled, till the moon paled and the stars faded and the bright sun rose and gave the hunted man a gleam of courage; but his fearful glance behind him still showed the grim figure of him who followed.

"He could not tell what instinct had guided him back to camp; but all through that awful day he had stumbled on through the roasting heat of the dunes, till late at night when I had seen him and gone to meet him as I described.

"All this he told me that night in the tent, now and again starting and glancing fearfully out and across the sands to point out the dread watcher he believed hovered near him. I tried to soothe him, to laugh away his fears, to tell him it was all a dream. And then? Well, he fumbled in his shirt and drew forth a little package tied up in a rag, and with many a fearful glance his trembling fingers undid it, and there poured forth a little cascade of magnificent diamonds—far finer than anything I had ever seen before or since in German West: a fortune in fact! I sat astounded, for I had not dreamed of this. Where they came from there must be more—a fortune for us all! Then I found my tongue. 'Carfax, man; I said, 'this is wonderful! Can you find your way back? It will make us all rich.'

"He shuddered. 'No! no!' he said, his hands pressed to his eyes as though to shut out the scene of horror; 'he is there! No, he cannot be; he is watching here for me—he will follow me always! Oh! Jason, don't leave me alone, old man; don't leave me; we'll get away when the boat comes! There's enough for us both! Don't leave me!'

"After a time he sank into a deep sleep; but to me sleep was now out of the question. Where on earth had he found the diamonds? They, at least, were real. Had he really found a spot where the terrific gale had shifted the sand and laid bare a treasure and tragedy of long ago? Such things might be. I had seen dead men in the dunes myself, and the overwrought state of Carfax, due to his sufferings, would account for the rest. If only he could find his way back when he came to his proper sense again!

"Thus musing I paced up and down outside the tent in the bright moonlight. Carfax was still sleeping, but uneasily, and muttering a lot in his sleep. There across the dunes the diamonds must be—there somewhere. He had come from yonder towards the big dune. And almost mechanically my footsteps wandered away from the tent towards where I had met Carfax. Here was the spot, here was the place where he had half scared me with his weird story of being followed, and where I had half believed myself that I had seen the follower. Here, for the wind had once more blown the sand from the filled-in footprints, were our spoors—mine meeting his; here we turned back; but why was this? *Whose* spoor was this, that followed upon our own, back towards where the tent stood?

"My hair rose on my head as I looked. The ghastly white moonlight showed the other spoor quite plainly—the print of a broad, square-toed, low heeled shoe.

"Every man of us wore *veldtschoens*; there was not a heel among the four of us, and as I marveled and superstitious fear crept upon me there came scream after scream of terror from the direction of the tent; and as I looked Carfax, barefoot as he had slept, came flying from the tent, his ghastly face contorted with horror, glancing behind him as he ran, and holding out his arms as though to ward off a pursuer.

"Past me he flew, straight across the sand towards the dunes from which he had lately come, his shrieks getting fainter and fainter as he sped until they ceased, and the faint breeze that heralded the dawn brought back the sound of mocking laughter.

"Fear held possession of me, for something had passed me in pursuit of the haunted man, and with terror gripping my faculties, I scarce dared turn my eyes to where the fresh spoor of Carfax's naked feet showed in the sand. Yes! It was there; a heavy, broad, square-toed print following and treading over Carfax's own and showing the signs of a mad pursuit.

"Did I follow them? No! I'm not ashamed to say I did not—at any rate not then. Instead, I walked down to the shore, where the solemn breakers offered some sort of companionship, and prayed for morning to come and blot out the ghastly moon and all it had shown me, and save my reason.

"The sun came at last, and with it an awful hurricane that equalled that of the previous week, and I was hard put to it to save our few belongings from being swept away and from being myself overwhelmed. In the evening came the calm, and with it the boat; and thank

God! I had not to face the moonlight again alone.

"Yes, we searched; but the storm had changed the whole aspect of the dunes, and the spoors lay buried under many feet of sand, and—well, Carfax was never seen again!"

Jason ended his narrative abruptly, and, rising, lit his pipe with an ember from the dying fire and stood gazing across the river to where the vague mysterious dunes of German West showed silver-white beyond the farther bank. "Good country to be out of!" he said with a shiver. "Come, boys, you'd better turn in. I can't sleep when there's a moon."

IN THE INTERESTS OF SCIENCE
THE STORY OF A BURGLARY
by
ANONYMOUS

Despite my best efforts I have been quite unable to discover the author of this darkly humourous tale, which was published anonymously in The Strand Magazine *(Vol. III., January to June) in 1892.* In the Interests of Science *was apparently translated from its original German and that's about all I can tell you.*

If you enjoy your chuckles on the dark side, then this story is for you. If nothing else this tale, whoever the author was, stands as a wonderful reminder that, despite some well-worn stereotypes, Victorians, and indeed Imperial era Germans, really did have a fine sense of humour.

* * *

Although I had known George Martin a long time, he had only lately initiated me into the mysteries of his life. I knew well that he had been guilty of many kinds of excesses and indiscretions in his youth, nevertheless I was not a little astonished to hear that he had once sunk so low as burglary. Without further remark I here relate the chief episode out of the remarkable career of this strange man:—

"Yes," said he, "I had a hard time of it in those days, and finally I became a—burglar. When Robert Schmiedlein proposed to me that we should break in to the somewhat retired house of two doctors, Dr. Engler and Dr. Langner, I thoughtlessly agreed. Both doctors were well known on account of their scientific researches, and one of them especially for his eccentric manner.

"Well, the night fixed for the carrying out of our design arrived, and we went to work with the greatest confidence, for all the circumstances were favourable for a burglary. It was pitch dark, neither moon nor stars visible and in addition a strong west wind was blowing, which was very welcome to us, as it promised to drown every sound, however slight.

"It was towards two in the morning as we, assuming all was safe began by filing through a chain which fastened a ladder to the wall. The ladder we placed under a window in the first story on the left side of the house. In less than five minutes we had opened the window, and, hearing nothing, Schmiedlein climbed through it and I followed him. After carefully reclosing the venetians we ventured to light a lantern, and then discovered that we were in a kind of lumber-room, the door of which was locked.

"After picking the lock, we determined first to explore the rooms on the ground floor, thinking we should thus run less risk of waking the inhabitants of the house.

"To our no little astonishment we perceived, as we crept downstairs, a light shining under the door of one of the rooms at the back of the building.

"At first we were both for beating a hasty retreat. Schmiedlein soon recovered himself, and proposed we should force our way into the room, bind and gag every occupant and then obtain by threats all desirable information.

"I agreeing, we approached the door. While carefully throwing the light round, noticed, about seven feet from the floor, a wire which appeared to pass through the door we were approaching, and on pointing it out to my companion, he thought it would be connected with some bell.

"I replied in a whisper that we should try and avoid an alarm by cutting the wire, and as I could just reach it with my hands I would hold it firm whilst Schmiedlein cut it between my hands, and thus prevent it jerking back and ringing the bell.

"Setting the lantern on the floor, I seized the wire, whilst Schmiedlein drew a pair of pincers out of his pocket. But the moment I touched it I felt a frightful shock which quivered through and through me, so that I fell all of a heap, tearing the wire down with me. I remember hearing the loud ringing of a bell, whilst Schmiedlein—whom, moreover, I have never seen since—disappeared like lightning into the darkness and escaped, very likely by the way we had come.

"On falling down I struck my head violently against the opposite wall and became unconscious, whilst the electric bell—at that time a novelty—rang unceasingly.

"Regaining my senses, I found myself bound and helpless, which after all did not surprise me, as I concluded I had been caught where I fell. It soon struck me, however, that there were some peculiar circumstances connected with my captivity.

"I was nearly undressed and lay on a cold slate which was about the height of a table from the ground, and only a piece of linen protected my body from immediate contact with the stone. Straight above me hung a large lamp, whose polished reflector spread a bright light far around, and when I, as far as possible, looked around, I perceived several shelves with bottles, flasks, and chemical apparatus of all kinds upon them. In one corner of the room stood a complete human skeleton, and various odds and ends of human bodies hung here and there upon the walls. I then knew I was lying on the operation—or dissecting—table of a doctor, a discovery which naturally troubled me greatly; at the same time I perceived that my mouth also was firmly gagged.

"What did it all mean? Had some accident befallen me, so that a surgical operation was necessary for my recovery? But I remembered nothing of the kind, and also felt no pain; nevertheless here I lay, stripped and helpless, on this terrible table... gagged and bound, which indicated something extraordinary.

"It astonished me not a little that there should be such an operation-room in such a house, until I remembered that Dr. Langner, as the district physician, had to carry out the post-mortem examinations for the circuit, and that in the small provincial town no other room was available for such a purpose. I felt too miserable, however, to think anything more about it. But I soon noticed, after another vain effort to free myself, that I was not alone in the room, for I heard the rustling of paper, and then someone said in quiet, measured tones:—

" 'Yes, Langner, I am quite convinced that this man is particularly suited for the carrying out of my highly important experiment. How long have I been wishing to make the attempt—at last, to-night, I shall be able to produce the proof of my theory.'

" 'That would indeed be a high triumph of human skill, I heard a second voice reply; 'but consider, dear doctor, if that man there were to expire under our hands—what then?'

" 'Impossible!' was the quick reply. 'It is bound to succeed, and even if it did not, he will die a glorious death in the interests of science; whilst, if we were to let him go he would sooner or later fall into the hands of the hang-man.'

"I could not even see the two men, yet their conversation was, doubtless, about me; and, hearing it, I shuddered from head to foot. They were proposing some dangerous operation on me, not for my benefit, but in the interests of medical science!

"At any rate, I thought, they won't undertake such a thing without my sanction; and what, after all, was their intention? It must be something terrible, for they had already mentioned the possibility of my succumbing. I should soon know the fearful truth, for, after a short pause, they continued—

" 'It has long been acknowledged that the true source of life lie in the blood. What I wish to prove, dear Langner, is this. Nobody need die from pure loss of blood, and yet such cases occur only too often, whilst we must all the time be in possession of means to renew this highly important sap of life and thus avoid a fatal result. We read of a few, but only a few, cases of a man who for some reason or other has lost so much blood that his death appeared inevitable, if some other noble-hearted man had not offered his own blood, in order to let it flow from his veins into the vein of the dying man. As you are aware, this proceeding has always had the desired effect. I consider it, however, a great mistake to deprive a fellow-being of necessary blood, for the one thereby only gains life and strength at the cost of another, who offers himself for an always dangerous sacrifice.'

" 'Yes, I do not think that right either,' replied Dr. Langner. 'And, moreover, how seldom is a man found at the critical moment, ready to submit himself at once to such a dangerous loss of blood.'

" 'That is very natural; no one lightly undertakes such a thing,' continued the other. 'So much greater will be our triumph if the operation succeeds. I hope to show you, dear colleague, that although we are thinking of taking that man's blood, even to the last drop, in a few hours we shall set him on his feet again.'

" 'Just so! I do not see why we should not succeed. At any rate, in the interests of science we should prove in a practical manner the correctness of our theory.'

" 'And this proof, dear friend, we will undertake without delay. Let me just repeat my instructions, for we cannot go to work too carefully to preserve the life of this man. I will open a vein in his thigh, and measure exactly the quantity of blood which flows out, at the same time watching the beating of the heart. Under ordinary circumstances nothing could possibly save him; but just before the extinction of the last spark of life, we will insert the warm blood of a living rabbit into his veins as we have already arranged. If my theory is right, the pulsation of the heart will then gradually increase in strength and rapidity. At the same time, it is important to protect his limbs from cold and stiffness, which will naturally take place with the loss of all arterial blood.'

"The conversation of the two doctors overwhelmed me with deadly terror. I could scarcely believe I was really awake, and not the victim of some cruel nightmare.

"The fact remained, however, that I lay helpless on the dissecting-table, that a threatening skeleton stood in the corner of the room, and, above all, that terrible conversation which I had to listen to in silence filled me with a fear such as I had never before experienced. Involuntarily the thought forced itself upon me that I was at the mercy of two infatuated doctors, to whose mad theory I should here fall the victim.

"I said to myself that no doctor with a sound mind would propose such a frightful and murderous experiment upon a living man.

"The two doctors now approached the dissecting-table, and looked calmly into my face; then, smiling, took off their coats, and tucked up their sleeves. I struggled to get free, as only a desperate man under such extraordinary circumstances could have struggled. In vain. Their long-acquired experience knew how to render me completely helpless, and, to their satisfaction, I could not even make a sound.

"Dr. Engler now turned to a side-table, and I saw him open a chest of surgical instruments and take out a lancet, with which he returned to me. He at once removed the covering from my right thigh, and although I lay bound to the table in such a way that I could not see my limbs, I was able to watch the doctor busied with his preparations.

"Directly after removing the cloth I felt a prick in the side of my leg, and at once felt the warm blood rush forth and trickle down my leg. The conviction that he had opened the principal vein in the thigh would have sufficed to shake the strongest nerves.

" 'There is no danger,' said Dr. Engler, looking into my staring, protruding eyes with terrible calmness. 'You will not die, my good man. I have only opened an artery in your thigh, and you will experience all the sensations of bleeding to death. You will get weaker and weaker, and finally, perhaps, lose all consciousness, but we shall not let you die. No, no! You must live, and astonish the scientific world through my great discovery!'

"I naturally could say nothing in reply, and no words can adequately express what I felt at that moment. I could, in one breath, have wept, implored, cursed, and raved.

"Meanwhile I felt my life's blood flowing, and could hear it drop into a vessel standing under the end of the table. Every moment the doctor laid his hand on my heart, at the same time making remarks which only increased my horror.

"After he had put his hand on me for at least the twentieth time, and felt the beating of the heart, he said to his assistant—

" 'Are you ready with your preparations, Langner? He has now lost an enormous quantity of blood and the pulsation is getting weaker and weaker. See, he is already losing consciousness,' and with these words he took the gag out of my mouth.

"A feeling of deadly weakness, as well as of infinite misery, laid hold of me when the physician uttered these words, and on my attempting to speak, I found that scarcely a whispering murmur passed my lips. Shadowy phantoms and strange colours flitted before my eyes, and I believed myself to be already in a state past all human aid.

"What happened in the next few minutes I do not know, for I had fainted. When I reopened my eyes I noticed I no longer lay on the dissecting table, but was sitting in an arm-chair in a comfortable room, near which stood the two doctors looking at me.

"Near me was a flask of wine, several smelling-salts, a few basins of cold water, some sponges and a galvanic battery. It was now bright daylight, and the two doctors smiled as they looked at me.

"When I remembered the terrible experiment, I shuddered with horror, and tried to rise. I felt too weak, however, and sank back helpless into the chair. Then the circuit physician, in a friendly but firm voice, addressed me—

" 'Compose yourself, young man. You imagined you were slowly bleeding to death; nevertheless, be assured that you have not lost a single drop of blood. You have undergone no operation whatever, but have simply been the victim of your own imagination. We knew very well you heard every word of our conversation, a conversation which was only intended to deceive you as much as possible. What I maintained was, that a man's body will always completely lie under the influence of what he himself firmly believes, whilst my colleague, on the other hand, held the opinion that the body can never be hurt by anything which only exists in imagination. This has been an open question between us, which, after your capture, we at once determined to decide. So we surrounded you with objects of a nature influence your imagination, aided further by our conversation; and, finally, your conviction that we would really carry out the operation of which you heard us speak, completed the deception.'

" 'You have now the satisfaction of knowing that you are as safe and sound as ever you were. At the same time we assure you that you really showed all the symptoms of a man bleeding to death, a proof that the body can sometimes suffer from the most absurd unreality that the mind can imagine.'

"Astonishment, joy, and doubt at finding myself neither dead nor dying struggled within me, and then rage at having been subjected to such an awful and heartless experiment by the two doctors, overcame me. I was quickly interrupted by Dr. Engler, however, on trying to give free scope to my indignation.

" 'We had not exactly any right to undertake such an experiment with you,' he said; 'but we thought you would pardon us if we delivered you from certain punishment, instead of having to undergo a painful trial and a long imprisonment for burglary. You are certainly at liberty to complain about us; but consider, my good fellow, if such a step is in your interests? I do not think so. On the other hand, we are quite willing to make you a fitting compensation for all the agony you have suffered.'

"Under the circumstances," continued George Martin,

"I considered it wise to accept their proposal, although I have not to this day forgiven the two men for so treating me.

"The doctors kept their promise. They made me a very handsome present, and troubled themselves about me in other ways, so that since that time I have been a more fortunate, and, I hope, a better man. Still, I have never forgotten the hour when I lay on the dissecting-table—the unexpected victim of a terrible experiment—in the interests of science, as Dr. Engler explained."

Such was the strange story of my friend. His death, which recently took place, released me from the promise of secrecy given to him about an event, which he could never recall, even after a lapse of thirty years, without a feeling of unabated horror.

THE PAINTED COIN
by
GUY THORNE

Guy Thorne was the pen name of Cyril Arthur Edward Ranger Gull (1875-1923), who also wrote under the names C. Ranger Gull and Leonard Cresswell Ingleby. A journalist and novelist, Thorne is best known for the novel When It Was Dark: The Story of a Great Conspiracy *(1903).*

After attending Oxford University, Thorne spent a few years on the staff of the Saturday Review, *as well as writing for* The Bookman *and* The Academy. *He was editor of* London Life, *and also worked for the* Daily Mail *and* Daily Express. *Guy Thorne published his first novel,* The Hypocrite: A Novel of Oxford and London Life, *anonymously in 1898 and one can only assume it was a success because from that point on he maintained a steady output of fiction, publishing 125 novels and an impressive array of short stories.*

First printed in The Pall Mall Magazine *(1911),* The Painted Coin *is a striking story with a cheeky* deus ex machina *that, while rather familiar these days, may have seemed quite neat at the time.*

* * *

We were both quite unsuccessful painters. The general

public would have nothing of either of us.

A few critics, writing in very 'superior' papers indeed, hailed us as the most brilliant exponents of realistic painting that the world had ever seen. We enjoyed an obscure celebrity. There were houses in Chelsea and Bedford Park where we were addressed as "Dear Master." We walked and talked—and tried to look—as if we were great. But the truth was that nobody bought our pictures.

Drawing-room praise and unnoticed paragraphs were our sole reward for extraordinary labors, a real and honest love for the work we were doing, a whole-hearted devotion to the special branch of art we had made our own, and in which (I am really not exaggerating) we were supreme.

Both Folliot and myself were absolutely certain that we were right in our own theories. We hated the romantic and the idealistic in art as in life. Anything romantic or visionary we laughed to scorn. Any sort of future life we agreed to be the hysteria of ill-regulated minds, or the cowardice of those who were afraid to enjoy themselves in this. Love, we said, was merely an affair of the senses; honor, a contention which it was as well to observe for the sake of convenience; and if we had troubled to define our general attitude in a single sentence, it would probably have been "Let us eat, drink, and paint, for tomorrow we die."

We flattered ourselves that any pictures signed 'John Folliot' or 'Charles Tremayne' were literal and accurate estimates. When either of us painted a portrait, nothing in the face was hidden, idealised, or improved. We painted as we saw. Every tell-tale wrinkle, every shifty look in the eyes, each suggestion of sin or sorrow that lurked in the corners of the mouth, was set down with absolute fidelity. The result, of course, was that neither of us got many portrait commissions. I remember Mostyn, a very successful portrait-painter, and a man of great personal charm, once having an argument with us on the subject.

Folliot and I were staying down in Cornwall at the artist colony of Portalone, a lovely and beautiful fishing village on the Atlantic, not far from Land's End.

There is a quaint and very ancient little inn there, which is known as 'The Brigantine.' The artists have decorated the walls of one of the rooms with paintings, and they meet together there, using the place as a sort of informal Bohemian club.

There we sat, one soft spring morning, Mostyn, Folliot, and myself, and the conversation was of extreme importance, in view of the weird and astounding story I have to tell.

I can see it all now, the scene is as fresh and vivid in my memory as if it had happened yesterday.

The old-fashioned parlor of the inn was panelled in oak, black with the passing of many years. Upon the panels hung innumerable paintings in slim gold frames— all of them presented to the landlord, old Billy Trewhella, by the artists of the colony.

The sun poured in through the leaded window-panes, and outside came a cheerful noise from the little harbor as the herring-boats disgorged their catches of the night before. Mostyn, big, blonde, distinguished, leant over the heavy table and emphasised his remarks to Folliot with knockings of his well-worn briar upon the wood.

Folliot listened calmly enough. He was a dark, hawk-faced man, with a saturnine and rather contemptuous smile, tall, thin, and muscular, though restless in all his movements and with an occasional wildness in his black eyes which puzzled people.

"You and Tremayne," Mostyn said, looking at both of us, "are brilliant painters. Your technique is wonderful, no one has ever denied it, but you haven't got the vision, the artistic vision, and that's where you fail."

"We see things as they are," I answered, "that is all," and Folliot nodded in confirmation.

"No, you don't," Mostyn answered, "and that's just where you make your mistake. You only see the surface of things. You steadfastly refuse to look below. You have just finished your portrait of old Baragwanetti, the smack owner, Folliot. It's a marvellous piece of brushwork, but you have painted a picture of a devil! Old Baragwanetti is an old scamp, I admit. He was a wrecker in his youth, he is suspected of being a smuggler now; he is a picturesque, sly, greedy, foul-mouthed old beast. But there's good in him too. There is good in his face if you look for it with sympathy and the desire to see it there! There is humor, geniality, a certain generosity, no meanness. I've been studying him too. You've missed all that. You've painted the mask only."

Folliot laughed rather contemptuously. "I've painted what I saw," he said.

"Exactly," Mostyn replied rather coldly, and rising from his seat as he did so; "pray Heaven to lighten your darkness, Folliot." And with that the big man nodded and left the room.

I confess that, for my part, Mostyn's words had rather gone home to me. Folliot was a man of forty; his convictions were fixed and settled, nothing would move them. I, on the other hand, was but five and twenty. Folliot was my master. I had eagerly adopted his theories and carried them out in my work. I painted as well as he did, but it was his influence that had determined the bent of my art. And there was another fact in our relations. My friend was rich; he was the son of a well-known mechanical engineer, who had left him a considerable fortune. My own means were wretchedly small, and

THE PAINTED COIN

Folliot had been very good to me.

But as Mostyn went away—and I knew well what a fine fellow he was—I caught myself wondering if he were not right after all. Might I myself not be merely a shadow of another man? A mirror in which the opinions of a stronger brain were reflected? A man who had unhesitatingly accepted the view of a friend because he was too mentally lazy to thresh out any of his own? All that day I wondered.

At this time I was rather at a loose end as far as work was concerned. A fit of idleness was upon me, which the soft and drowsy Cornish spring did but little to remove, and I hardly knew what to turn to next.

The morning after the talk with Mostyn, Folliot went up to London for a day or two. I saw him off at the little station—from where a single line ran to the main Penzance route—and then, with my box of paints slung over my shoulder, went down to the foreshore, intending to sketch for an hour or two. I sat on the little granite breakwater for a time, but found little to interest me. The fishermen were all at sea, and there was no one to talk to, while for some reason or other—perhaps it was too early—none of the other artists were out painting.

I strolled into 'The Brigantine,' ordered a glass of beer, and began to talk to old Billy Trewhella, the landlord. After a few minutes he was called away, and I was left alone in the mellow old oak room. The sun streamed into the place; and I sat back idly upon the settle thinking of nothing at all.

Then I saw that my change lay upon the table—I had paid Billy with a half-sovereign. A sunbeam fell with special radiance upon one half-crown; an idea came to me—an idea of idleness and childishness.

I got out my palette and brushes, and, using the half-crown as a model, began to paint an exact replica of it upon the polished surface of the table. Such a thing—whether it was worth doing or not—is no trick, but requires a vast amount of technical skill. Not one painter in five hundred could do it with any approach to reality; probably no one in England just then could have done it as well as I did— except Folliot, of course. I thought of the Hans Memling pictures at Bruges, and chuckled with sheer delight at my own skill as the thing grew.

When it was finished, although, of course, the paint was wet, there to all intents and purposes lay a genuine silver coin. Anybody would want to try to pick it up. I called Billy in and showed it to him. The old fellow was lost in admiration, and promised himself many jokes later on in the day.

While he was laughing and chuckling, steps were heard in the sanded passage outside, and a voice called for the landlord—a gentleman's voice, and one I did not know.

Billy hurried out, and I heard him showing some stranger the various other rooms of the quaint old inn, which really was a show place in its way and mentioned in all the guide books to Cornwall.

Finally, he ushered in a tall, elderly man with a red face and a white moustache—obviously a soldier—and showed him the landscapes upon the walls, and then, much to my amusement, pointed out my little *tour de force* upon the table.

"Mr. Tremayne 'e done this just now, sir!" said old Billy, in high delight. "You'd be long to think you could pick en up and spend en, couldn't you, sir? Mr. Tremayne's one of our leading artists in Portalone."

The stranger bowed and examined my effort with considerable interest. Then he sat down and at once began to talk. "Now that, sir," he said, "is what I call real art! It is the thing represented as it is! One could almost pick it

THE PAINTED COIN

up and put it in one's pocket, by Jove! I don't pretend to be a judge of these matters—indeed, most modern pictures puzzle me—but this, sir, is first-rate!"

I could not help being rather pleased at his simple and kindly criticism. The man was obviously a gentleman, and obviously a soldier too. I have always been fond of soldiers. My father was an officer in the Rifle Brigade, and as we fell into conversation I mentioned the fact. The newcomer introduced himself at once as Colonel Decies, of the —th. I gave him my own card, and to my pleasure—though hardly to my surprise, for the military world is a small one—I found he had known my father quite well. They had been brigaded together at Aldershot and had belonged to the same club for years.

Colonel Decies, it turned out, had taken a house at Portalone for six months, and had arrived three or four days ago with his daughter. He was a widower and she was his only child.

He promptly asked me to lunch that very morning, and I gladly accepted. We mounted the hill together towards the villa he had taken, which overlooked the bay.

It was a perfect morning. The sea was absolutely smooth and glowed like a vast sapphire. The sky was all blue and gold, gold upon blue! The wandering airs were soft and sweet as we came into the garden of the colonel's house.

"Come in, my dear boy," he said, "and I will introduce you to Helena and tell her that our first guest in Portalone has arrived!"

And I think those words and this episode may fitly close the introductory part of the extraordinary and sinister story I have to tell.

I had met many girls in my life. They had amused me—some of them; they had interested me—others of them. Like any other young man, I had flirted when the opportunity came. But I had always had rather a contempt for women. I was cynical about them with the cynicism of a young and cock-sure man. They were amusing creatures to meet and beautiful creatures to paint! That was my attitude, and it was fostered and encouraged in every way by my friend and master, Folliot.

And then on that bright morning I met Helena Decies.

Her hair was like ripe corn, her eyes were as brown—deep and translucent—as a forest pool shot with sunlight, her mouth was a scarlet eloquence of humor and simplicity. I knew that there was nobody like her in the whole world, there never had been, never could be!

The dreams of youth when it first meets the golden girl!...

Colonel Decies commissioned me to paint Helena's portrait. She used to come to my studio—in the free and informal fashion of Portalone—for a couple of hours three days a week, and gradually upon the canvas there grew a masterpiece.

I can say this now without fear of being thought conceited. That picture hangs in the Luxembourg at Paris now. All the world has seen it, but at the present time, ten years afterwards, a critic occasionally says that the "portrait of a lady which first brought fame to Tremayne has not yet been surpassed by the maturer work of the master."

I lived in a dream. Helena did also—she has told me so—and a fortnight had hardly passed before we were deeply and irrevocably in love with each other.

It was on the day the portrait was finished that I asked my dear if she would marry me. The afternoon sun was pouring into the old studio—it had been a boat-house once—and we stood together before the easel.

"It is wonderful!" she said, in a hushed voice, "but I

do not really look like that! You have made an ideal girl. The picture throbs with idealism and poetry—ah! If only I looked like that, Mr. Tremayne!"

Then I turned to her. I caught her in my arms and covered her face with kisses. "My love! My lady!" I cried. "I am only a realist and paint as I see, that is all!" I have painted you with brushes dipped in love and adoration—I love you! I love you! Dearest and best, say that you are for me. Tell me, oh, tell me!"

Hand in hand, our eyes radiant with the glorious knowledge that had come to us, we were sitting upon the old, battered studio sofa; it was growing dusk, though one last, long beam of sunlight shot down from the glass roof and bathed Helena's portrait with splendor.

Then the door opened with a sudden jerk, and a tall, dark figure swung into the room. It was Folliot, just returned from London, looking for me.

He did not see us at first. The irradiated picture caught his eye and he stopped before it with a deep breath.

I saw his face quite distinctly—wonder, astonishment froze it into rigid lines.

"Charles has done this!" he whispered to himself; "his brush cannot lie! Then who is she?—where?—where?—"

He turned and saw us, sitting hand-in-hand upon the sofa, and as I introduced him to my darling he moved and spoke like a man but newly waked from sleep.

A month passed. Without doubt it was the happiest month of my life. My love for Helena, and hers for me, irradiated everything; the meaning of life was altered.

But the most extraordinary thing of all was that my art underwent an absolute change and revolution. It was as though a blind had rolled up from before my eyes. I saw everything differently. My passion for hard, cold realism left me. I still painted things as I saw them, but how differently I saw them! The world was full of poetry and goodness now, the ideal was mixed with the colors of my palette, for the first time in my life. I really loved, and for the first time I really saw!

It was a joy to tell my girl of the happy transformation she had wrought, to point out to her the change in my work. Her appreciation was complete, she realised and understood everything as if she had been a painter all her life. One day I took her to 'The Brigantine,' where I had first met her father. I showed her the landscapes of my colleagues which decorated the old room, and then I showed her the half-crown I had painted upon the table, which had first made Colonel Decies talk to me and ask me to his house. She had heard of the episode, of course.

Helena was carrying a little green purse in her hand—she had been shopping—and with a delightful blush she took a half-crown from it and gave it to me.

"Here is a real one, dear old boy," she said; "keep it always in memory. It will bring you luck!"

I took it, had a hole bored in it that evening, hung it off a thin chain, and wore it round my neck under my clothes. When I was not with Helena I liked to feel her fantastic present, the charm she had given to me. Of the luck—indeed 'luck' is the word—it was to bring I had no prescience at all.

During these first weeks of my engagement I saw much less of Folliot than before.

I was hard at work, painting in the new style which love seemed to have taught me. When I was not working I was with Helena and her father. I used to ride with them over the wild Cornish moors. Colonel Decies and Helena taught me to fence—my beautiful, supple darling was a mistress of the foils. The days went by very swiftly.

Always morose to most people, a man living a strange, eccentric life of his own, Folliot now began to treat me much as he treated the rest of the world. Our old, intimate friendship of the past was quite interrupted, if not broken.

On the few occasions when he came to my studio and saw the work I was doing his face became positively malignant. Once, with a wild and unrestrained passion, his lips white and twitching, his eyes glittering, he poured out a stream of mad reproaches upon me.

I was a traitor to my art, I had thrown away my heritage—I should suffer torture some day for what I had done!

I did not take very much notice, I was too happy. Colonel Decies liked Folliot, they got on very well together, though the old gentleman more than once hinted to me that my friend and late master was 'peculiar,' to say the least of it.

"I like him and he amuses me," said the colonel, "but he's as mad as a hatter all the same!"

Helena, on the other hand, disliked Folliot intensely. He had made some sketches of her, promising a portrait some day, though it never seemed likely to be finished.

"I am always civil to him." she said to me, "because he is your friend, Charlie, and, of course, he is very clever. But somehow he frightens me. He impresses me with a sense of danger!"

I thought little of this, and, shortly after she had said it, Folliot took an old deserted farmhouse on the moor, fitted up his studio there, and came rarely into Portalone.

He was making experiments in painting by artificial light, so it was understood, and it was known that he had fitted up a complete acetylene gas installation and was carrying out extensive improvements in his new home.

He was, as I think I have said, an expert mechanical engineer.

One evening, about six o'clock, I was alone in my

rooms. It was a thunderous evening, grey, warm, and menacing.

Folliot suddenly turned up. He was pale and nervous—we had not met for quite three weeks—but more kind and friendly than he had been ever since I had first become engaged.

We had the usual argument, though quite friendly and quiet this time, and then he suggested I should walk out to the moor and sup with him. "And if my arguments can't convince you and bring you back to real art, then I think a picture I have to show you may!" he said, as we strode away together through the gathering storm.

We dined alone. There seemed no servant about, and the grim old stone building, two miles from any other habitation, seemed sinister and forlorn in the gathering storm. More than once I thought of Edgar Poe's ghastly story, 'The Fall of the House of Usher,' and shuddered.

Folliot's manner was increasingly curious. He talked extravagantly about realism in art, always seeming to be leading up to some climax and ever breaking away from it, feverishly, unnaturally. At last we rose from the table. He placed his hand upon my shoulder, and I felt it tremble.

"Come," he cried; and there was now a note as if of impending triumph in his voice. "Come and learn once for all what real art is!"

I followed Folliot down a long, silent passage, at the end of which was a door. Opening this, he showed a flight of steps, carpeted with felt, leading downwards into darkness. He lit a candle he was carrying.

"The old farmhouse cellars," he said; "smuggled goods were hidden here in the old days. Now I have fitted them up as studios for my experiments in painting by gaslight."

I followed him down many steps into the dark, and

then along a narrow, vaulted passage of stone, chill and silent.

Folliot unlocked a door. "Here we are!" he said; "and now for the picture which will bring you back to your allegiance."

We entered the small room, square in shape, as far as I could see in the light of the candle. Then Folliot struck a match, and in a few minutes the place was brilliantly illuminated by acetylene. It was a strange room to find underground in this ancient and deserted Cornish mansion.

A carpet of black felt was upon the floor. The walls were entirely draped by curtains of black velvet. At one end was a curtain of brilliant scarlet running on rings, obviously concealing the picture I had come to see.

In front of this, though not more than a yard away, there stood a massive chair of wood, painted black, with long projecting arms.

"To get the full effect," Folliot said—and his voice was now suddenly quiet and satisfied—you must sit in that chair, when I will pull the curtain. The thing is like Hans Memling; it is designed for the closest inspection."

I sat down in the chair; even as I did so the face of the man before me changed.

There was a sudden whirr of machinery, three or four sharp clicks, and a collar of steel shot out from the high back of the chair and snapped round my neck. My arms, which were lying along the chair-arms, were confined at the wrists by bands of rigid metal; a box-like arrangement rose from the floor and gripped my legs.

I was caught, trapped, absolutely powerless, and, to complete my immobility, Folliot ran an iron bar from side to side of the chair, where my legs joined the trunk.

I could not move an inch. I might have been a man of stone. I said nothing, I had seen the man's face. I was caught like a rabbit by this madman. Then he drew the curtain.

I saw the infamous masterpiece which all England has since seen, and my blood ran cold within me.

Close in front of me, life-size, a triumph of technique almost unequalled in the whole history of painting, was a portrait of Helena. The figure was in the padded coat, short serge skirt, and black stockings of a girl's fencing costume. It was lunging straight out of the picture with marvellous reality, and the point of the rapier was directed straight at the spectator's heart.

The face was covered by the wire mask used in foil play, but with extraordinary ingenuity the painter had contrived that the features behind the mask were clearly seen. Feature for feature they were those of my darling, but distorted into a mocking malignity, a smile of hate.

I gave a hollow cry. It was echoed by horrid laughter.

"A fine piece of realism, Tremayne; I see you appreciate it. You have need to, for it is the last thing on which you will look! There is your pretty darling! You will observe the position of her foil. Well, she has pierced your heart before; she will do it again now! I wish you a long good-night, Charles Tremayne—convert to the real in art!"

He laughed horribly, shaking in a paroxysm of insane and evil merriment. Then he went out of the room, shut the door and locked it, leaving me alone.

Rigid, motionless, like a man of marble, I stared at the dreadful wonder before me... there was a sudden, sharp, metallic sound—click!

From out the picture the sharpened point of a shining steel rapier was now projecting an inch or more. It seemed exactly as if the mocking figure of the portrait was advancing it towards my heart.

Click! Another warning note in the dreadful

machinery of my doom, another inch of the shining steel, and now I knew!

So this was how I was to die, in hellish and fantastic torture, at the hands of a raging and cunning maniac. A deep groan burst from me. There was no help that I knew; I was no victim of an elaborate practical joke. Folliot was mad, stark, staring mad; his precautions were taken with coldblooded certainty. Click!

There were four inches of the steel now; the cruel, mocking face of the marvellous portrait, like and yet so unlike, grinned horribly at me through the mesh of the mask.

Click! It was to be soon then! I shouted aloud; wild, despairing cries and calls filled the black-hung chamber of death. I struggled in my gyves till every limb was wounded and torn... Click!

Peace came upon me. It was all over, revolt and struggle passed away. I was to die, thus it was God's will. I began to pray, humbly resigning myself, praying for forgiveness—praying for Helena.

Click! The long whip of steel was almost touching my waistcoat, over the heart. A few minutes now and all would be over. I called out on the name of God and resigned myself. "Helena, dearest, good-bye! I die loving you; we shall meet again!"

The sharp point had pierced cloth and flannel; one more movement...

Click! I heard the noise, felt the deadly steel push through, and then—what was this? There was a sharp, hard pressure on my flesh, but no dreadful, agonising piercing of the skin! I held my breath, and then in an instant I knew what had happened.

The point of the steel had struck upon the coin I wore upon a chain—my darling's love gift!

Click! And now the pressure increased intolerably,

and I braced myself to meet it. Once again, and the steel of the rapier bent upwards like a bow.

Click! My heart seemed enclosed in an iron band, and I saw the glittering steel projecting from the picture rise up into a half-hoop. My sight began to fail; there was a noise in my ears like sudden drums at midnight; and then, with a loud clanging jar, the foil snapped under the pressure. The end part whipped up to the ceiling, cutting my face in a deep line: my breath came back to me, and I swooned into a deep and tranquil sleep.

Late that night they found me, rigid, half-conscious, a prey to shrieking terror, led by the maniac himself, raving with glee at what he had done, in a ghastly and horrified rush over the moor.

Folliot died raving three days afterwards. My wife keeps the half-crown now, and as for the one painted on the table of 'The Brigantine,' it is covered over with glass, and no offers for it can tempt old Billy Trewhella.

THE CORNER HOUSE
by
BERNARD CAPES

Bernard Capes wrote five collections of strange stories in the late 1890s and early 1900s and was ignored by anthologists from then on. This could hardly have been because of the quality of his work.

Capes, who was born in London in 1854, died in 1918 of heart failure compounding influenza. His writing career, as far as books were concerned, spanned only twenty years, yet he was one of the era's most prolific authors. He contributed stories to at least twenty-one of the magazines then prevalent, very often with a dozen appearances in the same journal over the years. His most popular work was probably the novel The Lake of Wine *(1898) and all told he produced over thirty-five books, the last being the posthumous* The Skeleton Key *(1919).*

The Corner House *appeared first in Capes' 1913 collection* Bag and Baggage *and has not been seen in an anthology since.*

Bernard Capes was undoubtedly one of the Victorian age's great fantasists and it is a shame that for a long while he was not given the recognition due him.

* * *

Some three years ago two men, both preoccupied in

thought, went by one another on Vauxhall Bridge. The next instant, the one making for the Surrey side halted on a subconscious recognition, wheeled about, and, returning hurriedly on his tracks, accosted the back of the retreating figure:

"Is that you, Gethin?"

The other started, turned round, and uttered a pleased exclamation:

"O, Acheson! I didn't see you. What good luck!"

"Eh? O, yes, of course!"

"I'm on my way to look for lodgings. You can come and advise me."

The first speaker hesitated, glanced at his watch, and raised a lean anxious face, the lenses of whose spectacles, catching the just kindled lamplight at an angle, looked suddenly like dead, upturned eyes.

It was a dripping, sodden November evening. Rain fell drearily; every buttress and lamp-post had its fibrous reflection underfoot, as if the pavement had grown transparent, revealing the deep roots of the things embedded in it. The heavy air floated with umbrellas, like a last swarming of antediluvian bats; labouring omnibuses were packed to suffocation; to anyone looking over the parapet, the barges slowly forging through the arches below appeared like submarines crawling dim and phantom-like in abysmal waters. A dull depressing squalor characterised everything—the faces of passers-by, the sordid brick of the houses, the streaming windows of the cheap shopfronts. In the dropping mist of the rain one could see myriads of blacks being slowly precipitated to the pavement. It seemed impossible that a feeling of solidity could ever be restored to the texture of things.

Acheson looked at his watch again before he returned it to his pocket.

"Why, the fact is," he said, "I—I was going home to tea."

He was a small spare man, more callow than clean shaved, with a sensitive neurotic face and a hungry expression. He looked older than his friend, though, as a matter of fact, the two were much of an age, young men of twenty-five or thereabouts. He was as boneless as the other was compact and strong-ribbed. Friendship could not have offered a greater physical contrast. The handbag which Gethin carried with ease would have weighed Acheson to the earth. Holding that in one hand, and his umbrella in the other, the former had nothing but a foot to kick out in invitation.

"Come and have tea with me?" he said. "You won't abandon an ancient chum, unassisted, to these wildernesses?"

A vision of a cosy fireside in the Wandsworth Road, of a singing kettle, and a dish of hot poached eggs, to be discussed over a volume of Myers's *Human Personality*, passed wistfully for one moment before Acheson's consciousness. He yielded it, the next, with a sigh. Curiosity, after all, was a dominant factor in his being; and he wanted to hear what had brought Gethin so unexpectedly from his native Woking to seek lodgings in this unattractive quarter of London. He succumbed, with a feeble grace.

"O, certainly!" he said. "Where shall we go?"

The other shrugged his shoulders.

"Where?" he said. "I am a stranger—a country cousin. I leave myself in your hands."

Crossing to the Middlesex shore, and chatting somewhat spasmodically under the general weight of things, they soon found a humble caravanserai, which was at least good enough to offer them warmth, dryness, and a sufficiency of creature comfort. But they were both men of small means, and accustomed to accept the amenities of existence as they could afford them.

It had been in the mind of each, perhaps, to postpone all intimate discussion until they were thus snugly ensconced and isolated; but, now that the moment was come, a mutual consciousness of something difficult and rather barren in the situation stepped between. They talked, after the first brief exchange of enthusiasms, in that rather forced galvanic way which often characterises the re-meetings of once intimate friends, whose interests and sympathies have long ceased to be one. Goodwill could not quite restore a confidence which had been largely due to circumstance and environment; nor could the fire of an ancient devotion penetrate through this distance of time with more than a very qualified warmth. As they secretly recognised the shadow, Gethin and Acheson yielded themselves a little sarcastically to its chill.

They had once been fellow-draughtsmen in a local architect's office, and Acheson had been the first to break away. That was some five years since, when a measure of interest, together with his own personal tastes and qualifications, had procured him the post of free-librarian in an important London centre. That was the best he had coveted, or ever intended to covet. He had no ambitions, but a vast psychologic curiosity, and the post assured him a perpetual sufficiency of the means to feed his intellect, and keep his body going. Years of study had not tended, perhaps, to qualify him for the continued friendship of the athletic, somewhat grim young giant by his side. He was painfully conscious of the fact as he glanced furtively from time to time Gethin's face, and calculated the effect upon it should he suddenly rise and declare the necessity of his getting on homewards.

"You haven't told me yet," he said presently, in his

high, rather strained voice, "what has brought you from home, looking for lodgings in this particular part of London?"

"Why not this as well as any other, Acheson?"

"O, well, if you put it that way, really I don't know."

Gethin Laughed.

"As far as I know my London geography, it's handy for me."

"O!" said Acheson. "Why is it?"

Gethin laughed again annoyingly. He was rather inclined to that form of humour which sees fun in perfectly natural ignorances.

"Isn't Victoria Street in this neighbourhood?" he said.

"Yes, but——"

"And isn't Wrexham's in Victoria Street? That's to be my office for the future—I *hope*."

"Architects?"

"Yes, architects."

"You've left Pettigrews, then?"

"Yes, I've left them. What was there to keep me, when a better berth offered? I've had to wait longer for one than you."

"Well, I can only hope it's as satisfactory, now it's come"

"O, as to that, old man, *my* ambitions always widen with my prospects! But I'm only on probation for the moment. It's an opportunity, and—well, I've got to find lodgings for a month."

"If you want an inexpensive quarter——"

"I do."

"Then this is certainly as good as any."

"So I supposed. But there was just one other reason—ridiculous, but enough to influence me."

"What was that?"

Gethin leaned over the table, his arms crossed, a

curious smile on his face.

"Acheson," said he, "do you still make a hobby of all that supernatural business?"

"I don't know what you mean by a hobby. I assume the necessary interest of the subject to any intelligent mind."

"I see. You are still a corresponding member of the Psychical Research Society?"

"O, yes!"

"Well, do you know you gave me quite a turn, meeting me on the bridge like that."

"Did I? Why?"

"Because, as it happens, a friend and neighbour was the last person who met my father before he disappeared for ever—and it was on Vauxhall Bridge."

Acheson nodded surprisedly, but he was patently not much impressed by the coincidence.

"O, I don't say there's anything in it," said Gethin; "only it struck me. It was the memory of that first meeting, in point of fact, which led me, absurdly enough, perhaps, to seek this way round to my improved fortunes. *He* was going to look for work, too. I dare say you remember something of the story."

"Something. Tell it me again."

"There's not much to tell. It's fifteen years ago, and I was a boy at the time—a boy at school. We had been in fair circumstances, and then it all stopped suddenly. Canstons, the big Army contractors, smashed up, and my father was in it, and his savings were in it. We were near ruined, in fact, and I don't think my mother took it very well. Between ourselves, there were scenes at home. He left that, at last, on the chance or offer of work in London—went off one day after tiffin, and never turned up again. From that moment to this we have never set eyes on him, or gathered by so much as a word a clue to his whereabouts. He just disappeared from mortal ken."

He paused, and there followed a short silence.

"They vanish sometimes," said Acheson presently. "There have been authentic cases."

"Relations came forward," continued Gethin, as if he had not heard him; "I had to put my young shoulder to the wheel, and we scraped along. But it was funny."

"Was he—have you any reason——" began the librarian; but the other took him up.

"The last man in the world to commit suicide—a cheery soul, like his son; indomitable, I might call him, without conceit. Besides, the neighbour who saw him, who met him on that bridge, testified to his buoyant, hopeful mood. He was on his way then, like myself, to look for lodgings. Acheson"—he bent forward very earnestly and touched his friend on the arm—"it was a wet November evening, like this."

He waited for the inevitable comment, a little surprised that his friend did not immediately respond, as expected. Acheson chewed the offered coincidence again, reflective; and his verdict once more was that it was untenable.

"If my studies teach me anything," he said, "it is the folly of jumping in such matters to hasty conclusions. A tempered scepticism is the first equipment of your rational psychist. Coming from Woking, if you don't go on to Waterloo, you must get out at Vauxhall. In electing deliberately to do so, you made your own coincidence."

"But the date and the weather, man?"

"Both suggested that course to you. Now, if some accident had turned you out at——"

"And the meeting on the bridge?"

"No analogy whatever. You have asked me to help you to find lodgings, you see; and, if you are serious—"

"You bet I am. *I* don't want to vanish, like the baseless

fabric of what-d'ye-call-it."

"You see? Localised from the outset. No; depend upon it, Gethin—you'll forgive my saying it—there was some perfectly human and natural explanation of your father's conduct."

"O, of course, you mean some discreditable attachment. I shouldn't have believed it of him, but I confess that that's the view my mother took."

"H'm, I take it for granted that every enquiry——"

"Yes, yes. O, yes; of course!"

He answered a little impatiently, and sat frowning, and drumming his fingers on the table.

"Well, if you are ready," he said suddenly, looking up.

"Quite ready," said Acheson, with a sigh of relief, and got to his feet.

Gethin paid the reckoning, lifted his bag thoughtfully, and they passed out into the street together. Swift darkness had descended while they loitered, and the rain was falling more hopelessly than ever. There was no wind, but the air was opaque with a very fog of water, through which the flare of the shops and the jets of the lamps burned with a dull miasmatic glow, which, in the light of passing vehicles, seemed to be constantly throwing off from itself a multitude of little travelling globes, which sped on like fen-candles into the murk, and were one by one extinguished. The houses looked gigantically tall and unreal; there was little human in suggestion about the shapes of the few foot-passengers, as they hurried past them, muffled, grey and dripping, into their dreary selves. Gethin gave a gasp of disgust.

"Look here," he said; "I'm lost. I hold by you to convoy me into some harbour of refuge."

Acheson considered a moment.

"There are plenty enough of every sort," he said, "both right and left. It's a heterogeneous quarter. Mansions rub shoulders with dosshouses hereabouts. But we must strike a line and take our chance. Your first point is a lodging for the night. If it doesn't suit, you can look again to-morrow. Supposing we turn down here for an experiment. It's sure, by its looks, to reveal a harvest of lodging-cards as thick as blackberries. Shall we go?"

"O, anywhere!" said Gethin, in a depressed voice.

They turned into a blank little street, making in the Horseferry Road direction. Quiet and dismality swallowed them almost on the instant. The sound of traffic died down behind them; their own footsteps spoke louder; the rain and the fog claimed them to complete isolation. Not a creature seemed to be abroad here; and the squalid ranks of houses they passed were, for the most part, lightless and lifeless in suggestion. They plodded along, painstakingly scrutinising the fronts. The crop of cards, if it had ever existed, was gathered or rotted away. Not a casual invitation greeted their groping eyes; but, one by one, as they advanced, the recurrent lamps brightened to a nucleus, made dismally emphatic the meanness of their surroundings, and drowsed and dulled again as they fell behind. They turned off at an inviting angle, and again turned, and yet once more.

"Where are we?" said Gethin suddenly.

His companion stopped.

"Why, that's the funny part of it," he said, in a most unhumorous voice.

"You don't know?"

"The rain and this obscurity are so very confusing," pleaded Acheson. "If we could only find a policeman, now——"

They stood, as he spoke, at the corner opening of a frowsy, melancholy little square, with a patch of degraded garden in its midst—at least, so it looked. Opposite them was the blank side-wall of a house—the first, it seemed, of a terrace. A street-lamp diffused its melancholy halo at the kerb of the pavement hard by.

"Perhaps the name's written up there," said Gethin. "I'll go and look."

He crossed the splashy road and went round to the front of the house. "Here we are," he called across to Acheson. "Come over. A chance, anyway."

Acheson followed and stood beside him.

"Where?" he said. The light from the lamp fell full upon the corner house. It was one of a four-square terrace, as they had supposed. A shallow flight of steps led up to its door; the sill of its ground-floor window stood about level with the tops of the area-railings in front.

" 'Lodgings for a single gentleman,' " said Gethin, "and a reassuring light behind the blind. It doesn't look too pretentious. Shall I try?"

"Lodgings!" said Acheson stupidly. "There?"

"Can't you see it?" answered Gethin impatiently. "Shall I try, I say?"

"O, there's no harm in trying," said Acheson. His voice sounded quite strange to himself.

With something of a flounce, Gethin ran up the steps. As he did so, Acheson backed to the lamp-post, and put an arm involuntarily about it. Standing thus, the falling curtain of light dazzled his eyes, and blinded them for the moment to what followed. He was aroused by hearing his friend speak close beside him.

"It's all right. She can take me in provisionally, anyhow. I'm about done, and I shall chance it. What's the matter with you? Has the tea got into your head?"

Acheson came away from his support, reeling a little.

"No, no," he said. "I'm glad—I won't detain you." And he fairly bolted away into the darkness.

Gethin looked after him a moment; then shrugged his

shoulders, and turned to his new quarters. "Poor old Peter," he muttered. "What's come to him? I don't believe he's quite all there."

His landlady was waiting for him at the door. She was a little lean woman, haggard to deathliness. The wolf of hunger, it was evident, had gnawed her ribs and nozzled in the blue places of her eyes. She was all spoiled and drawn in appearance, and her voice was as lifeless as her face. She motioned him into the hall, coughing in a small distant way.

He entered, with a cheery stamp. Half-perished oilcloth was on the floor, and a cheap paraffin-lamp burned sickly on the wall.

"A beastly night," he said. "Which way, Mrs. Quennel?"

She took the lamp from the wall, and, holding it high, revealed the foot of a squalid stairway going up into darkness."

"On the first floor, Mr. Gethin," she said, holding her other hand before her mouth to cough.

He followed her up, commanding his nerves with an effort. Fatality had evidently appropriated to him a refuge in the last stage of decline. But it was a refuge, and cheap.

He was satisfied so far. The room was poor, and its appointments refined to attenuation. But the linen on the little iron bedstead was fresh, and the small grained washing-stand scrubbed to barrenness. There were a cane-bottomed chair or two, and some dingy lithographs on the walls.

"A sittin'-room?" said the landlady weakly, behind her hand.

"We'll discuss that to-morrow," answered Gethin.

"Meals?"

"Not now," said the lodger. "I'm going to turn in and go to sleep, early as it is. I've had a tiring day."

She went to strike a light and kindle a candle on the little dressing-table. Her movements were as bodiless as her voice. Gethin, watching her blankly, was urged to ask a question:

"Any other lodgers?"

She turned, with the lamp again in her hand. Her fragment of a face appeared, in its glow, to jerk and waver in the oddest way.

"One, Mr. Gethin," she said. "But he keeps to his room when he's at home, and locks it when he goes out. You won't be troubled by him."

He was about to disclaim any *arrière pensée* in his enquiry, but desisted in sheer depression. He wanted somehow to get rid of her, and be alone. She chilled him.

And, almost before he realised it, she was gone, and the door shut.

He undressed wearily, extracted his nightshirt from the bag, and dived under the sheets. They were thin but innocuous. Then, leaving, for some unconfessed reason, his candle burning by his side, he settled himself to sleep, and opened his eyes again suddenly, with a start.

"She called me by my name," he whispered, "and I'll swear I never told it her!"

In the discussion of that amazing problem, his mind swayed, flickered, and suddenly went out. Health and bodily fatigue were on his side, and he sank into a profound sleep.

He was awakened suddenly—it might have been after many hours—by a consciousness of voices murmuring in his neighbourhood. Alert on the instant, he sat up, in immediate possession of his full faculties, and waited, listening. Two people, he was convinced, were talking just outside his room door—one, his landlady; the second, by his full hoarse intonation, a man. Gethin held his breath.

"My God," the deep voice was saying, as he first realised it, "I daren't do it!"

"Be a man!" answered the other, shrill and sibilant, fearful in its tenseness. "Break it in before it's too late, and save us from death and ruin!"

"I daren't," repeated the former speaker. "It might happen on the moment. I'll go for the police. Come away, Martha, in God's name!"

"And leave the new lodger?"

"I'll wake him first."

Gethin sprang out of bed, as the door was flung wide; and there was the figure of a great, white-faced, shadowy man standing in the opening. Wild fear was in his eyes, entreaty in his shaking hands. The lodger had only time to notice that he was bulky in his build, in suggestion something like a respectable ex-butler, and that he was in hat and overcoat, when the figure had withdrawn, and was appealing to him from the outer darkness.

"Come along, sir, in God's name, and run for it!"

On the instant Gethin was out, and in the passage. Breathing, sobbing, palpitating forms seemed to urge and shoulder him this way and that.

"What is it?" he cried. "What's the matter? I don't know where I am—I don't know what you are talking about!"

"You'll soon know unless you hurry up," said the man's quavering voice in the darkness.

Gethin, groping out, felt the wall, and put his back against it.

"I'll not move," he said loudly, "until I know what all this means!"

The woman's thin hurried voice took up the tale, small and toneless, as if she were speaking the other side of glass:

"It's Danby, the lodger, sir. He's one of those

dynamiters, it seems. We never knew or guessed—he kept himself so secret in his room, and locked it when he went out. He was arrested this very evening, with an infernal machine in his possession. George, my husband here, saw him taken with his own eyes."

The wall felt suddenly cold against Gethin's back.

"What dynamiters?" he said. "I didn't know there were any of them about now." He set his teeth.

"But in any case," he added, "if he's taken, he's taken, and there's an end of him."

The woman trembled on:

"The thing, it seems, sir, went by clockwork—*and there's a ticking going on in his room now.* You can hear it quite plain if you put your ear to the door."

Gethin laughed—on a rather hollow note.

"Is that all? Why, you don't suppose, even if it was true, that he would go out and leave one of those things maturing in his absence?"

"Some accident may have started it, sir—a rat or a mouse. There's plenty hereabouts."

"Come," said Gethin decidedly; "we'll break in. That's nonsense, you know. If he was such a fool——"

"They're all fools, sir."

"We'll break in, I say. Where's that big husband of yours? Now, Mr. Quennel?"

"I won't go near it!" said the hoarse frightened voice from the stairhead.

"Then, here goes," said Gethin. "Where's the room?"

He came away from the wall—felt himself quickly and softly induced, rather than directed, towards a door. Touching it, he bent his ear, and listened. Sure enough, a little sharp regular pulsation came from within, indefinite in quality, but quite appreciable in that still fog-ridden house.

"It's inconceivable," he whispered, "but we'll soon

solve the mystery."

The lock was a cheap affair; the door, which opened inwards, of the flimsiest; the lodger muscular. He put his broad shoulder to the essay, and, getting purchase with his bare feet, bore on the wood with one mighty heave. There followed a crack, a ripping sound, and, to Gethin, a sudden wink of light and a jerk—nothing more. But the sensation was so instant, and so physically and mentally disintegrating, that, for the moment, he could conceive no thought of himself but as a sort of pyrotechnic bomb, which had been shot into mid-air, had burst, and was slowly dropping a multitude of coloured stars. These, as they fell, went out one by one, and, with the quenching of the last, consciousness in him ceased altogether.

Somebody was speaking to him; some application, distinctly physical in its nature, was being made to his body. It felt like a boot. He opened his eyes languidly, and encountered the vision of a face bent above him. It was an official face, and mature, surmounted by a blue helmet, and the expression on it was unsympathetic, not to say threatening.

"Come, sir, what are you doing here?" said the police sergeant. "You must get up, please, and give an account of yourself."

Gethin, accepting the offer of a proffered arm like a bolster, scrambled to his feet in a hurry. He understood on the instant what had happened. The bomb had actually exploded as he broke in the door, and he had been knocked insensible. A mercy, at least, that it was no worse. He clung on to his support a little, feeling somewhat dazed and shocked. It occurred to him, then, with a thrill of gratification, that he must have the constitution of a cat, not only to have survived that appalling experience, but to be standing, as he was, in his normal condition of body. And then something tickled him suddenly, and he lapsed into a shaking giggle. To have been asked to give an account of himself sounded so inexpressibly funny under the circumstances. It was as if *he* had manufactured the bomb. But, in the midst, the element of tragedy in the business struck and sobered him. He backed, and shook himself into reason.

"What about the other two?" he said. "Are they hurt?"

"Eh?" said the officer blankly.

"The others," persisted Gethin—"the landlord and his wife, who were with me when I broke open the door? Are they maimed—mutilated? Good God, man! They aren't killed?"

The sergeant, curiously contemplative of the speaker, stood, one thumb hooked into his belt, the other hand slowly fondling his chin.

"If I was you," he said at length, thoughtfully and oddly irrelevantly, "I'd, take a red-herring and soda-water for my breakfast.

Gethin stared, flushed, and put the question a second time:

"I ask you, are they killed?"

"O, yes! They're dead all right—dead and buried, too."

"Buried!"

Gethin clapped a hand to his head. Had he been insensible longer than he supposed? But, in that case——

"When?" he asked faintly.

"It will have been in '85," said the officer, watchful of him.

Gethin's brain seemed to stagger, and recover itself with a crick. For the first time a sense of something unspeakable in his surroundings was beginning to penetrate it. Weak dawn, while he lay, had come into the house, revealing its structure. Now, in a moment, he understood that there was more of that visible than was compatible with decency or reason. The whole interior of the building; seen from his place in the passage, seemed a shattered ruin. Walls were broken, ceilings torn, doors sprawling dismembered, lights blown out of windows, stair-rails snapped, black abysses formed in the flooring. All that, in itself, was comprehensible. The odd thing was that an indescribable air of antiquity seemed to characterise the wholesale dilapidations.

"This house was blown to pieces," was all he could think of saying.

"Blown to pieces," echoed the sergeant; and added remonstrantly: "Come now, sir, pull your wits together!"

"When?" said Gethin.

"Fifteen years ago, to a day."

"To a day?"

"To a day. I ought to remember. I was on duty hard by at the time."

Gethin felt suddenly sick. He leaned back against the wall.

"I suppose I got muddled up in the fog," he said faintly, "and took refuge in this house, and went to sleep and had a dream."

"That was it, sir, no doubt," said the sergeant encouragingly.

"Untenanted, eh?" said Gethin.

"Avoided like," said the sergeant. "It's never got cured of its bad name."

"For fifteen years? Great God!"

He came away from the wall.

"I think I should like to get out of it—into the air," he said.

"There's your bag and umbrella," said the officer, "at the door of that room. Ain't you going to take them?"

He accompanied Gethin down the stairs. In the lower

quarters, age-long dust and grime showed visible on all sides. The very edges of the shattered panes were green with decay; canopies of cobweb festooned the ceilings. Gethin breathed out a volume of relief as he found himself in the square, looking up awestruck at the blackened deserted building.

"How did you suspect me?" he asked the sergeant.

"Saw the front door ajar, and muddy footsteps going through the hall and up the stairs."

"You think I was drunk, don't you?"

"We'll call it a bit taken, sir."

"A small offence?"

"Very like," said the officer drily. "I hope you enjoyed yourself."

Gethin, biting his lip, looked at him a little pallidly.

"I wish you'd tell me," he said. "Who was it blew that up?"

"Name of Danby," said the sergeant promptly, relieving his throat and coming erect again: "a dynamiter, one of the 'eighties lot. He was the cause of it, anyway—left a charged machine working in his room there, while he went out to deposit another, a blind one, which he'd picked up by mistake. They arrested him with it on him."

Gethin found a momentary difficulty in asking his next question:

"Any lives lost—here, I mean?"

"They accounted for three," said the sergeant; "those two Quennels that you spoke of, and a third, unidentified. He was supposed a chance lodger; but he was mutilated beyond recognition, and none ever claimed him. They say you can see the marks of his blood on the wall now. I don't know; I never had the curiosity to look."

"Thanks," said Gethin. He turned away, quite white. "I don't know where I am," he said. "I suppose you won't mind taking half a crown to put me on my way, and in recognition of your services?"

Weeks later, Gethin ran across Acheson in Victoria Street, and accosted him. Acheson had a queer look to greet him with, guilty and anxious in one.

"Probation satisfactorily over?" he asked.

"That's all right," said Gethin. "I stopped you to tell you something, and to ask a question. I've found out what became of my father."

Acheson gasped, and murmured something inarticulate.

"Acheson," said his friend, "what was the matter with that corner house the other night?"

The large spectacles seemed to disc as Acheson looked up.

"Don't you know, Gethin?"

"What did you see in it, I say?"

"Why—why, I didn't see what you saw, that's all."

"Not the lights and the bill? Well, good-bye, Acheson."

The librarian ran after him.

"Gethin! Would you mind telling me? The P.R.S.—I'm a corresponding member—I——"

Gethin shook him off good-humouredly:

"Not a bit of it, my friend. You lost a rare chance of securing evidence at first-hand when you deserted me so basely that time. You're not a practical psychist, Acheson—too much of the tea-and-crumpet ghost-seer about you. You prefer to take your spirits on trust. Besides, you libelled my father. Goodbye!"

THE HEADLESS LEPER
by
FREDERICK COWLES

The early death of Frederick Cowles (1900-1948) cut short a career which had included lecturer, traveller, antiquarian, bibliophile and prize winning author. Folklore was one of his specialities and his published works on the subject include The Fairy Isle *(1935) and* Romany Wonder Tales *(1935).*

Another of his specialities was ghost stories and here he was surprisingly neglected by anthologists for many years until his inclusion in Hugh Lamb's second anthology A Wave of Fear *(1973). Cowles' two collections of ghost stories* The Horror of Abbot's Grange *(1936) and* The Night Wind Howls *(1938) contain some very good tales and he has since been deservedly republished.*

Cowles was for many years a librarian at Swinton Library, in Yorkshire, England. During these years he edited the library newsletter in which he first began publishing his ghost stories. He also indulged in some ghost-hunting of his own and is said to have encountered the sound of ghostly footsteps on an empty staircase.

Cowles, perhaps unsurprisingly, was a fan of M. R. James and the pair met on at least one occasion. He also named Stoker, Algernon Blackwood and Sheridan LeFanu as inspiration for his work.

THE HEADLESS LEPER

The Headless Leper *was first published in the anthology* Nightmares: A Collection of Uneasy Tales *(1933), part of Charles Birkin's* Creeps *series, before appearing in subsequent Cowles anthologies. The story is markedly short but contains imagery that will burn itself into the mind for days afterwards.*

* * *

Nearly fifteen years have passed since I first visited the little ruin around which this story centres. I was then a lad of thirteen—rather quieter than most boys are at that age, and given much to wandering away on solitary rambles.

I was on a visit to my grandparents, who lived in a little East Anglian market town, and, one day, I left the place by a road which was new to me. The outskirts of the town were squalid and dirty: a huge clay-pit yawned by the roadside, but, in the distance, I could see meadows golden with buttercups and hedges white with may.

The highway led over a railway bridge, on the other side of which I was surprised to see a tiny ruined chapel standing alone in a field. To the casual wayfarer there would be nothing untoward in this event, but, to my romantic mind, the sight of the lonely ruin became a great adventure—a living link with the historic past. My imagination soon reared a stately abbey around the little chapel, and it was with an eager thrill in my heart I climbed the fence which separated the field from the main road.

Once in the meadow the sordid realities became more apparent, for, by the east wall of the building, was a pigsty, and the chapel itself was evidently used as a barn.

I tried the door, but it was locked. The long, narrow windows were beyond my reach, but I was determined to see the interior of the chapel, and so walked round to investigate. On the north side was a haystack, and, by climbing on a part where the hay had been cut away, I found I could see through a window above the choir. At first I could see little, but as my eyes became more accustomed to the gloom I was able to make out a few trusses of hay on the floor. There also seemed to be the remains of a stone altar. What a pity, I thought, that such a delightful little chapel should be so desecrated.

It was pleasant on the haystack, and I must have been rather tired after my walk. I settled down and made myself so comfortable that I was soon asleep. When I awakened the sun had set, and it was already twilight.

I was just preparing to descend from my couch when I smelt a most offensive odour. At first I thought it came from the pigsty, but no pigsty on this earth could ever smell so utterly foul and corrupt.

Soon I discovered that the odour appeared to come from the chapel, and, boy-like, I put my head through the window to see what it could be. The smell was certainly inside—a sickly, nauseous stench that almost made me faint.

I was turning to the fresh air again when I thought I saw something move in the semi-darkness of the chapel. I looked again, half fascinated, half afraid, and saw that something was certainly moving—what I had previously taken to be trusses of hay were men in soiled, yellow robes, and they knelt on the hard floor with heads bowed.

I looked towards the east end of the building, and there, to my amazement, two candles were burning on the altar, and before it stood a vested priest. He knelt on one knee as I watched him, and lifted, high above his head, the white wafer of the Eucharist. In the chapel the heads of the yellow-robed men bowed even lower and, as they moved, little bells tinkled. I looked for the bells and found that they were attached by cords to the necks of the worshippers. The priest again prostrated himself, and again rising lifted the silver chalice that all might adore. Again came the doleful sound of the tuneless bells tinkling in the shadows.

Suddenly one of the bowed figures scrambled to its feet, and moved towards the window by which I stood. A terror filled my heart, but I was rooted to the spot. The figure came nearer to me, and raised its hand to the window-sill, and they were white, like white clay, and their whiteness was a mass of living sores. A great sickness made me dizzy, and I looked down. Then my heart seemed to stop beating, for my eyes beheld the greatest horror of all—the figure before me was headless. With a wild yell I fled from the terrible scene, but something followed me through the little meadow and down the main road—almost to my very door—a thing with terrible white hands and no head.

Long after I had been safely sitting by the fire in my grandparents' home the nameless horror haunted me, and in bed that night I hid my head under the clothes, and dared not look out. Even in the years that followed the terror still haunted my dreams, and I no longer went alone into the country.

It was twelve years later when I visited the little town again. My grandparents had both died, and I stayed with some old friends. The terrible experience of my boyhood was only a hazy memory, and the town held no unpleasant associations.

One of my friends, knowing my taste for archaeology, took me to visit most of the churches in the vicinity, and it was near the end of my stay when he informed me I was to see, that day, a gem of Norman work—an old chapel recently restored for worship.

As we passed out of the town the road seemed to be vaguely familiar. Near the roadside was a great lake, and my friend informed me that this had once been a clay-pit, but had had to be abandoned as the water rose so rapidly. Some memory stirred, but even then I did not realize to where we were going until we actually stood before the little chapel in which I had seen the terrifying apparition twelve years previously. It was, as my friend had said, a perfect specimen of Norman architecture. It had been refitted for worship in a modest way, but none of its charm had been destroyed.

"By the way," I inquired, "is this one of the chapels of a great monastery?"

"Good Lord! No," was the matter-of-fact reply, "I thought you knew. It is the chapel of the Leper Hospital of St Mary of Pity."

As my friend spoke I felt a feeling of fear and nausea coming over me. With a great effort I managed to shake off the feeling and advanced to the altar-rails. I stopped, just at the entrance of the sanctuary, to inspect the choir arch. My friend was looking at some inscription at the back of the chapel.

Suddenly the terror gripped me again; the ground beneath my feet seemed to go damp and sticky. I heard the dull sound of the tinkling bells, and, by my side, stood the headless figure with the white hands. What happened after that I cannot say—except that I fainted. My friend was very solicitous about me, but I managed to convince him that my faintness was caused by the close atmosphere inside the chapel.

As we were proceeding homewards my host said, "There is a queer story about that chapel. I don't think many people know it, but I have copy of one of the old books of the Hospital in which it is set out in detail. I will let you see it after dinner."

You may guess that I was very eager to hear or see anything that might throw some light upon my experiences in the chapel.

After the meal he took me into his study, and placed a transcription of a medieval manuscript before me. "There," he said, "is a copy of the accounts of the Almoner of the Leper Hospital of St Mary of Pity. The building you have seen today was the Norman chapel of the place, but it was not used after 1298."

"How was that?" I queried.

"A murder was committed in it," was the blunt reply. "A murder so terrible that, rather than reconsecrate the building, the monks erected another chapel. Why the old one was never pulled down I cannot make out—anyway, it has outlived the new." He touched the manuscript. "On page forty-two you can read the record of the desecration as the Almoner set it down."

He left me, and I eagerly settled myself to read the old Norman-French writing. Briefly, the scribe related how a certain Raymond of Low, a leper, was housed at the Hospital. He was a mild and gentle man, and very popular with the Brothers. One day a newcomer knocked at the gate. The stranger was a leper from Yorkshire, and the loathsome disease was already turning his brain. For some unaccountable reason the new guest took a violent dislike to the inoffensive Raymond.

No details of the event were given—only the bald statement that, at an early Mass, on the 22nd of June 1298, the lepers being in the chapel, the newcomer attacked Raymond of Low with a sickle, which he had hidden in his robes, and, before he could be restrained, had, with a tremendous blow, severed his unfortunate victim's head from his body.

I closed the book, and, as I replaced it on the desk, I seemed to see the whole of that terrible scene. The priest, pale and terror-stricken, crouching by the altar; the tall Yorkshireman held fast by the horrified lepers; and, on the floor, the headless body with the white hands bent in the agony of death, lying in a pool of blood.

About a week ago an extract from an East Anglian daily paper was sent to me. The report may have some connexion with the ghastly apparition in the chapel, and so I reprint it here:

Our readers have doubtless watched with interest the restoration and refurnishing of the ancient chapel of the Leper Hospital of St Mary of Pity. Much beautiful Early Norman work has been brought to light, together with a number of church ornaments: but a discovery, made during excavations in the interior of the chapel this week, is of exceptional interest. Whilst seeking to find the original level of the floor a workman struck some hard substance near the entrance to the chancel. Upon investigation this proved to be the lid of a coffin which was sunk only a few inches under the floor.

In the presence of the authorities the coffin was raised and the lid removed. Inside was the skeleton of a man, but the skull, instead of being in place, was resting at the feet, and the head had evidently been roughly severed from the body. It would seem that this fact indicated that the bones were those of some State prisoner who had been beheaded, but in the coffin was also found a small brass bell such as those worn at the neck by lepers.

OUR SCIENTIFIC OBSERVATIONS ON A GHOST
by
GRANT ALLEN

Canadian-born Grant Allen (1848-1899) graduated from Oxford after education in America and France. He followed a scientific and teaching career, and his first published writings were scientific articles. Once, in order to promote a particular scientific argument, he cast it in the form of a story, which was so successful that he was asked to write more fiction. These first stories were published under a pseudonym but eventually Allen published his first collection of tales under his own name, Strange Stories *(1884) and that same year saw publication of his first novel* Philista. *From then on, he produced equal quantities of short story collections and novels. Few of his philosophical essays and scientific articles have survived but a brief selection appeared posthumously in* The Hand of God *(1909).*

Our Scientific Observations On a Ghost, *which was included in* Strange Stories, *was first published in* Belgravia *magazine in 1878. Bringing his scientific background to bear on his supernatural fiction, Allen created something that is both humorous and fascinating as two eager scientists put an agreeable spirit through its paces.*

***

"Then nothing would convince you of the existence of ghosts, Harry," I said, "except seeing one."

"Not even seeing one, my dear Jim," said Harry. "Nothing on earth would make me believe in them, unless I were turned into a ghost myself."

So saying, Harry drained his glass of whisky toddy, shook out the last ashes from his pipe, and went off upstairs to bed. I sat for a while over the remnants of my cigar, and ruminated upon the subject of our conversation. For my own part, I was as little inclined to believe in ghosts as anybody; but Harry seemed to go one degree beyond me in scepticism. His argument amounted in brief to this,—that a ghost was by definition the spirit of a dead man in a visible form here on earth; but however strange might be the apparition which a ghost-seer thought he had observed, there was no evidence possible or actual to connect such apparition with any dead person whatsoever. It might resemble the deceased in face and figure, but so, said Harry, does a portrait. It might resemble him in voice and manner, but so does an actor or a mimic. It might resemble him in every possible particular, but even then we should only be justified in saying that it formed a close counterpart of the person in question, not that it was his ghost or spirit. In short, Harry maintained, with considerable show of reason, that nobody could ever have any scientific ground for identifying any external object, whether shadowy or material, with a past human existence of any sort. According to him, a man might conceivably see a phantom, but could not possibly know that he saw a ghost.

Harry and I were two Oxford bachelors, studying at the time for our degree in Medicine, and with an ardent love for the scientific side of our future profession. Indeed, we took a greater interest in comparative physiology and anatomy than in physic proper; and at this particular moment we were stopping in a very comfortable farm-house on the coast of Flintshire for our long vacation, with the special object of observing histologically a peculiar sea-side organism, the Thingumbobbum Whatumaycallianum, which is found so plentifully on the shores of North Wales, and which has been identified by Professor Haeckel with the larva of that famous marine ascidian from whom the Professor himself and the remainder of humanity generally are supposed to be undoubtedly descended. We had brought with us a full complement of lancets and scalpels, chemicals and test-tubes, galvanic batteries and thermo-electric piles; and we were splendidly equipped for a thorough-going scientific campaign of the first water. The farm-house in which we lodged had formerly belonged to the county family of the Egertons; and. though an Elizabethan manor replaced the ancient defensive building which had been wisely dismantled by Henry VIII, the modern farmhouse into which it had finally degenerated still bore the name of Egerton Castle. The whole house had a reputation in the neighbourhood for being haunted by the ghost of one Algernon Egerton, who was beheaded under James II for his participation, or rather his intention to participate, in Monmouth's rebellion. A wretched portrait of the hapless Protestant hero hung upon the wall of our joint sitting-room, having been left behind when the family moved to their new seat in Cheshire, as being unworthy of a place in the present baronet's splendid apartments. It was a few remarks upon the subject of Algernon's ghost which had introduced the question of ghosts in general; and after Harry had left the room, I sat for a while slowly finishing my cigar, and contemplating the battered features of the deceased gentleman.

As I did so, I was somewhat startled to hear a voice at my side observe in a bland and graceful tone, not unmixed with aristocratic *hauteur*, "You have been speaking of me, I believe,—in fact, I have unavoidably overheard your conversation,—and I have decided to assume the visible form and make a few remarks upon what seems to me a very hasty decision on your friend's part."

I turned round at once, and saw, in the easy-chair which Harry had just vacated, a shadowy shape, which grew clearer and clearer the longer I looked at it. It was that of a man of forty, fashionably dressed in the costume of the year 1685 or thereabouts, and bearing a close resemblance to the faded portrait on the wall just opposite. But the striking point about the object was this, that it evidently did not consist of any ordinary material substance, as its outline seemed vague and wavy, like that of a photograph where the sitter has moved; while all the objects behind it, such as the back of the chair and the clock in the corner, showed through the filmly head and body, in the very manner which painters have always adopted in representing a ghost. I saw at once that whatever else the object before might be, it certainly formed a fine specimen of the orthodox and old-fashioned apparition. In dress, appearance, and every other particular, it distinctly answered to what the unscientific mind would unhesitatingly have called the ghost of Algernon Egerton.

Here was a piece of extraordinary luck! In a house with two trained observers, supplied with every instrument of modern experimental research, we had lighted upon an undoubted specimen of the common spectre, which had so long eluded the scientific grasp. I was beside myself with delight. "Really, sir," I said, cheerfully, "it is most kind of you to pay us this visit, and I'm sure my friend will be only too happy to hear your remarks. Of course you will permit me to call him?"

The apparition appeared somewhat surprised at the philosophic manner in which I received his advances; for ghosts are accustomed to find people faint away or scream with terror at their first appearance; but for my own part I regarded him merely in the light of a very interesting phenomenon, which required immediate observation by two independent witnesses. However, he smothered his chagrin—for I believe he was really disappointed at my cool deportment—and answered that he would be very glad to see my friend if I wished it, though he had specially intended this visit for myself alone.

I ran upstairs hastily and found Harry in his dressing gown, on the point of removing his nether garments. "Harry," I cried breathlessly, "you must come downstairs at once. Algernon Egerton's ghost wants to speak to you."

Harry held up the candle and looked in my face with great deliberation. "Jim, my boy," he said quietly, "you've been having too much whisky."

"Not a bit of it," I answered, angrily. "Come downstairs and see. I swear to you positively that a Thing, the very counterpart of Algernon Egerton's picture, is sitting in your easy-chair downstairs, anxious to convert you to a belief in ghosts."

It took about three minutes to induce Harry to leave his room; but at last, merely to satisfy himself that I was demented, he gave way and accompanied me into the sitting-room. I was half afraid that the spectre would have taken umbrage at my long delay, and gone off in a huff and a blue flame; but when we reached the room, there he was, *in propriâ personâ*, gazing at his own portrait—or should I rather say his counterpart?—on the wall, with the utmost composure.

"Well, Harry," I said, "what do you call that?"

Harry put up his eyeglass, peered suspiciously at the phantom, and answered in a mollified tone, "It certainly *is* a most interesting phenomenon. It looks like a case of fluorescence; but you say the object can talk?"

"Decidedly," I answered, "it can talk as well as you or me. Allow me to introduce you to one another, gentlemen:—Mr. Henry Stevens, Mr. Algernon Egerton; for though you didn't mention your name, Mr. Egerton, I presume from what you said that I am right in my conjecture."

"Quite right," replied the phantom, rising as it spoke, and making a low bow to Harry from the waist upward. I suppose your friend is one of the Lincolnshire Stevenses, sir?"

"Upon my soul," said Harry, "I haven't the faintest conception where my family came from. My grandfather, who made what little money we have got, was a cotton-spinner at Rochdale, but he might have come from heaven knows where. I only know he was a very honest old gentleman, and he remembered me handsomely in his will."

"Indeed, sir," said the apparition coldly. "*My* family were the Egertons of Egerton Castle, in the county of Flint, Armigeri; whose ancestor, Radulphus de Egerton, is mentioned in Domesday as one of the esquires of Hugh Lupus, Earl Palatine of Chester. Radulphus de Egerton had a son——"

"Whose history," said Harry, anxious to cut short these genealogical details, "I have read in the Annals of Flintshire, which lies in the next room, with the name you give as yours on the fly-leaf. But it seems, sir, you are anxious to converse with me on the subject of ghosts. As that question interests us all at present, much more than family descent, will you kindly begin by telling us whether you yourself lay claim to be a ghost?"

"Undoubtedly I do," replied the phantom.

"The ghost of Algernon Egerton, formerly of Egerton Castle?" I interposed.

"Formerly and now," said the phantom, in correction. "I have long inhabited, and I still habitually inhabit, by night at least, the room in which we are at present seated."

"The deuce you do," said Harry warmly. "This is a most illegal and unconstitutional proceeding. The house belongs to our landlord, Mr. Hay: and my friend here and myself have hired it for the summer, sharing the expenses, and claiming the sole title to the use of the rooms." (Harry omitted to mention that he took the best bedroom himself and put me off with a shabby little closet, while we divided the rent on equal terms.)

"True,' said the spectre good-humouredly; "but you can't eject a ghost, you know. You may get a writ of *habeas corpus*, but the English law doesn't supply you with a writ of *habeas animam*. The infamous Jeffreys left me that at least. I am sure the enlightened nineteenth century wouldn't seek to deprive me of it."

"Well," said Harry, relenting, "provided you don't interfere with the experiments, or make away with the tea and sugar, I'm sure I have no objection. But if you are anxious to prove to us the existence of ghosts, perhaps you will kindly allow us to make a few simple observations?"

"With all the pleasure in death," answered the apparition courteously. "Such, in fact, is the very object for which I've assumed visibility."

"In that case, Harry," I said, "the correct thing will be

to get out some paper, and draw up a running report which we may both attest afterwards. A few simple notes on the chemical and physical properties of a spectre will be an interesting novelty for the Royal Society, and they ought all to be jotted down in black and white at once."

This course having been unanimously determined upon as strictly regular, I laid a large folio of foolscap on the writing-table, and the apparition proceeded to put itself in an attitude for careful inspection.

"The first point to decide," said I, "is obviously the physical properties of our visitor. Mr. Egerton, will you kindly allow us to feel your hand?"

"You may *try* to feel it if you like," said the phantom quietly, "but I doubt if you will succeed to any brilliant extent." As he spoke, he held out his arm. Harry and I endeavoured successively to grasp it: our fingers slipped through the faintly luminous object as though it were air or shadow. The phantom bowed forward his head; we attempted to touch it, but our hands once more passed unopposed across the whole face and shoulders, without finding any trace whatsoever of mechanical resistance. "Experience the first," said Harry; "the apparition has no tangible material substratum." I seized the pen and jotted down the words as he spoke them. This was really turning out a very full-blown specimen of the ordinary ghost!

"The next question to settle," I said, "is that of gravity—Harry, give me a hand out here with the weighing-machine—Mr. Egerton, will you be good enough to step upon this board?"

Mirabile dictu! The board remained steady as ever. Not a tremor of the steelyard betrayed the weight of its shadowy occupant. "Experience the second," cried Harry, in his cool, scientific way: "the apparition has the specific gravity of atmospheric air." I jotted down this note also, and quietly prepared for the next observation.

"Wouldn't it be well," I inquired of Harry, "to try the weight in vacuo? It is possible that, while the specific gravity in air is equal to that of the atmosphere, the specific gravity in vacuo may be zero. The apparition—pray excuse me, Mr. Egerton, if the terms in which I allude to you seem disrespectful, but to call you a ghost would be to prejudge the point at issue—the apparition may have no proper weight of its own at all."

"It would be very inconvenient, though," said Harry, "to put the whole apparition under a bell-glass: in fact, we have none big enough. Besides, suppose we were to find that by exhausting the air we got rid of the object altogether, as is very possible, that would awkwardly interfere with the future prosecution of our researches into its nature and properties."

"Permit me to make a suggestion," interposed the phantom, "if a person whom you choose to relegate to the neuter gender may be allowed to have a voice in so scientific a question. My friend, the ingenious Mr. Boyle, has lately explained to me the construction of his air-pump, which we saw at one of the Friday evenings at the Royal Institution. It seems to me that your object would be attained if I were to put one hand only on the scale under the bell-glass, and permit the air to be exhausted."

"Capital," said Harry: and we got the air-pump in readiness accordingly. The spectre then put his right hand into the scale, and we plumped the bell-glass on top of it. The connecting portion of the arm shone through the severing glass, exactly as though the spectre consisted merely of an immaterial light. In a few minutes the air was exhausted, and the scales remained evenly balanced as before.

"This experiment," said Harry judicially, "slightly modifies the opinion which we formed from the preceding one. The specific gravity evidently amounts in itself to nothing, being as air in air, and as vacuum in vacuo. Jot down the result, Jim, will you?"

I did so faithfully, and then turning to the spectre I observed, "You mentioned a Mr. Boyle, sir, just now. You allude, I suppose, to the father of chemistry?"

"And uncle of the Earl of Cork," replied the apparition, promptly filling up the well-known quotation. "Exactly so. I knew Mr. Boyle slightly during our lifetime, and I have known him intimately ever since he joined the majority."

"May I ask, while my friend makes the necessary preparations for the spectrum analysis and the chemical investigation, whether you are in the habit of associating much with—er—well, with other ghosts?"

"Oh yes, I see a good deal of society."

"Contemporaries of your own, or persons of earlier and later dates?"

"Dates really matter very little to us. We may have Socrates and Bacon chatting in the same group. For my own part, I prefer modern society—I may say, the society of the latest arrivals."

"That's exactly why I asked," said I. "The excessively modern tone of your language and idioms struck me, so to speak, as a sort of anachronism with your Restoration costume—an anachronism which I fancy I have noticed in many printed accounts of gentlemen from your portion of the universe."

"Your observation is quite true," replied the apparition. "We continue always to wear the clothes which were in fashion at the time of our decease; but we pick up from new-comers the latest additions to the English language, and even, I may say, to the slang dictionary. I know many ghosts who talk familiarly of 'awfully jolly hops,' and allude to their progenitors as 'the governor.' Indeed, it is considered quite behind the times to describe a lady as 'vastly pretty,' and poor Mr. Pepys, who still preserves the antiquated idiom of his diary, is looked upon among us as a dreadfully slow old fogey."

"But why, then," said I, "do you wear your old costumes for ever? Why not imitate the latest fashions from Poole's and Worth's, as well as the latest cant phrase from the popular novels?"

"Why, my dear sir," answered the phantom, "we must have *something* to mark our original period. Besides, most people to whom we appear know something about costume, while very few know anything about changes in idiom,"—that I must say seemed to me, in passing, a powerful argument indeed—"and so we all preserve the dress which we habitually wore during our lifetime."

"Then," said Harry irreverently, looking up from his chemicals, "the society in your part of the country must closely resemble a fancy-dress ball."

"Without the tinsel and vulgarity, we flatter ourselves," answered the phantom.

By this time the preparations were complete, and Harry inquired whether the apparition would object to our putting out the lights in order to obtain definite results with the spectroscope. Our visitor politely replied that he was better accustomed to darkness than to the painful glare of our paraffin candles. "In fact," he added, "only the strong desire which I felt to convince you of our existence as ghosts could have induced me to present myself in so bright a room. Light is very trying to the eyes of spirits, and we generally take our constitutionals between eleven at night and four in the morning, stopping at home entirely during the moonlit half of the month."

"Ah, yes," said Harry, extinguishing the candles; "I've read, of course, that your authorities exactly reverse our own Oxford rules. You are all gated, I believe, from dawn to sunset, instead of from sunset to dawn, and have to run away helter-skelter at the first streaks of daylight, for fear of being too late for admission without a fine of twopence. But you will allow that your usual habit of showing yourselves only in the very darkest places and seasons naturally militates somewhat against the credibility of your existence. If all apparitions would only follow your sensible example by coming out before two scientific people in a well-lighted room, they would stand a much better chance of getting believed: though even in the present case I must allow that I should have felt far more confidence in your positive reality if you'd presented yourself in broad daylight, when Jim and I hadn't punished the whisky quite as fully as we've done this evening."

When the candles were out, our apparition still retained its fluorescent, luminous appearance, and seemed to burn with a faint bluish light of its own. We projected a pencil through the spectroscope, and obtained, for the first time in the history of science, the spectrum of a spectre. The result was a startling one indeed. We had expected to find lines indicating the presence of sulphur or phosphorus: instead of that, we obtained a continuous band of pale luminosity, clearly pointing to the fact that the apparition had no known terrestial element in its composition. Though we felt rather surprised at this discovery, we simply noted it down on our paper, and proceeded to verify it by chemical analysis.

The phantom obligingly allowed us to fill a small phial with the luminous matter, which Harry immediately proceeded to test with all the resources at our disposal. For purposes of comparison I filled a corresponding phial with air from another part of the room, which I subjected to precisely similar tests. At the end of half an hour we had completed our examination—the spectre meanwhile watching us with mingled curiosity and amusement; and we laid our written quantitative results side by side. They agreed to a decimal. The table, being interesting, deserves a place in this memoir. It ran as follows:—

Chemical Analysis of an Apparition.

Atmospheric air	96·45 per cent.
Aqueous vapour	2·31 ,,
Carbonic acid	1·08 ,,
Tobacco smoke	0·16 ,,
Volatile alcohol	A trace
	100·00 ,,

The alcohol Harry plausibly attributed to the presence of glasses which had contained whisky toddy. The other constituents would have been normally present in the atmosphere of a room where two fellows had been smoking uninterruptedly ever since dinner. This important experiment clearly showed that the apparition had no proper chemical constitution of its own, but consisted entirely of the same materials as the surrounding air.

"Only one thing remains to be done now, Jim," said Harry, glancing significantly at a plain deal table in the corner, with whose uses we were both familiar; "but then the question arises, does this gentleman come within the meaning of the Act? I don't feel certain about it in my own mind, and with the present unsettled state of public opinion on this subject, our first duty is to obey the law."

"Within the meaning of the Act?" I answered; "decidedly not. The words of the forty-second section say distinctly 'any *living* animal.' Now, Mr. Egerton, according to his own account is a ghost, and has been dead for some two hundred years or thereabouts: so that we needn't have the slightest scruple on that account."

"Quite so," said Harry, in a tone of relief. "Well then, sir,' turning to the apparition, "may I ask you whether you would object to our vivisecting you?"

"Mortuisecting, you mean, Harry," I interposed parenthetically. "Let us keep ourselves strictly within the utmost letter of the law."

"Vivisecting? Mortuisecting?" exclaimed the spectre, with some amusement. "Really, the proposal is so very novel that I hardly know how to answer it. I don't think you will find it a very practicable undertaking: but still, if you like, yes, you may try your hands upon me."

We were both much gratified at this generous readiness to further the cause of science, for which, to say the truth, we had hardly felt prepared. No doubt, we were constantly in the habit of maintaining that vivisection didn't really hurt, and that rabbits or dogs rather enjoyed the process than otherwise; still, we did not quite expect an apparition in human form to accede in this gentlemanly manner to a personal request which after all is rather a startling one. I seized our new friend's band with warmth and effusion (though my emotion was somewhat checked by finding it slip through my fingers immaterially), and observed in a voice trembling with admiration, "Sir, you display a spirit of self-sacrifice which does honour to your head and heart. Your total freedom from prejudice is perfectly refreshing to the anatomical mind. If all 'subjects' were equally ready to be vivisected—no, I mean mortuisected—oh,—well,—there," I added (for I began to perceive that my argument didn't hang together, as "subjects" usually accepted mortuisection with the utmost resignation), "perhaps it wouldn't make much difference after all."

Meanwhile Harry had pulled the table into the centre of the room, and arranged the necessary instruments at one end. The bright steel had a most charming and scientific appearance, which added greatly to the general effect. I saw myself already in imagination drawing up an elaborate report for the Royal Society, and delivering a Croonian Oration, with diagrams and sections complete, in illustration of the "Vascular System of a Ghost." But alas, it was not to be. A preliminary difficulty, slight in itself, yet enormous in its preventive effects, unhappily defeated our well-made plans.

"Before you lay yourself on the table," said Harry, gracefully indicating that article of furniture to the spectre with his lancet, "may I ask you to oblige me by removing your clothes? It is usual in all these operations to—ahem—in short, to proceed *in puris naturalibu*s. As you have been so very kind in allowing us to operate upon you, of course you won't object to this minor but indispensable accompaniment."

"Well, really, sir," answered the ghost, "I should have no personal objection whatsoever; but I'm rather afraid it can't be done. To tell you the truth, my clothes are an integral part of myself. Indeed, I consist chiefly of clothes, with only a head and hands protruding at the principal extremities. You must have noticed that all persons of my sort about whom you have read or heard were fully clothed in the fashion of their own day. I fear it would be quite impossible to remove these clothes. For example, how very absurd it would be to see the shadowy outline of a ghostly coat hanging up on a peg behind a door. The bare notion would be sufficient to cast ridicule upon the whole community. No, gentlemen, much as I should like to gratify you, I fear the thing's impossible. And, to let the whole secret out, I'm inclined to think, for my part, that I haven't got any independent body whatsoever."

"But, surely," I interposed, "you must have *some*

internal economy, or else how can you walk and talk? For example, have you a heart?"

"Most certainly, my dear sir, and I humbly trust it is in the right place."

"You misunderstand me," I repeated: "I am speaking literally, not figuratively. Have you a central vascular organ on your left-hand side, with two auricles and ventricles, a mitral and a tricuspid valve, and the usual accompaniment of aorta, pulmonary vein, pulmonary artery, systole and diastole, and so forth?"

"Upon my soul, sir," replied the spectre with an air of bewilderment, "I have never even heard the names of these various objects to which you refer, and so I am quite unable to answer your question. But if you mean to ask whether I have something beating just under my fob (excuse the antiquated word, but as I wear the thing in question I must necessarily use the name), why then, most undoubtedly I have."

"Will you oblige me, sir," said Harry, "by showing me your wrist? It is true I can't *feel* your pulse, owing to what you must acknowledge as a very unpleasant tenuity in your component tissues: but perhaps I may succeed in *seeing* it."

The apparition held out its arm. Harry instinctively endeavoured to balance the wrist in his hand, but of course failed in catching it. We were both amused throughout to observe how difficult it remained, after several experiences, to realize the fact that this visible object had no material and tangible background underlying it. Harry put up his eyeglass and gazed steadily at the phantom arm; not a trace of veins or arteries could anywhere be seen. "Upon my word," he muttered, "I believe it's true, and the subject has no internal economy at all. This is really very interesting."

"As it is quite impossible to undress you," I observed,

turning to our visitor, "may I venture to make a section through your chest, in order, if practicable, to satisfy myself as to your organs generally?"

"Certainly," replied the good-humoured spectre; "I am quite at your service." I took my longest lancet from its case and made a very neat cut, right across the sternum, so as to pass directly through all the principal viscera. The effect, I regret to say, was absolutely nugatory. The two halves of the body reunited instantaneously behind the instrument, just as a mass of mercury reunites behind a knife. Evidently there was no chance of getting at the anatomical details, if any existed, underneath that brocaded waistcoat of phantasmagoric satin. We gave up the attempt in despair.

"And now," said the shadowy form, with a smile of conscious triumph, flinging itself easily but noiselessly into a comfortable arm-chair, "I hope you are convinced that ghosts really do exist. I think I have pretty fully demonstrated to you my own purely spiritual and immaterial nature."

"Excuse me," said Harry, seating himself in his turn on the ottoman: "I regret to say that I remain as sceptical as at the beginning. You have merely convinced me that a certain visible shape exists apparently unaccompanied by any tangible properties. With this phenomenon I am already familiar in the case of phosphorescent gaseous effiuvia. You also seem to utter audible words without the aid of a proper larynx or other muscular apparatus; but the telephone has taught me that sounds exactly resembling those of the human voice may be produced by a very simple membrane. You have afforded us probably the best opportunity ever given for examining a so-called ghost, and my private conviction at the end of it is that you are very likely an egregious humbug."

I confess I was rather surprised at this energetic

conclusion, for my own faith had been rapidly expanding under the strange experiences of that memorable evening. But the visitor himself seemed much hurt and distressed. "Surely," he said, "you won't doubt my word when I tell you plainly that I am the authentic ghost of Algernon Egerton. The word of an Egerton of Egerton Castle was always better than another man's oath, and it is so still, I hope. Besides, my frank and courteous conduct to you both to-night, and the readiness with which I have met all your proposals for scientific examination, certainly entitle me to better treatment at your hands."

"I must beg ten thousand pardons," Harry replied, "for the plain language which I am compelled to use. But let us look at the case in a different point of view. During your occasional visits to the world of living men, you may sometimes have travelled in a railway carriage in your invisible form."

"I have taken a trip now and then (by a night train, of course), just to see what the invention was like."

"Exactly so. Well, now, you must have noticed that a guard insisted from time to time upon waking up the sleepy passengers for no other purpose than to look at their tickets. Such a precaution might be resented, say by an Egerton of Egerton Castle, as an insult to his veracity and his honesty. But, you see, the guard doesn't know an Egerton from a Muggins: and the mere word of a passenger to the effect that he belongs to that distinguished family is in itself of no more value than his personal assertion that his ticket is perfectly *en régle*."

"I see your analogy, and I must allow its remarkable force."

"Not only so," continued Harry firmly, "but you must remember that in the case I have put, the guard is dealing with known beings of the ordinary human type. Now, when a living person introduces himself to me as Egerton of Egerton Castle, or Sir Roger Tichborne of Alresford, I accept his statement with a certain amount of doubt, proportionate to the natural improbability of the circumstances. But when a gentleman of shadowy appearance and immaterial substance, like yourself, makes a similar assertion, to the effect that he is Algernon Egerton who died two hundred years ago, then I am reluctantly compelled to acknowledge, even at the risk of hurting that gentleman's susceptible feelings, that I can form no proper opinion whatsoever of his probable veracity. Even men, whose habits and constitution I familiarly understand, cannot always be trusted to tell me the truth: and how then can I expect implicitly to believe a being whose very existence contradicts all my previous experiences, and whose properties give the lie to all my scientific conceptions—a being who moves without muscles and speaks without lungs? Look at the possible alternatives, and then you will see that I am guilty of no personal rudeness when I respectfully decline to accept your uncorroborated assertions. You may be Mr. Algernon Egerton, it is true, and your general style of dress and appearance certainly bears out that supposition; but then you may equally well be his Satanic Majesty in person—in which case you can hardly expect me to credit your character for implicit truthfulness. Or again, you may be a mere hallucination of my fancy: I may be suddenly gone mad, or I may be totally drunk, and now that I look at the bottle, Jim, we must certainly allow that we have fully appreciated the excellent qualities of your capital Glenlivat. In short, a number of alternatives exist, any one of which is quite as probable as the supposition of your being a genuine ghost; which supposition I must therefore lay aside as a mere matter for the exercise of a suspended judgment."

I thought Harry had him on the hip, there: and the

spectre evidently thought so too; for he rose at once and said rather stiffly, "I fear, sir, you are a confirmed sceptic, upon this point, and further argument might only result in one or the other of us losing his temper. Perhaps it would be better for me to withdraw. I have the honour to wish you both a very good evening." He spoke once more with the *hauteur* and grand mannerism of the old school, besides bowing very low at each of us separately as he wished us good-night.

"Stop a moment," said Harry rather hastily. "I wouldn't for the world be guilty of any inhospitality, and least of all to a gentleman, however indefinite in his outline, who has been so anxious to afford us every chance of settling an interesting question as you have. Won't you take a glass of whisky and water before you go, just to show there's no animosity?"

"I thank you," answered the apparition, in the same chilly tone; "I cannot accept your kind offer. My visit has already extended to a very unusual length, and I have no doubt I shall be blamed as it is by more reticent ghosts for the excessive openness with which I have conversed upon subjects generally kept back from the living world. Once more," with another ceremonious bow, "I have the honour to wish you a pleasant evening."

As he said these words, the fluorescent light brightened for a second, and then faded entirely away. A slightly unpleasant odour also accompanied the departure of our guest. In a moment, spectre and scent alike disappeared; but careful examination with a delicate test exhibited a faint reaction which proved the presence of sulphur in small quantities. The ghost had evidently vanished quite according to established precedent.

We filled our glasses once more, drained them off meditatively, and turned into our bedrooms as the clock was striking four.

Next morning, Harry and I drew up a formal account of the whole circumstance, which we sent to the Royal Society, with a request that they would publish it in their Transactions. To our great surprise, that learned body refused the paper, I may say with contumely. We next applied to the Anthropological Institute, where, strange to tell, we met with a like inexplicable rebuff. Nothing daunted by our double failure, we despatched a copy of our analysis to the Chemical Society; but the only acknowledgment accorded to us was a letter from the secretary, who stated that "such a sorry joke was at once impertinent and undignified." In short, the scientific world utterly refuses to credit our simple and straightforward narrative; so that we are compelled to throw ourselves for justice upon the general reading public at large. As the latter invariably peruse the pages of "BELGRAVIA," I have ventured to appeal to them in the present article, confident that they will redress our wrongs, and accept this valuable contribution to a great scientific question at its proper worth. It may be many years before another chance occurs for watching an undoubted and interesting Apparition under such favourable circumstances for careful observation; and all the above information may be regarded as absolutely correct, down to five places of decimals.

Still, it must be borne in mind that unless an apparition had been scientifically observed as we two independent witnesses observed this one, the grounds for believing in its existence would have been next to none. And even after the clear evidence which we obtained of its immaterial nature, we yet remain entirely in the dark as to its objective reality, and we have not the faintest reason for believing it to have been a genuine unadulterated ghost. At the best we can only say that we saw and heard Something, and that this Something differed very widely from almost any other object we had ever seen and heard before. To leap at the conclusion that the Something was therefore a ghost, would be, I venture humbly to submit, without offence to the Psychical Research Society, a most unscientific and illogical specimen of that peculiar fallacy known as Begging the Question.

MIRACLE IN SUBURBIA
by
THOMAS BURKE

Thomas Burke's life would seem to have been as colourful and thrilling as those of the protagonists in his stories. That is, at least, if Thomas Burke's own biographical embellishments are to be believed.

What we do know is that Sydney Thomas Burke was born in Clapham Junction in 1886, but was sent to live with his uncle in Poplar, East London, after the untimely death of his father. In 1901, while working as an office boy, Burke published his first professional piece, The Bellamy Diamonds, *in* Spare Moments *magazine and in 1915 published his observations of the working-class London he so loved in* Nights in Town: A London Autobiography.

In 1916 he published his first anthology, Limehouse Nights, *and it was this that gained Burke some accolade as either an author ('the laureate of London's Chinatown') or, to some, an unhelpful propagator of racist 'Yellow Fever' fantasies.*

Burke's 1935 anthology Night-Pieces: Eighteen Tales, *from which the following story is taken, was a striking collection of the weird and macabre, all centered, of course, around the dark underbelly of his beloved London.* Miracle in Suburbia *has a deliciously dark sting in its tail.*

Whether or not Thomas Burke actually 'sat at the feet of Chinese philosophers who kept opium dens to learn from the lips that could frame only broken English, the secrets, good and evil, of the mysterious East' we may never know.
But probably not.

* * *

In a back room of one of the many old houses still left along London's southern riverside, an elderly man and a youth sat at a table and looked at each other. The man had a bird profile and a probing eye, and the hands that were clasped on the table were large and thin and white. The youth had no profile, and his hands were neither thin nor white, but large and red. They appeared to worry him. Once or twice he put them on the table, in imitation of the man's easy pose. Then he seemed to see them in comparison with the man's, and hid them. From time to time, as though they were forgetful of their unseemliness, they came again to the table, clasping and unclasping.

The room, too, seemed to worry him. It was an odd room; out of character with that stretch of the riverside; such a room as the youth had never seen there or elsewhere. He had seen museums and their contents. This room contained none of the things he had seen in museums, but it was filled with things that were not everyday furniture—queer things; and it had the feeling of a museum. He could not give names to the things; he knew only that he had never seen them in the British Museum or in South Kensington. Weird-looking things. Queer-shaped jars. Wooden sticks. Circular things. Triangular things. Yellow paper with all sorts of squiggles on them. He didn't like the look of them, but his eyes continued to rove about the room and return to them.

The man noted his uneasiness. "Have a drink?" He went to a sideboard, and began to get out some bottles.

The youth said hastily: "No thanks. No thanks. I—I'm not thirsty." He was not averse from a drink. He liked a drink with his friends. But he did not want a drink in this room with this man. Under his reason, under even his sense, he was aware that he was being warned not to have a drink here, not to stay here. The table warned him. The things hanging on the wall warned him. The window-curtains warned him. The very nostrils of the man talking to him warned him. The room seemed to be murmuring with distant drums. All the objects in it were throwing off something that went to the secret corners of his being and said, "Have nothing to do with this place. Get out while you can."

But he couldn't be so silly as to make a sudden bolt; neither the man nor the room had so far afforded any reason for that. He would obey the feeling so far as to refuse a drink—you never knew with drinks; so easy to put something in 'em—but that urge to get out was probably just nerves. The man seemed quite a nice chap, and he couldn't *see* anything wrong with the room. There was no danger anywhere; nobody was threatening him. If the man tried to attack him, that would be different. That'd be a reason for getting out. But a mere 'feeling' was silly, and the feeling that he had about this room was probably due to his not having seen a room like it before. He must fight it down. The man had said he had a proposal to make which might be profitable to the youth, and the youth could do with a proposal or two of that sort. He mustn't allow 'feelings' to interfere with business.

"Well, if you won't have a drink," the man was saying, "let's get on with our talk. I spoke to you in the coffee-shop just now because you looked a likely lad for the work I want done. A simple piece of work, and I'd pay well. H'm."

"I could do with a job. Been out nearly a year now. Tramping about every day looking for something. Can't find anything, though."

"No? I thought that was the case. Well, now, I just want a little bit of work done, and I'll pay for it what you'd probably have to work half a year for in the ordinary way. For this piece of work, which you can do in an hour or two, I'll pay you—fifty pounds."

"Fifty pounds?"

"Fifty pounds."

The youth seemed to try to visualize fifty pounds—fifty pounds all at once. The picture, and the effort to produce it, made him frown. He became suspicious. "Fifty pounds... Must be something queer if you'd pay all that. Fifty pounds... Must be something not right."

The man smiled. "I like your recoil. I appreciate it. But you need have no hesitation on that score. The answer to your remark is, in a sense, yes and no. That is, a little technical point of what is called wrong-doing is involved. But not the kind of technical point that could get you into trouble. Just a matter of—" he laughed—"taking something from somebody. But listen!" He held up a hand to stop the youth's protest. "Taking something from somebody who stole it. A perfectly honourable proceeding. An act that a dozen men of spotless respectability would be willing to perform, if they were young enough and agile enough. And I'm willing to pay fifty pounds—sums of money convey little to me, though I realize that they mean something to others—because I need a young man whom I can trust. A young man to whom fifty pounds would be a symbol of a vow of silence. That was why I picked on you. It's like this."

He leaned back in his chair and held the youth with his

eyes. The youth frowned again in the effort of concentrating on what might be a complicated story. "A very valuable relic has been taken from a museum with which I'm connected. If we make the loss public we're likely to lose it. It will go abroad. We want no publicity; no scandal. We want simply to get it back. We know who has it and where it is. And a smart young man could get it without any trouble. And would do a service to society. And—further—without any danger to himself whatever."

"Oh..." The youth pondered. It sounded all right, but coming from this particular man It didn't seem quite as right as it sounded. He was an honest youth, and never would have eased his troubles even by the lightest of crimes. Yet this man's eyes and voice swayed him. It seemed that he was asked to perform a straightforward, but not quite proper, service, and was to be handsomely paid for it and protected from all risk. Well, if it *was* all right, fifty pounds was fifty pounds. Without that handsome reward he would have said no to the proposal, even if the act was a service to society. He was not a hero, and saw no reason for implicating himself in other people's troubles. On the other hand if it was not all right, a reward of a thousand pounds and complete immunity would not have tempted him to common theft. He couldn't quite 'get' this man. His chief feeling was that it wasn't all right, but under this man's eyes he couldn't feel that it was wrong. It seemed to be a private row about public property, and if that was so his moral sense told him that he would be justified in accepting the job and restoring the thing, whatever it was, to its owners. Still, there were one or two funny points about it.

"But if it's all right and above board, and as easy as you say, why are you paying all that money for the job?"

"I've told you. Fifty pounds probably seems a lot of money to you, but it's nothing to the historic value of this relic. Anyway, I should not be paying that money for the mere job. I should be paying it, as I said, for a man's honesty and for his keeping quiet. This matter must not be talked about to anybody. It's a delicate matter. Might lead to trouble with other countries. You understand? That's why I need somebody who knows nothing of the circumstances surrounding the affair and somebody who will forget it after he has performed his service. Somebody who will never mention that service—nor what the object of the service was. Particularly that. No mention of the nature of the relic.

"I'm not much of a talker at any time."

"I've observed that on my visits to the coffee-shop."

"But what's this about no trouble and no danger? How can that be? If I'm taking something from another chap, he naturally wouldn't let me. Or what about a copper seeing me do it?"

"Even if you were seen taking it, nobody could harm you. You will be protected. You will approach that man freely and you will come away freely. I have power to protect you, and my power will accompany you all the time."

"Power? You mean some of your people—some of those interested in the thing?"

The man smiled. "I see you don't understand. And perhaps it's as well you don't. You will be more efficient for the work. But there are powers other than the powers of the hands and limbs. There are powers other than the powers of the brain. There is a power of the spirit. That is the power that will protect you."

"Mmm... Sounds all right. So do lots o' things. But if you got all this—what you call power, I should think you could get it back easy enough yourself. Just say, 'Presto, come over here,' like the conjurers." He giggled. Was this old chap drunk—him and his talk about taking things from people and being protected by power?"

"I see you don't understand. And don't believe. We who have this power may not use it ourselves. We may use it only through an instrument. *Then* it is effective. And no harm can come to our instrument. We can place our protective power around him."

"How d'you make that out? S'posing the chap that's got this thing goes for me, and——"

"If he does, no harm can come to you. You do not believe, and it is not really necessary that you should. But perhaps I may convince you. Look, I am putting my power around you now. I am calling up the power within you. Now!"

He pushed back his chair and stood erect, looking down at the youth. For some seconds they stared at each other. In the moment of his rising the man's body seemed to fill the room and to be bursting from it. The lamp on the mantelshelf threw its shadows enormously on the wall, and the shadows copied their movements and became a secondary couple engaged in silent, sinister business. The youth was faintly sensible of some disturbance of the air; then of some change in himself—a feeling of confidence and strength.

The first instinct was that the man was putting something over on him. He resented this and wasn't going to have it. He was glad he hadn't had that drink. But with the feeling of confidence his resentment passed. This was good. This wasn't the hypnotism he had heard about. He wasn't this man's dumb servant; he was his equal. He felt that all the things he had often seen himself doing, he could do; that he had abilities which he hadn't even guessed at but which this man perceived. He felt as though up to now he had been tied up; an inarticulate, ineffectual youth; and that this man had released him. He stretched both hands on the table, no longer ashamed of them, leaned back, and stared at the man.

"You feel something? Ah.... That is my power meeting your power—blending with it and clothing you. You doubted what I said. It is natural that you should. These things are known to few. But now you are doubting your own doubts. My power is over you. And you are aware of it. Now I will convince you utterly that if you serve me in this matter you will be protected from every kind of harm. See!"

In one rhythmic movement the man swung to the wall, tore down from it a naked Turkish sword, whirled it above his head with a long arm, and brought its edge, full swing, down upon the youth's right wrist.

The youth said "Oo, I say!"

"Hurt you?"

"No. Give me a start, like. Wasn't expecting you to do that."

"Ha! Look at that blade's edge. Feel it."

"Jee! Blooming razor." Then he seemed to realize that something odd had happened. His voice rose to a squeak. "Here—but—but you slashed that across my wrist with all your might. You—you—A thing like that'd cut through a table. And you——"

"I did. Look at your wrist."

The youth examined the wrist. "Can't see anything. Not a mark even."

"Of course not. Didn't I tell you that my power was protecting you? Give me one of those logs from that box by the fire."

The youth took up an oak log-wedge of twelve-inch thickness—and placed it on the table."

"Now see. My power is not protecting that log, and so——" He made a second swing of the sword and brought it down on the log. The log fell in two pieces.

The youth stared. "Jee!"

"That sword, as you say, would cut through a table. But it cannot cut through you. Nothing could. Nothing can in any way harm you. Between danger and you stands my power. And so you can do this little business for me—er—and my colleagues with no more risk than you would face in walking from here to your home. Does this evidence convince you?"

The youth's face was blank. His sense and brain were in effervescence. "Well, if blooming miracles is evidence..."

"It was not a miracle—in your sense. It was a fact. What is commonly called a miracle is only a fact of applied knowledge. Now, will you do a little bit of work for us?"

"Well, if it's absolutely straight—yes. But I don't want to be mixed up in any funny stuff."

"It *is* absolutely straight. The circumstances of the affair prevent my giving you proof of that. You must take my word for it. That you will be guaranteed against all danger I have already proved. Nobody need be ashamed of performing such a service as this—the recovery of a valuable relic for its owners..."

"Well, what do you want me to do? And what is this thing?"

"The thing—" the man lowered his voice, and for a moment seemed to lose the suggestion of bulk—"the thing is a porcelain goblet."

"Porce—*what*?"

"A por—a china jar. A simple china jar. But very old. And of great historic value. You will simply take it from the man and bring it here."

"Simply take it... And what'll he do?"

"He may make some resistance, but no matter what he does he cannot harm you. I thought I had made that clear."

"Yes... yes... er... I see. You mean there might be a schemozzle but me being like I am now, his stuff won't come off. Like the sword? That's it, eh?"

"That's it exactly."

"Don't hardly seem able to believe it. More like a dream."

"Well, you have had proof with the sword. And you will have further proof. Now follow your instructions... At half-past eleven to-night a man will come from a house in Sloane Street and walk along Sloane Square. A short man in spectacles, wearing a fawn overcoat and bowler hat. He will be carrying an attache case. If he is not carrying a case the—er—jar will be in his overcoat pocket. He will go through that narrow street by the District station—he will be making for Pimlico Road. When he is in that narrow street, you will approach him and snatch the case, or take the jar from his pocket, and bring it here to me."

The youth, stirred by this picture of daring doings, giggled. "Sounds easy."

The man folded his arms and looked at him with cold eyes. "It *will* be easy."

The youth got up. "Y'know, I believe it will. You could make a chap believe anything in this room. I don't understand it, but after that sword..."

"Good. I see that you believe, and that you know you can do what I want. Here—" He put a hand inside his coat and brought out a bundle of treasury notes. "Fifty, if you count them, I think."

The youth stared. "Caw! This is a rum joint. Paying me before I've earned it. Before I've done the job."

"You will earn it. I am passing this over as proof of my good faith. Your good faith will be proved by your performance."

"But s'pose I was to bunk with the bag?"

"You will not bunk with the bag. For one thing, you are not that kind of young man. I know you. Anyway, the bag would not be worth five shillings, and the—the china jar has no commercial value. You could not sell it. But I——" For a moment he forgot the youth, and again he seemed to fill the room. "I, with that goblet, am lord of all beauty. With the Bool Museum goblet, I am lord of all——"

"You're how much?"

He recovered himself. "Er—I said claiming that goblet is a laudable duty."

"But s'pose I was copped by a motor-bus and smashed up?"

He made a *tch* of irritation. "How many times am I to tell you that so far as this matter is concerned, you are under protection. Now and always. You cannot be harmed by anything arising from this matter—neither now nor at any time. I am protecting you. Now are you ready?"

The youth made but a momentary hesitation. Then— "Yes, I'll do it."

"Good. It is now half-past ten. You have plenty of time for the journey to Sloane Square. You have your instructions. Make no mistake in them. I shall expect you back soon after twelve." He opened the door and led the way into the passage, and so to the front door.

The youth walked out with light step and swinging shoulders. His gaze was direct and his movements sharp. Within the last hour he had developed a profile. He was not aware of this himself; he was aware only that he was 'feeling fine.' Whether this was due to the fifty pounds in his pocket, to the thing he had witnessed in that room, or to something else he did not know. He was content to feel fine and to go upon his errand.

As he went, he chuckled in self-communion. "Jee!

Talk about the age of miracles. If anybody'd told me I'd a-seen a thing like that in these streets... He's a Dr. Caligari, he is. Almost frightens you, seeing a thing like that. And yet it don't. I don't feel that way at all. Going to do a hold-up and get away with it. Still, he says it's all right. Only taking something from a thief for them it belongs to. Wonder if it does belong to 'em? Still, he seems all right. And I made it clear I wouldn't touch it if it wasn't straight. I got a clear conscience on that. And I got me fifty pounds anyway. Better drop that at home on me way. Case there's anything sticky about the business, and it goes wrong. Then at least they'll have that to help 'em. But I reckon it'll be all right. He *makes* you feel everything's all right."

At half-past eleven he was waiting in the shadow by the Sloane Square District station. He had been there for fifteen minutes, waiting for the half-hour with no more trepidation than if he were waiting for a bus. He was wondering no more about the business; he seemed to be outside it, half-asleep. His mind would not be interested in it; even when the man appeared his pulse remained unchanged.

The man appeared at three minutes past the half-hour. He came into the Square from Sloane Street—a small man in spectacles, wearing a fawn overcoat and bowler hat, and carrying an attache case. He walked softly, his eyes primly fixed on the pavement. He passed the youth without raising his eyes, and turned into the side-street. The youth followed, as casually as though he were merely walking that way, too.

Then, in the middle of the street, where the light was dim, he moved more quickly. A few paces brought him right behind the man. One hand, with a clean flash, grabbed the man's wrist; the other snatched the case.

That was easy. What would happen next he did not

know, but he turned to make swiftly, without running, for Sloane Square. But this was not to be so easy. Before he had taken three paces the man was upon him. Two iron arms, unexpected from so slight a man, went round him. He staggered on his heels. One of the arms slid down his arm to reach the case. He closed his fingers over its handle, and gave a violent backward kick. It met a shin, and with its impact, there was a moment's easing of the arms. The youth took that moment to slip through the arms downward to the ground.

With his free arm he caught the man behind the knees, and they came down together. Silent, save for their gasping, they rolled on each other across the pavement. The man did not strike him but fought for the hand that held the case. The youth held to it fiercely, struggling to rise. Then, with a sudden movement from the man, he found himself underneath, lying on his back with his neck against the curb. He made a few sharp struggles to reverse the positions, but within a second or so he saw that they were useless, and his throat went dry.

The dim light had shown him the man's hand shooting to his coat. Next moment he saw the hand lifted, and alongside the hand the dim light was caught by the blade of an open razor.

The youth's left hand still clutched the case. With his right he made a feeble effort to hold the man away, but the man, with his strong left, bent the arm back. The youth saw the razor sweeping down. Instinctively he shut his eyes. He felt the razor slash across his neck. He felt it go deep into each side. He gurgled and was aware of floating away.

It was a mere muscular movement that caused him to open his eyes, and it was then that he remembered what he had momentarily forgotten—that he was under protection. He opened his eyes to see that the man, half-squatting, had drawn back from him and was staring at him—at his neck—with eyes in which was a light of horror. With another instinctive movement the youth put his hand to his neck. His neck was whole. No wound. No pain. The man still held the open razor and looked stupidly at it. It was spotless.

Gripping the case, the youth rolled over and got to his feet. The man scrambled up with him and held out a hand. "Here—my case—my case." It was a plea more than a demand. The youth ignored it. He moved away, and the man with the strong arms put out a weak hand to detain him. "My case—my case."

Round the corner came a constable. He looked at their dusty clothes and torn collars.

"What's all this? What's this?"

The youth answered him. "It's all right. Just a private dust-up. We're moving on now."

"Do it then."

The man tried to say something. "He—he—he——" and seemed unable to find further words.

"Well, what did he do?"

"He—he—he——"

"Now come on. Pack up and get home. And take more water with it."

The youth said, "All right," and went easily toward Sloane Square with the case. Behind him he heard the little man saying "No, but he—he—he——" and the constable saying, "Come on now—take a walk." He saw the constable wave the little man toward Pimlico Road, and he saw the little man tamely go.

On the platform of the District station he waited for an east-bound train. Four times while waiting he said, "Jee!" Not in a mood of chuckling but in a mood of awe. He felt a little sick—not because he had been wounded but because he hadn't been wounded.

Half an hour later he delivered the case to the old man and went home. He got into bed with a blunt prayer—Jee!

For the next week life was good to him. Out of his vast store of fifty pounds, he used half-crowns and five-shillings at a time, presenting them to his mother as wages he had received for odd jobs. He took in delicacies for her tea. He bought his young sister a needed pair of boots. He saw prosperity ahead. Before it was exhausted he would certainly get a job; one bit of luck always led to another. Or with that capital he might start a little business. Or with ten or fifteen pounds of it he might go into partnership with a stall-holder.

Anyway, he was on his feet again, and all through meeting that—he almost thought of him as That Old Bonehead—a name which he and his friend, Fred, had used when discussing the old man in the coffee-shop. But after what had happened he couldn't use that term. He was a little afraid; it would be like mocking thunder and lightning. Something more respectful was needed, but he couldn't think of any word that would fit such an overwhelming man. The only events he knew comparable with what had happened were those he had learned of in religious lessons in school—making the sun stand still and those chaps that walked in the furnace. And you couldn't quite put a man who lived three streets away from you in an everyday suburb, in that class. That was Holy, and this man wasn't Holy. On the other hand he must certainly be the most wonderful man in the world. He compromised by thinking of him as The Wonderful Old Man.

Once or twice during the week he felt a little twinge in his neck. But when he examined it in the mirror there was nothing to be seen; just a clean white neck, as usual. He concluded that the little man must have gripped his neck before he struck, and given a slight sprain to a small bone. You got that kind of thing sometimes at football on Saturdays and often didn't feel it till the middle of the next week. After the second twinge, he ignored it, and went cheerfully about his plans for laying out his money.

Nine days after his little adventure he had his seven-o'clock tea, with two kippers, and then went into the parlour of their little four-room home, to read the evening paper and a book he had borrowed from the Free Library—a book which he found hard to read but which he wanted to read: a book on the Magic of the Ancients.

Half an hour later his friend Fred called. The youth's mother opened the door to him. "Hullo, Fred."

"Hullo, Mrs. Brown. Joe in?"

"Yes. He's in the parlour, reading, I think."

"Got a bit of news for him. He ever tell you about an old man we've met in Harry's coffee-shop?"

"No. Not that I remember."

"Ah. You hear a bang just now?"

"Might have. Yes, I believe I did. But there's all sorts of bangs around here. Lorries back-firing and that. You don't notice 'em."

"Well, the old man's blown himself up."

"Blown himself up?"

"Yes. Making some experiment, I suppose, and blown the house and himself all to bits The whole front of the house. Blown clean out. I just come from it. There's crowds staring at it. Thousands. I thought Joe might like to come and have a look."

"Ah. Well, you'll find him in there. I must get on with me washing."

Fred opened the parlour door and stepped in, beginning his story with "I say, Joe, there's a——" And then Mrs. Brown heard a scream. She bustled into the passage "What's the matter, Fred? Whatever's the matter?"

Fred stepped back into the passage with white face and open jaws. He put out an arm "Don't go in. Don't go. Keep out."

"Why—why? What—what is it?"

But Fred could only say—"Don't—don't go in. His throat! His throat!"

EGO SPEAKS
by
J. H. PEARCE

J. H. Pearce received glowing reviews for his short story book Drolls From Shadowland *(1893). The* New York Mail *and* Express *said it contained 'genius of an uncommon kind'; the* Boston Traveller *described the stories as 'beautiful to read from their deep imagination and haunting in their allegorical depth'; in Britain the* Illustrated London News *commented: 'his is imagination of a fine kind'. Yet, for all this praise, and that afforded his other work in this vein* Tales of the Masque *(1894), Pearce faded into obscurity after what appears to be his last work* The Dreamer's Book *(1905).*

Joseph Henry Pearce was born in 1856 and his writing career started in 1891 with the novel Esther Pentreath. *He wrote several Cornish novels, and all told published nine books in fourteen years.*

It is from Tales of the Masque *that* Ego Speaks *is drawn, and, much like* Marie St. Pierre *earlier in this collection, it is a dark and troubling view of the end of life.*

* * *

EGO SPEAKS

Fragments of a confidence.

I

The dear, dear Earth, our mother and protector, who feeds us with the known and establishes our strength with the familiar, who is always with us whoever leaves us, and who holds our bodies till they are dust: her attractions for us are infinite and her love is inexhaustible: she is our dear, dear mother, and we are her children to the end.

But when Death's lean fingers finally close upon us and the familiar swiftly and irrevocably recedes; when the sensations are unravelled and the weft of them ruined fatally, and the consciousness crumbles drowsily and the heart stands still; ah! then, when the soul is flung out into the darkness, what Power is there that shall comfort us, and to what shall we gravitate in our need?

II

I pass over the maddening agony of my murder. To lie there helpless in the darkened lane and have the life beaten savagely out of my body, was an experience grim and appallingly gruesome. The tramp, to whose greed and ferocity I had succumbed, I would have murdered myself, had I only had the power. But my body lay there wrecked and dead: and the unseen Ego was adrift in the world.

The unfamiliar—the unfamiliar!—I had always hated it. I had no strength of imagination to array my sympathies in line with it, and no unsatisfied hunger that made me crave to pierce its core. I had always hated death for its secrecy and its strangeness, for the things it concealed and the new experiences it would compel one to: and here was I dead and the book of the familiar closed irrevocably!

If only annihilation might have followed the stoppage of the pulse!

III

And now my grisly experiences began.

Up to the moment when the shrine of my personality was shattered; I had been a quiet, well-behaved, tax-paying citizen: a married man with a wife and a couple of children, and with a small circle of intimate acquaintances, whose respect, if not their active affection, I was presumed to have secured and retained permanently.

The Ego, as it finally was dislodged from the body, had vitality enough to take the world by the beard, so proud and energetic and self-sufficient did it seem. But even while it gathered up the world in its glance, it was conscious of a certain drain of vitality in less than an instant after it was dislodged.

With the loss of its body it had lost more than its protection: it had lost the kernel and crown of its consequence as well. And it seemed to me, unless I misinterpret, that its health and strength were not inherent, but depended on the attitude of its fellows towards it, so that, practically, from the moment it was dislodged from its envelope it began fatally to shrivel and collapse.

I watched the tramp empty and toss away my purse, take my watch and chain and scarf-pin and even the pencil-case I carried, and then, with a grunt at the smallness of his booty, he dragged my body among the ferns that grew rankly against the hedge and, looking around hurriedly, took to his heels.

I was distracted with a multiplicity of emotions. I wished to watch the body; I wanted to dog the heels of the murderer; and I desired to see my wife to inform her of the deed and of where she might find the body and of how she might find the man.

Finally I decided to follow the murderer for the present; lest the man should escape my vengeance after all.

But, to my dismay, the man kept steadily plodding onward. He had soon left the scene of the murder miles behind him, and evidently had settled down to an all-night tramp. He appeared to me to be bound for London, which was distant from here about fifty miles.

At last I gave up the wearying pursuit and rapidly flitted to the neat little villa which my consciousness had called *home* while it had a body at command.

A more lame and impotent conclusion to an errand had never befallen me in the whole of my experience.

I was absolutely powerless to do anything. There was I in the house, unseen and unrecognised, and unable to communicate, even in the most rudimentary fashion, with those who were nearest and dearest to me on earth.

To add to my bewilderment and appalling loneliness, the part which the body had played in my life began to be apparent to me at last. Without it I found I was barred, most effectually, from definite communication with those still alive. I might manage in some way to impress a consciousness—might communicate to it an indeterminate impulse, or arouse in it a transient hallucination—but the capture of the attention, as by personal magic, I was henceforth absolutely powerless to effect. Neither through the eye, nor the ear, nor even through the touch, could I manage to impress a being still alive. And shut out from communication by any of these avenues, I found myself now as impotent as a dream.

Once or twice I managed to arouse in my wife a casual uneasiness as to my prolonged absence. But she was a placid-natured woman, not in the least sentimental, and in the cosy domestic atmosphere the husband was not missed.

In vain I endeavoured to directly reach her thoughts: to convey to her some definite, unmistakable idea, such as a man may convey by a phrase or even a glance. She leaned back in the armchair dandling her infant placidly and cooing to it in the most matter-of-fact way in the world.

The sense of my isolation, and of my absolute helplessness, was an experience far more appallingly cruel than you who are alive can in any way comprehend.

The expulsion of the Ego from its battered fleshy tenement, grisly though it was, was less gruesome than this. To be a helpless sheaf and tangle of memories, with nothing but the fragile knot of consciousness to bind them into a temporary whole; and to feel the knot loosening and the sheaf falling asunder—falling into a ruin profound and irremediable—this, indeed, was the very bitterness of death. I would have welcomed instant annihilation as a boon.

As the hours lengthened my wife grew restless, and by midnight she had at last become thoroughly alarmed.

The next morning my absence had grown portentous, and the police were communicated with and set on the quest.

The body was soon discovered and carried home: but the murderer had by this time escaped securely, and—to make a long story short—he still remains uncaught.

IV

At the funeral, so great was the interest this aroused, Ego swelled with life almost to its old dimensions.

The horses, with their plumes of feathers and their

velvet trappings, paced slowly through the streets with the hearse behind them. Through the glass sides of the hearse one could see the long oak coffin resting on the shining brass supports and almost smothered in wreaths of hothouse flowers. But the dim form seated at the head of the coffin—the Ego from whom the veil had fallen for ever—this the living could not see, however closely they might look.

The streets were fuller, however, of dead folks than they were of the living, and the former, as they glided along dumb and invisible, glanced sadly at the wan and marrowless figure and bowed their heads to it as those who understood.

The journey through the noisy, crowded haunts, from which I was now for ever exiled, was a time of strange experiences as I sat crouched on the coffin. To think the bounds of my knowledge were enlarged so inconceivably, yet I was crippled so fatally and cut off cruelly from so much!

I was taking my last tithe of interest from humanity. This drive through the streets in the awful solitude of the hearse, with the trappings on the horses and the wreaths on the coffin... and then the pit in the graveyard for the abandoned body, and for the spirit the vast black pit of the past!

V

When the funeral was over and the murder had become forgotten—swept out of memory by the press of other incidents—Ego found its life oozing steadily away.

My wife that had been—my widow that was—was fairly young and reasonably attractive, and before her year of conventional mourning had expired she was again a wife, and I was to her but a memory: and a very thin and bloodless memory too.

Even the children ceased to trouble much about 'father' now they had a newer flesh-and-blood father to make pets of them: and Ego shrivelled daily, and is shrivelling still.

I had fancied, while I was still clothed with a body, that, if I were freed from the material thraldom of the flesh, I would roam about the world feasting hungrily on its scenes until I was thoroughly sated with whatever it had to offer.

But what are art and literature, or scenery however beautiful, to the unhoused Ego with no register for its experiences, with its capacities like slipping sand, and the walls of its treasure-house broken down? The experiences of the senses—how could I garner them? The experiences of the soul—wonderful and terrible though I know them—how could I store them up except in the terms of the senses? How could I hold them to ponder over? How could I share them if I wished?

I found the homeless Ego so helpless in itself—so dependent on those who had known of its existence and to whom alone it could turn for consideration—that I was practically rooted to the habitat of my memories; and only there, and along these lines, could I exist.

VI

Today I am still feebly existent. Tomorrow I may be wholly forgotten: and shall have ceased.

THE PHANTOM SHIP
by
WILLIAM HOPE HODGSON

William Hope Hodgson (1875-1918) was a man who influenced many other authors of the macabre, and yet remained in relative obscurity for years.

The son of an Essex clergyman, Hodgson left home at an early age and spent eight years at sea. This experience provided him with the background for his most successful tales. He obtained a commission with an artillery regiment on the outbreak of World War I, and was killed while on duty as an observation officer.

He left behind a small but brilliant output of some of the finest macabre tales ever written, and is best known for his Sargasso Sea *tales and the series featuring* Carnacki The Ghost Finder. *And it is his sea-faring tales which really chill the blood, blessed as they are with the authenticity of experience (you may find many of the nautical terms bewildering but that does not spoil the enjoyment) and Hodgson's talent for giving you just enough detail to fill in the blanks yourself to terrifying effect.* The Phantom Ship, *which did not see publication until 1973 (in* Shadow: Fantasy Literature Review*), is a classic example.*

Hodgson had been grossly underrated for many years but was finally recognised as the master of the genre that he undoubtedly was.

* * *

We were in the Southern Pacific, just within the tropics. It was the the second dog watch when, away on our starboard beam, distant some three or four hundred yards, we saw a large ship sliding slowly along in the same direction as ourselves. We had come up with her during the previous watch, but the wind failing, our speed had dropped and we were doing no more than keep abreast of her.

The Mate and I were watching her curiously; for to all our signals she had paid not the slightest heed. Not even a face had peered over her rail in our direction; though—save once or twice when a curious thin haze had seemed to float up from the sea between the two ships—we were plainly able to see the officer of the watch pacing the poop, and the men lounging about her decks.

Stranger than this was our inability to catch any sound from her—not even an occasional order or the stroke of the bells.

"Sulky beasts!" said the Mate expressively. "A lot of darned uncivil Dutchmen!"

He stood for a couple of minutes and eyed them in silence. He was very much annoyed at their persistent disregard of our signal, yet I think that, like myself, he was even more curious to know the reason of it; for his very bafflement on this point only served to increase his irritability.

"Pass out that trumpet, Mr. Jepworth," he said, turning to me. "We'll see if they have the manners to notice that."

Going to the companionway I unslung the speaking trumpet out of its becketts and brought it to him.

Taking it quickly he raised it to his lips and sent a loud 'ship ahoy' across the water to the stranger. He waited a few minutes, but there was no sign to show that he had been heard.

"Blast them!" I heard him mutter. Then he lifted the trumpet again. This time he hailed the other craft by name which was plainly visible on the bow. "*Idortzeztus* ahoy!"

Again he waited. Still there was no sign to show that they had either heard or seen us.

"The devil fly away with you!" he shouted, lifting the trumpet and shaking it towards the strange vessel.

"Here, take this back, again, Mr. Jepworth," he growled. "If ever I came across a lot of petticoated skunks it's them!"

For the space of an hour we continued to watch the strange ship at intervals through our glasses; but we failed to discover that they had become even aware of our presence.

Then, as we watched her, there appeared suddenly a great show of activity aboard of her. The three royals were lowered almost simultaneously, and in a minute the t'gallen' sails followed them. Then we saw the men jump into the rigging and aloft to furl.

"I'm damned if they're not going to shorten her down!" cried the Mate. "What the devil's the matter with them——"

He stopped short as though a sudden idea had come to him.

"Run below," he called to me, without removing his gaze from the other packet, "and take a look at the glass."

Without wasting time I hurried below, returning in a minute to tell him that the glass was perfectly steady.

He made no reply to my information; but continued to stare across the water at the stranger.

"Look here, Mr. Jepworth," he said at last, "I'm just beggared that's what I am. I can't make head nor tail of it. I've never seen the likes of it all the time I've been 'fishing'."

"Looks to me as though their skipper was a bit of an old woman," I remarked. "Perhaps——"

"Lord!" he cried impiously. "And now they're taking the courses off her. Their Old Man must be a fool!"

He had spoken rather loudly, and in the silence that followed his words I was startled to hear a voice at my elbow say:

"Whose Old Man is a fool?"

It was our skipper who had come on deck, unobserved. Without waiting for a reply he inquired if the other packet had deigned to notice our signals yet.

"No, Sir," the Mate answered. "We might be a lump of dirt floating about for all the notice they take of us."

"They've shortened her down to topsails, Sir," I said, offering him my glasses.

"Can't understand it at all," I heard him mutter. "Pass me out the telescope," he said.

With this he studied the stranger awhile, but there was nothing that would explain the mystery.

"Most extraordinary!" he exclaimed. Then he pushed the telescope in among the ropes on the pinrail, and took a few turns up and down the poop.

The Mate and I continued to scrutinise the strange vessel; but all to no purpose. Outwardly, at least, she was an ordinary full-rigged ship; and save for her inexplicable silence and the furling of her sails, there was nothing to distinguish her from any chance windjammer one might happen to fall across in the course of a long sea voyage.

The Captain ceased to pace up and down, and stood by the Mate, staring curiously across at the silent ship on our starboard beam.

"The glass is as steady as a rock," he remarked presently.

"Yes," the Mate assented. "I sent Mr. Jepworth to give

a look as soon as I saw they were going to shorten down."

"I can't understand it!" said the Captain again with a sort of puzzled irritability. "The weather's just grand."

The Mate made no immediate reply, but pulled a plug of ship's tobacco out from his hip pocket, and took a bite. He replaced it, expectorated, and then expressed his opinion that they were all a lot of Dutch hogs.

The Captain resumed his walk, while I continued to scan the other vessel. A little later one of the 'prentices went aft and struck eight bells. A few seconds later the Second Mate came up on to the poop to relieve the Mate.

"Have you got the lady to speak yet?" he inquired, referring to the unsociable craft away on our beam.

The Mate almost snorted. I didn't hear his reply; for at that moment, unbelievable as it may seem, I saw Things coming out of the water alongside the silent ship. Things like men they were, with a strange misty, unreal look. For the minute I thought I must be going dotty, until I glanced round and saw the Mate staring over my shoulder, his face thrust forward and his eyes fixed in their intensity. Then I saw that these queer shapes were climbing up the other hooker's side—thousands of them.

We were so close to the vessel that I could see the officer of the watch lighting his pipe. He stood leaning up again the port rail, facing to starboard. I saw the chap at the wheel wave his arms, and the officer move quickly towards him. The helmsman pointed, and the officer turned about and looked at what he was pointing at.

In the dusk and at that distance I could not distinguish his features; but I knew by his attitude that he had seen. For one short instant he stood motionless; then he made a wild dash for the break of the poop, gesticulating. He appeared to be shouting. I saw the 'lookout' seize a capstan bar and pound on the fo'cas'le head. Several men ran out from the port doorway. And then, all at once, sounds came to us from the hitherto silent ship. At first, muffled, as though from miles away. Quickly they grew plainer. And so, in a moment, as though an invisible barrier had been torn down we heard a multitudinous shouting of frightened men. It rolled over the sea to us like the voice of Fear clamouring.

A minute passed—it seemed an age. A thick haze grew up out of the sea and closer about the hull of the strange ship, leaving only her spars to be seen. Out from the mist there still drove that Babel of hoarse cries and shouting.

Almost unconsciously my glance roved among the spars and rigging that rose straight up into the sky out of that weird clot of mist on the sea. Suddenly my wandering gaze was arrested. Through the calm evening air I saw a movement among the stowed sails. Gaskets were being cast adrift, and against the darkening skies I made out dim ghostlike shapes working fiendishly.

With a slow rustle first, and then a sudden flap, the bellies of the three t' gallan' sails fell out of the bunt gaskets and hung. Almost immediately the three royals followed. And all this while the confused noises continued. Now, however, there was a sudden lull of silence; and then, simultaneously, the six yards began to rise amid a perfect quietness save for the chafing of the ropes in the blocks, and the occasional squeal of a parrel against a mast.

We on our deck made no sound; said nothing. There was nothing to be said. I—for one was temporarily speechless. The sails continued to rise with the steady, rhythmic, pull-and-heave movement peculiar to sailormen. A minute went by, then another. Then the leeches of the sails tautened, and the hauling eased. The sails were set.

The mist still clung about the hull, a little hill of cloud, hiding it completely as well as a portion of the lower masts, though the lower yards with the courses made fast upon them were plainly visible.

And now I became aware of ghostly forms at work upon the gaskets of the three courses. The sails rustled upon the yards. Scarcely a minute it seemed, and the mainsail slid off the yard and fell in loose festoons, followed, almost immediately by the fore and crossjack.

From somewhere out of the mist there came a single strangled cry. It broke off instantly; yet it seemed to me as though the sea echoed it remotely.

For the first time I turned and looked at the Old Man who was standing a little to my left. His face was expressionless. His eyes were fixed with a queer stony stare upon that mist-enshrouded mystery. It was only a momentary glance I gave, and then I looked back quickly.

From that other ship there had come a sudden squeal and rattle of swinging yards and running gear, and I saw that the yards were being squared in swiftly. Very quickly this was accomplished, though what slight airs there were came from the south west, and we were braced sharp up on the port tack to make the most of them. By rights this move on the part of the other packet should have placed her all aback and given her sternway. Yet, as I looked with incredulous eyes, the sails filled abruptly bellying out as though before a strong breeze, and I saw something lift itself up out from the mist at the after end of the ship. It rose higher and grew plainer. I saw it then, distinctly. It was the white painted 'half-round' of the stern. In the same moment the masts inclined forward at a distinct angle that increased till the top of the chart house came into view.

Then, deep and horrible, as though lost souls cried out, there came a hoarse, prolonged cry of human agony.

The ship's stern rose higher out from the mistiness,

and for one single instant I saw the rudder move blackly against the evening sky. The wheel spun sharply, and a small black figure plunged away from it helplessly, down into the mist and noise.

The sea gave a sobbing gurgle, and there came a horrible bubbling note into the human outcry. The foremast disappeared into the sea, and the main sank down into the mist. On the after mast the sails had slatted a moment, then filled, and so, under all sail, the strange ship drove down into the darkness. A gust of crying swept up to us for one dreadful instant, and then only the boil of the sea as it closed in over all.

Like one in a trance I continued to stare. In an uncomprehending way I heard voices down on the main deck—and echo of mixed prayer and blasphemy filling the air.

Out on the sea the mistiness still hung about the spot where the strange vessel had vanished. Gradually, however, it thinned away and disclosed various articles of ship's furniture circling in the eddy of the dying whirlpool. Even as I watched, odd wreckage rushed up out of the ocean with a plop, plopping sound.

Abruptly, the Mate's voice rasped across my bewilderment roughly, and the noise from the main deck had dropped to a steady hum of talk and argument.

He was pointing excitedly somewhat to the southward of the floating wreckage. I caught only the latter part of his sentence.

"...over there!"

Mechanically my eyes followed the direction indicated by his finger. For a moment they refused to focus anything distinctly, then suddenly there jumped into the circled blue of my vision a little spot of black that bobbed upon the water and grew plain. It was the head of a man who was swimming desperately in our direction.

At the sight of him the horror of the last few minutes fell from me and, thinking only of rescue, I ran towards the starboard lifeboat, whipping out my knife as I ran. Over my shoulder came the bellow of the skipper's voice:

"Clear away the starboard lifeboat! Jump along some of you!"

Even before the running men had reached the lifeboat I had ripped the cover off her and was busy heaving out the miscellaneous lumber that is so often stowed away into the boats of a windjammer. Feverishly I worked, with the help of half a dozen men, and soon we had the boat clear, and the running gear ready for lowering away. Then we swung her out, and I climbed into her without waiting for orders. Four of the men followed, while a couple of the others stood by to lower away.

A moment later we were pulling rapidly for the solitary swimmer, Reaching him we hauled him into the boat, and not a minute too soon, for he was palpably done up. We sat him on a thwart, and one of the men supported him. He was gasping heavily and gurgling as he breathed. Then he spoke for the first time.

"My God!" he gasped. "Oh, my God!" And that was all he seemed able to say.

Meanwhile I had told the others to give way, and we steered towards the wreckage. As we neared it the rescued man struggled suddenly to his feet, and stood swaying and clutching at the man who was supporting him, while his eyes swept wildly over the ocean. His gaze rested on the patch of floating hencoops, spars, and other lumber. He bent forward and peered at it as though trying in vain to understand what it meant. Then a vacant expression crept over his features and he slid down on to the thwart limply, muttering to himself.

As soon as I had satisfied myself that there was nothing living among that mass of floating stuff, I put the boat's head round and made for the ship with all speed. I was anxious to have the poor fellow attended to as soon as possible.

Directly we got him aboard he was turned over to the steward who made him up a bed in one of the bunks in a spare cabin opening off the saloon.

What happened afterwards was told to me by the steward.

"It was like this, Sir," he said. "I stripped him an' got him into the blankets which the doctor had made warm at the galley fire. The poor beggar was all of a shake at first, and I tried to get some whiskey into him, but couldn't do it no-how. His teeth seemed locked, an' so I just gave up an' let him bide. In a little, the shakes went off him, an' he was quiet enough. All the same, seein' him that bad I thought as I'd sit up with him for the night. There was no knowin' but that he'd be wanting somethin' later on.

"Well, Sir, all through the first watch he lay there, not sayin' nothin', nor stirin', but just moanin' quiet-like to himself. An', thinks I, he'll go off into a sleep in a bit, so I just sat there without movin'. Then, all of a sudden, about three bells in the middle watch he started shiverin' and shakin' again. So I shoved some more blankets on to him, an' then I had another try to get some whiskey between his teeth; but 'twas no use; an' then, Sir, all at once he went limp, an' his mouth come open with a flop. I ran for the Cap'n then, but the poor devil was dead before we got back."

We buried him in the morning, sewing him up in some old canvas with a few lumps of coal at his feet.

To this day I ponder over the thing I saw, and wonder, vainly, what he might have told us to help solve the mystery of that silent ship in the heart of the vast Pacific.

A TWILIGHT EXPERIENCE
by
MRS. BAILLIE REYNOLDS

Gertrude Minnie Robins (1861-1939) was born in Teddington, England, to a barrister father, Julian Robins. A natural story-teller, she began early in her life. According to the literary journal The Bookman *in 1907 'She began to invent stories as soon as she could talk, and to tell them to her mother before she could read.'*

As a teenager, Gertrude and her sister started their own magazine, which she illustrated herself, and her brother claimed that she 'made up a ghost story every week.'

Writing under several names, including both her maiden name G. M. Robins, and her married name, Mrs. Baillie Reynolds, she was extremely prolific. She wrote articles for magazines, published both novels and short stories and was comfortable in a wide variety of genres. During the Boer War she even wrote a hymn entitled Hymn for the War, *which became very popular both at home and on the front.*

The following story, an evocative and wistful tale set in the Dorset countryside, was taken from her wonderfully titled 1902 collection The Relations and What They Related and Other Weird Tales.

* * *

"Let me not slur over any of my weaknesses! Needs must I then begin with an admission that I do worse than write bad verses—I paint bad pictures.

"One cannot tell why. I am without the motive that inspired Dante on the historic occasion when he began to paint an angel. It is a mere superfluity of naughtiness, for which no excuse can be found, and for which indulgence must be humbly craved.

"There lies a district in the extreme west of Dorsetshire, near the coast, which appeals to my inmost being in a way I can only account for by supposing that it must have been the scene of a remote previous incarnation. It is beautiful, of course. The hills are wild, the combes deep, the poor soil only lavish of pine, larch, heather, and golden broom; but other places as beautiful make not the same appeal.

"This is a land desolate and forsaken, of dwindling villages, ruined cottages, vast tracts of solitude, and hints of bygone races in cairn and castrum.

"There is one particular spot which, when you reach it, at the summit of a sheer sharp climb, emerging from the dense shadow of a pine-hanger, gives the effect of a vast natural amphitheatre. Before you lies a circular basin of broken moorland; the opposite rim makes your horizon, lifting jagged edges like crenelations against the dead eastern evening sky.

"Rabbits and juniper, whortleberry and bramble, patches of heather, some bare sandy scars where the loose land has slipped a little—this is all; yet the effect is tremendous.

"It was sunset when I first reached it. Mrs. Vyell, the wife of the squire who owned the old red house in the fertile neighbouring combe, had given me the hint to seek it out.

"A spot more separate, more completely isolated from all life, one could not conjure up in thought. Sketching-material was with me; the place was absolutely unsketchable. But it held me with a powerful, compelling hand, the solitude reaching out mighty arms to clutch me. I sat down and drank in the impression of desolation, paint-box and palette idle beside me.

"Wild, sterile land! There was not even pasture for sheep. How few feet, since the dawn of history, must have trod its inhospitable acres! No trace of farming, no shed, no barn, not even a gate, wherever I turned my eyes.

"The sun went down as I sat lost in musings. I knew the moon would soon be up, and that she would rise in the east, right before me. It became a necessity to wait, gazing into the purple August twilight until the disc of yellowed silver should emerge, a radiant surprise, from behind the rim of my amphitheatre, to hang lamenting above the silence and emptiness.

"Just where would she appear? Behind that bit of crumbled wall? Behind the beech-clump next to it? Over the castellated edge of rabbit-levelled turf? I must wait and see. No human being could or would intrude. It led no whither, this wild cup in the heart of the hills. Loneliness had immemorially claimed it wholly; it belonged 'to darkness and to me' in the uttermost sense of those magic words.

"And even as the thought was framed, I became aware of some movement in the depth of the hollow beneath me, down far below, where winter torrents had washed and broken the ground into fantastic shapes, finding only partial outlet, and in summer settling down to be soft emerald morass.

"Something, someone, flitted behind a big bramble-bush, then emerged, and moved upwards, away from me, but nearer to the level of my line of vision. It was a man, carrying a bundle over his shoulder—a shepherd, as I guessed, slowly and with toil ascending the eastern slope of the amphitheatre, exactly opposite my point of view.

"I wondered whence he came and whither he went; and as the moon tarried and nothing else diverted my eye, I watched him with careful eagerness in the fading light, and it seemed that as he moved, a very narrow track which he was following became perceptible on the rugged slopes. Up he went, slowly but steadily, never glancing behind, making evidently for a given point; and now that the pink flush had wholly died away from the hillside, it suddenly became apparent that what had seemed only a bit of broken wall on the horizon line, was in fact a solitary dwelling—a cottage with a thatched roof. So soon had my fantastic conception of utter loneliness received its contradiction!

"That cottage was doubtless the wayfarer's bourne. Here, careless of the awful dead weight of isolation, unmoved by the power of the spirit of the hills, he dwelt, and brought up children, and rested, all unconscious of the awful forces of nature, and faced without flinching the terrors which were real to his forefathers, simply because he did not understand them.

"In a few minutes he would reach his home, and in a few minutes more a light would appear in that remote window, which I saw now only as a small square of shadow.

"Yes, I was right. He had reached the cottage; he had paused, or hesitated,—he was too far off for me to divine why,—and now he had gone in at the door.

"But all was still dark within. More and more densely the shadow of night fell upon the hills; the brooding peace was broken only by the wheeling flight of a white owl around my head. Ah, there at last! A bright gleam was shining through the window-square. It grew larger as I gazed; the aperture was very gradually filling with light—a dazzling, pure, white light.

"Something like a shock overcame me as I suddenly realised the truth. It was the moon I saw—the moon, which had stolen up behind the hill, and now showed me the weird fact that the cottage was a ruin, a hollow shell. Its broken lineaments were now plainly visible against the radiance behind.

"What did the shepherd seek there at this hour?

"An unaccountable tremor seized me—a desire for human society and a warm hearth; the spirits of the hills were too strong for me. The shepherd might have no nerves, but I was the child of my age, and I promptly packed up my things and went home through the murky recesses of the pine-hanger, and then by way of lanes which human feet had lately trodden, and where one saw occasionally behind drawn curtains the twinkle of a light more homely, if less brilliant, than that of the queenly moon.

"But next evening the influences of the place drew me there again at sunset; and again at the same hour I saw the same man taking the same course up the hillside to the cottage. It was, of course, later that evening before the moon came up; but though I waited till then, I did not see the man come out.

"I was consumed with a vast curiosity—a curiosity to know what he did there alone without a light in the ruin. I laughed at my own folly, too. He kept his tools there; he was storing peat, or bringing up a lamb by hand. But none of these obvious reasons satisfied me. Deep down in my heart blossomed the hope that he might turn out to be a recluse, a real lover of solitude, a person capable of sympathising with me.

"I formed a plan to intercept him. The next night I

would come early, walk round to the ruined cottage, confront him on his arrival, and have a talk—perhaps become the recipient of some quaint bit of history or folklore. The idea so formed was quickly carried out. The spell of glorious weather waxed with the waxing moon; nothing on the following day intervened to prevent my solitary evening ramble.

"The cottage was a long way off; it took a surprisingly long time to reach it. Perched on the brow of the hill, it overlooked another combe as desolate as this one, and also commanded a view of the sea.

"It had evidently been a dwelling-house; in a square walled-in garden-patch were still traces of cultivation. It was built of solid stone, but the decay of the roof had left it at the mercy of the wild weather, and it was sadly fallen to ruin. There were four rooms—two upstairs, two down. One walked straight into the kitchen, with its wide fireplace and mouldering remnant of dresser-shelves, and ladder-like stair giving access to the rooms above. From the kitchen a communicating doorway opened into an inner parlour.

"Among the scattered ashes on the hearth bloomed a yellow sea-poppy; no fire, then, had been recently kindled there. The soft summer breeze blew lightly through the hollow shell, and swayed a jagged end of rope that dangled in the doorway between kitchen and parlour.

"I tried the narrow stair. It creaked and groaned, but it was of Dorset oak and it bore my weight. Above were two bedrooms, empty and half unroofed. Nothing to be seen or found there. A search around the back of the premises revealed no more; there were no stores, no woodpile, no sign of human industry, no apparent reason of any kind why a man should visit the place.

"Piqued curiosity began to stimulate imagination, and sought to invent a motive for lonely twilight seeking of such a spot. It might be a tryst; there might be a second party, as yet unseen, who came over the brow of the hill to meet her lover as he ascended from the valley. Or it might be a place to hide treasure—though I could find no indication of a cellar. As gloaming fell, romance awoke, and various possibilities suggested themselves. It seemed very long before I saw the figure of my friend, as I secretly called him, working his way up the hillside, his bundle as usual on his shoulder.

"I had taken up my station in the little square bit of garden-ground in front of the cottage. The gate had entirely disappeared, the gateway through which the approaching figure must enter was about three yards to my left. I sat on the low stone wall, and watched him come.

"It was not dark. I could see him plainly; it followed, therefore, that he could see me also. But even when he drew near enough for his features to be recognisable, he took no notice.

"Pausing, he fumbled at the yawning gateway in the place where no latch was. Such light as remained was behind him, so his face was not distinctly visible. It was dark and bearded. He seemed a powerful man in the prime of life.

"His indifference was curiously annoying, I had been awaiting his appearance so long and so anxiously.

" 'Good evening, friend,' I said heartily. He neither started nor turned; he simply took no notice whatever.

"A queer feeling of chill crept over me. He had passed by in such a notable silence; his feet upon the weed-grown shingle pathway made no sound; he had slipped into the gloom of the interior like a shadow.

"Again the curious agitation of the nerves which had possessed me when first I saw the moonlight glint through the ruin!

"I had no matches with me, and I confess, to the detriment of my reputation for courage, that, until the moon rose, I simply dared not enter the cottage.

"There was no method of getting out at the back; he could hardly leave the place without my seeing him. My pipe, lit with my last match, was mercifully not out. I sat down to wait. No sound came from the darkness inside. It might have been hard to say which was the more completely silent, he within or I without.

"Slowly, slowly the showering radiance of the moonlight stole over the dusky wall. Her coming illuminated all things, sharp, well-edged, splendidly massed into lights and darks. I delayed no longer, but stepped up the pathway and looked into the cottage.

"All was still. In the kitchen there was not much light, for there was no window in the opposite wall; but to the right, beyond the doorway that led into the parlour, a vivid moonbeam streamed across the floor, throwing into dear relief some object that swung from the jagged rope's end—something drooping, limp, inhuman, with a head that lolled horribly to one side.

"I faced it for several appreciable seconds. I heard my own heart-beats as there gradually awoke a tingling repulsion, a rush of shame at my callous, cowardly waiting outside while inside this man had unhindered inflicted upon himself the death which apparently he had contemplated for the past two nights, without the courage to accomplish it. It was not cowardice, but an instinct stronger than I,—it may have been reverence,—that caused me to cover my eyes a moment before snatching out my knife and advancing.

"In that moment the delusion had vanished: no dark form hung in the void space where still the jagged rope's end swung to and fro on the idle breeze. I saw the empty oblong of the doorway, like a dark picture-frame, filled with moonlight. Some madness had seized my senses; there was nothing there.

"I made no further investigations, but just turned on my heel and hurried away—not to say bolted—over the hillside, plunging through the thick trees, down to where nestled the old red manor-house of Barton Fitzroy.

"It was late for a call, but the squire and Mrs. Vyell were kind enough to overlook the irregularity. It was explained that night had overtaken me rambling on the hillside; and when a glass of Madeira and a good cigar had tranquillised the nerves which, it must be owned, were somewhat jarred, and I felt pretty sure of being able to control the vocal chords, I said lightly:

" 'What a curiously solitary place is that little circular combe of which you told me!'

" 'Ah, you have been there!'

"Pretty Mrs. Vyell was interested.

" 'More than once,' I confessed, with eyes fixed upon my cigar.

" 'Did you happen to notice a ruined cottage on the brow of the hill?'

" 'Yes, I thought it the most lonely human habitation I have met with in England.'

" 'It has never been inhabited since I remember,' she said softly, gazing into the fire. 'About thirty years ago there was a tragedy there.'

" 'Will you tell me about it?'

" 'Francis knows more about it than I do,' she said, with a glance at her husband. 'He's a native of these parts, you see. Tell it, Francis. Mr. Rivers won't accuse a man of exaggeration; women have all the credit of a lively imagination.'

"The squire looked reminiscent for a few moments.

" 'There was a man in this village,' he suddenly began, 'when I was quite a youngster, named Israels. He was a miller's son, and they had Portuguese blood in them. Young Israels was a big, handsome fellow, but moody and restless, with the fever of the sea adventurer in his veins. He would have nothing to do with the mill, but was always a rover. When he was about thirty years old, he came home from a voyage, wooed Kitty Eusden, our local belle, and married her, under the very nose of Larking, a good, respectable fellow, to whom she was betrothed.

" 'Israels' marriage developed in him a new trait—a jealousy that was almost mania; he may have had more reasons for it than we knew of, but the fact is certain that the men of the village hardly dared pass the time of day with his wife, for fear of getting their teeth knocked down their throats.

" 'When they had been two or three years wed, the yearning to wander came upon him again. He was torn between the ever-growing restlessness and his fear of leaving his wife behind. So he set to work to build that cottage—far from the village—far from everything that might have helped her to bear her solitude; settled her in it, with provision of all he could think of for her comfort, and was off, leaving her, though this he did not know, within six months of becoming a mother for the first time.

" 'She was fond of him, and she was not a bad girl, not by any means, though shallow. Her conduct at first was exemplary, and had the baby lived I believe all might have gone well. But the baby died, and there came on the top of this desolation a period when she heard not a word from her absent husband. Her loneliness must have been hard to bear, and poor Larking used to go and see her.

" 'The place was so remote that nobody knew what was going on, until, when Israels had been two years absent, they went away together. A week after their departure the wanderer returned.

" 'He went up to the cottage, found it forsaken, and came down to the vicarage for information. All they could do was to show him his baby's grave in the churchyard, and tell him that his wife was gone. The vicar was a good man, but hard; he told Israels that he deserved his fate. The wretched creature went back to the deserted cottage on the hillside, and hanged himself in the doorway between the kitchen and the parlour. There, a month later, his corpse was found by Larking, who had come back to get some things for Kitty.

" 'Of course no one would rent the cottage after that. It was lonely before; now were added all the horrors of superstition, and people have been actually known to declare that Israels still haunts the hillside. A shepherd told me seriously about fifteen years ago that his dog saw him, and bolted off some miles across the countryside, half mad with fear. These superstitions come of living too far from a railway: the inhabitants of these combes live, as one might say, some centuries behind the times.'

"What could I say after that? I could not own to what I had seen. The squire would have been quite polite about it, but from that moment he would have considered me an unreliable person. One must preserve one's character for veracity even at the expense of truth," concluded the Minor Poet sadly. "Therefore I held my tongue; but for all that I did see what I have told you, and I consider it the most curious experience of my life."

FATHER MARTIN'S TALE
by
R. H. BENSON

No other family has approached the Bensons for sheer volume of printed words. Between them, Arthur Christopher Benson (1862-1925), Edward Frederic Benson (1867-1940) and Robert Hugh Benson (1871-1914) published over one hundred and fifty books, with E. F. Benson becoming the most well-known of the brothers. Ghost stories, incidentally, were just a fraction of their output.

The brothers were the children of the Archbishop of Canterbury, but Hugh Benson decided to turn away from the Church of England and instead embrace the Roman Catholic Church, rising to become a private chamberlain to Pope Pius X in Rome.

R. H. Benson's passion for his faith is evident not just in his non-fiction work and religious musings, but also in his fiction. Some have held Hugh's Catholicism as an inherent weakness in his storytelling but, as an avid follower of real-life hauntings, he clearly saw his supernatural tales as more than simply a pulpit for his faith.

Benson's second collection of ghost stories, A Mirror of Shallot *(1907), was an impressive publication of intertwined stories. First published in the* Ecclesiastical Review *and the* Catholic Fireside, *each tale is told by a different priest in a group, as they relate their supernatural experiences to each other.*

Less celebrated than many of its companion pieces, Father Martin's Tale *is nonetheless an eerie story, with a memorable ending.*

* * *

The Father Rector announced to us one day at dinner that a friend of his from England had called upon him a day or two before; and that he had asked him to supper that evening.

"There is a story I heard him tell," he said, "some years ago, that I think he would contribute if you cared to ask him, Monsignor. It is remarkable; I remember thinking so."

"To-night?" said Monsignor.

"Yes; he is coming to-night."

"That will do very well," said the other, "we have no story for to-night."

Father Martin appeared at supper; a grey-haired old man, with a face like a mouse, and large brown eyes that were generally cast down. He had a way at table of holding his hands together with his elbows at his side that bore out the impression of his face.

He looked up deprecatingly and gave a little nervous laugh as Monsignor put his request.

"It is a long time since I have told it, Monsignor," he said."

"That is the more reason for telling it again," said the other priest with his sharp geniality, "or it may be lost to humanity."

"It has met with incredulity," said the old man.

"It will not meet with it here, then," remarked

Monsignor. "We have been practising ourselves in the art of believing. Another act of faith will do us no harm."

We explained the circumstances.

Father Martin looked round; and I could see that he was pleased.

"Very well, Monsignor," he said, "I will do my best to make it easy."

When we had reached the room upstairs, the old priest was put into the arm-chair in the centre, drawn back a little so that all might see him; he refused tobacco, propped his chin on his two hands, looking more than ever like a venerable mouse, and began his story. I sat at the end of the semi-circle, near the fire, and watched him as he talked.

"I regret I have not heard the other tales," he said; "it would encourage me in my own. But perhaps it is better so. I have told this so often that I can only tell it in one way, and you must forgive me, gentlemen, if my way is not yours."

"About twenty years ago I had charge of a mission in Lancashire, some fourteen miles from Blackburn, among the hills. The name of the place is Monkswell; it was a little village then, but I think it is a town now. In those days there was only one street, of perhaps a dozen houses on each side. My little church stood at the head of the street, with the presbytery beside it. The house had a garden at the back, with a path running through it to the gate; and beyond the gate was a path leading on to the moor.

"Nearly all the village was Catholic, and had always been so; and I had perhaps a hundred more of my folk scattered about the moor. Their occupation was weaving; that was before the coal was found at Monkswell. Now they have a great church there with a parish of over a thousand.

"Of course, I knew all my people well enough; they are wonderful folk, those Lancashire folk, I could tell you a score of tales of their devotion and faith. There was one woman that I could make nothing of. She lived with her two brothers in a little cottage a couple of miles away from Monkswell; and the three kept themselves by weaving. The two men were fine lads, regular at their religious duties, and at Mass every Sunday. But the woman would not come near the church. I went to her again and again; and before every Easter; but it was of no use. She would not even tell me why she would not come; but I knew the reason. The poor creature had been ruined in Blackburn, and could not hold up her head again. Her brothers took her back, and she had lived with them for ten years, and never once during that time, so far as I knew, had she set foot outside her little place. She could not bear to be seen, you see."

The little pointed face looked very tender and compassionate now, and the brown, beady eyes ran round the circle deprecatingly.

"Well, it was one Sunday in January that Alfred told me that his sister was unwell. It seemed to be nothing serious, he said, and of course he promised to let me know if she should become worse. But I made up my mind that I would go in any case during that week, and see if sickness had softened her at all. Alfred told me too that another brother of his, Patrick, on whom, let it be remembered—" and he held up an admonitory hand— "I had never set eyes, was coming up to them on the next day from London, for a week's holiday. He promised he would bring him to see me later on in the week.

"There was a fall of snow that afternoon, not very deep, and another next day, and I thought I would put off my walk across the hills until it melted, unless I heard that Sarah was worse.

"It was on the Wednesday evening about six o'clock that I was sent for.

"I was sitting in my study on the ground floor with the curtains drawn, when I heard the garden gate open and close, and I ran out into the hall, just as the knock came at the back door. I knew that it was unlikely that any should come at that hour, and in such weather, except for a sick-call; and I opened the door almost before the knocking had ended.

"The candle was blown out by the draught, but I knew Alfred's voice at once.

"'She is worse, Father,' he said, 'for God's sake come at once. I think she wishes for the Sacraments. I am going on for the doctor.'

"I knew by his voice that it was serious, though I could not see his face; I could only see his figure against the snow outside; and before I could say more than that I would come at once, he was gone again, and I heard the garden door open and shut. He was gone down to the doctor's house, I knew, a mile further down the valley.

"I shut the hall door without bolting it, and went to the kitchen and told my housekeeper to grease my boots well and set them in my room with my cloak and hat and muffler and my lantern. I told her I had had a sick-call and did not know when I should be back; she had better put the pot on the fire and I would help myself when I came home.

"Then I ran into the church through the sacristy to fetch the holy oils and the Blessed Sacrament.

"When I came back, I noticed that one of the strings of the purse that held the pyx was frayed, and I set it down on the table to knot it properly. Then again I heard the garden gate open and shut."

The priest lifted his eyes and looked round again; there was something odd in his look.

"Gentlemen, we are getting near the point of the story. I will ask you to listen very carefully and to give me your conclusions afterwards. I am relating to you only events, as they happened historically. I give you my word as to their truth."

There was a murmur of assent.

"Well, then," he went on, "at first I supposed it was Alfred come back again for some reason. I put down the string and went to the door without a light. As I reached the threshold there came a knocking.

"I turned the handle and a gust of wind burst in, as it had done five minutes before. There was a figure standing there, muffled up as the other had been.

" 'What is it?' I said, 'I am just coming. Is it you, Alfred?'

" 'No, Father,' said a voice—the man was on the steps a yard from me—'I came to say that Sarah was better and does not wish for the Sacraments.'

"Of course I was startled at that.

" 'Why! Who are you?' I said. 'Are you Patrick?'

" 'Yes, Father,' said the man, 'I am Patrick.'

"I cannot describe his voice, but it was not extraordinary in any way; it was a little muffled: I supposed he had a comforter over his mouth. I could not see his face at all. I could not even see if he was stout or thin, the wind blew about his cloak so much.

"As I hesitated, the door from the kitchen behind me was flung open, and I heard a very much frightened voice calling:—

"'Who's that, Father?' said Hannah.

"I turned round.

"'It is Patrick Oldroyd,' I said. 'He is come from his sister.'

"I could see the woman standing in the light from the kitchen door; she had her hands out before her as if she were frightened at something.

"'Go out of the draught,' I said.

"She went back at that; but she did not close the door, and I knew she was listening to every word.

"'Come in, Patrick,' I said, turning round again.

"I could see he had moved down a step, and was standing on the gravel now.

"He came up again then, and I stood aside to let him go past me into my study. But he stopped at the door. Still I could not see his face—it was dark in the hall, you remember.

"'No, Father,' he said, 'I cannot wait. I must go after Alfred.'

"I put out my hand toward him, but he slipped past me quickly, and was out again on the gravel before I could speak.

"'Nonsense!' I said. 'She will be none the worse for a doctor; and if you will wait a minute I will come with you.'

"'You are not wanted,' he said rather offensively, I thought. 'I tell you she is better, Father: she will not see you.'

"I was a little angry at that. I was not accustomed to be spoken to in that way.

"'That is very well,' I said, 'but I shall come for all that, and if you do not wish to walk with me, I shall walk alone.'

"He was turning to go, but he faced me again then.

"'Do not come, Father,' he said. 'Come to-morrow. I

tell you she will not see you. You know what Sarah is.'

" 'I know very well,' I said, 'she is out of grace, and I know what will be the end of her if I do not come. I tell you I am coming, Patrick Oldroyd. So you can do as you please.'

"I shut the door and went back into my room, and as I went, the garden gate opened and shut once more.

"My hands trembled a little as I began to knot the string of the pyx; I supposed then that I had been more angered than I had known"—the old priest looked round again swiftly and dropped his eyes—"but I do not now think that it was only anger. However, you shall hear."

He had moved himself by now to the very edge of his chair where he sat crouched up with his hands together. The listeners were all very quiet.

"I had hardly begun to knot the string before Hannah came in. She bobbed at the door when she saw what I was holding, and then came forward. I could see that she was very much upset by something.

" 'Father,' she said, 'for the love of God do not go with that man.'

" 'I am ashamed of you, Hannah,' I told her. 'What do you mean?'

" 'Father,' she said, 'I am afraid. I do not like that man. There is something the matter.'

"I rose; laid the pyx down and went to my boots without saying anything.

" 'Father,' she said again, 'for the love of God do not go. I tell you I was frightened when I heard his knock.'

"Still I said nothing; but put on my boots and went to the table where the pyx lay and the case of oils.

"She came right up to me, and I could see that she was as white as death as she stared at me.

"I finished putting on my cloak, wrapped the comforter round my neck, put on my hat and took up the lantern.

"'Father,' she said again.

"I looked her full in the face then as she knelt down.

"'Hannah,' I said, 'I am going. Patrick has gone after his brother.'

"'It is not Patrick, she cried after me; 'I tell you, Father—"

"Then I shut the door and left her kneeling there.

"It was very dark when I got down the steps; and I hadn't gone a yard along the path before I stepped over my knee into a drift of snow. It had banked up against a gooseberry bush. Well, I saw that I must go carefully; so I stepped back on to the middle of the path, and held my lantern low.

"I could see the marks of the two men plain enough; it was a path that I had made broad on purpose so that I could walk up and down to say my office without thinking much of where I stepped.

"There was one track on this side, and one on that.

"Have you ever noticed, gentlemen, that a man in snow will nearly always go back over his own traces, in preference to any one else's? Well, that is so: and it was so in this case.

"When I got to the garden gate I saw that Alfred had turned off to the right on his way to the doctor; his marks were quite plain in the light of the lantern, going down the hill. But I was astonished to see that the other man had not gone after him as he said he would; for there was only one pair of footmarks going down the hill; and the other track was plain enough, coming and going. The man must have gone straight home again, I thought.

"Now——"

"One moment, Father Martin," said Monsignor leaning forward; "draw the two lines of tracks here." He put a pencil and paper into the priest's hands.

Father Martin scribbled for a moment or two and then held up the paper so that we could all see it.

As he explained I understood. He had drawn a square for the house, a line for the garden wall, and through the gap ran four lines, marked with arrows. Two ran to the house and two back as far as the gate; at this point one curved sharply round to the right and one straight across the paper beside that which marked the coming.

"I noticed all this," said the old priest emphatically, "because I determined to follow along the double track so far as Sarah Oldroyd's house; and I kept the light turned on to it. I did not wish to slip into a snowdrift.

"Now, I was very much puzzled. I had been thinking it over, of course, ever since the man had gone, and I could not understand it. I must confess that my housekeeper's words had not made it clearer. I knew she did not know Patrick; he had never been home since she had come to me. I was surprised, too, at his behaviour, for I knew from his brother that he was a good Catholic; and—well, you understand, gentlemen—it was very puzzling. But Hannah was Irish, and I knew they had strange fancies sometimes.

"Then, there was something else, which I had better mention before I go any further. Although I had not been frightened when the man came, yet, when Hannah had said that she was frightened, I knew what she meant. It had seemed to me natural that she should be frightened. I can say no more than that."

He threw out his hands deprecatingly, and then folded them again sedately on his hunched knees.

"Well, I set out across the moor, following carefully in the double track of—of the man who called himself Patrick. I could see Alfred's single track a yard to my right; sometimes the tracks crossed.

"I had no time to look about me much, but I saw now

and again the slopes to the north, and once when I turned I saw the lights of the village behind me, perhaps a quarter of a mile away. Then I went on again and I wondered as I went.

"I will tell you one thing that crossed my mind, gentlemen. I did wonder whether Hannah had not been right, and if this was Patrick after all. I thought it possible—though I must say I thought it very unlikely—that it might be some enemy of Sarah's—some one she had offended—an infidel, perhaps, but who wished her to die without the Sacraments that she wanted. I thought that; but I never dreamt of—of what I thought afterwards and think now."

He looked round again, clasped his hands more tightly and went on.

"It was very rough going, and as I climbed up at last on to the little shoulder of hill that was the horizon from my house, I stopped to get my breath and turned round again to look behind me.

"I could see my house-lights at the end of the village, and the church beside it, and I wondered that I could see the lights so plainly. Then I understood that Hannah must be in my study and that she had drawn the blind up to watch my lantern going across the snow.

"I am ashamed to tell you, gentlemen, that that cheered me a little; I do not quite know why, but I must confess that I was uncomfortable—I know that I should not have been, carrying what I did, and on such an errand, but I was uneasy. It seemed very lonely out there, and the white sheets of snow made it worse. I do not think that I should have minded the dark so much. There was not much wind and everything was very quiet. I could just hear the stream running down in the valley behind me. The clouds had gone and there was a clear night of stars overhead."

The old priest stopped; his lips worked a little, as I had seen them before, two or three times, during his story. Then he sighed, looked at us and went on.

"Now, gentlemen, I entreat you to believe me. This is what happened next. You remember that this point at which I stopped to take breath was the horizon from my house. Notice that.

"Well, I turned round, and lowered my lantern again to look at the tracks, and a yard in front of me they ceased. They ceased."

He paused again, and there was not a sound from the circle.

"They ceased, gentlemen. I swear it to you, and I cannot describe what I felt. At first I thought it was a mistake; that he had leapt a yard or two—that the snow was frozen. It was not so.

"There a yard to the right were Alfred's tracks, perfectly distinct, with the toes pointing the way from which I had come. There was no confusion, no hard or broken ground, there was just the soft surface of the snow, the trampled path of—of the man's footsteps and mine, and Alfred's a yard or two away."

The old man did not look like a mouse now; his eyes were large and bright, his mouth severe, and his hands hung in the air in a petrified gesture.

"If he had leapt," he said, "he did not alight again."

He passed his hand over his mouth once or twice.

"Well, gentlemen, I confess that I hesitated. I looked back at the lights and then on again at the slopes in front, and then I was ashamed of myself. I did not hesitate long, for any place was better than that. I went on; I dared not run; for I think I should have gone mad if I had lost self-control; but I walked, and not too fast, either; I put my hand on the pyx as it lay on my breast, but I dared not turn my head to right or left. I just stared at Alfred's tracks in front of me and trod in them.

"Well, gentlemen, I did run the last hundred yards; the door of the Oldroyds' cottage was open, and they were looking out for me and I gave Sarah the last Sacraments, and heard her confession. She died before morning.

"And I have one confession to make myself—I did not go home that night. They were very courteous to me when I told them the story, and made out that they did not wish me to leave their sister; so the doctor and Alfred walked back over the moor together to tell Hannah I should not be back, and that all was well with me.

"There, gentlemen."

"And Patrick?" said a voice.

"Patrick of course had not been out that night."

THE BEAD NECKLACE
by
ALICE PERRIN

Born Alice Robinson in Mussoorie, Colonial India, in 1867, Alice Perrin studied in England before returning and marrying engineer Charles Perrin in 1886. Bored with the limited life available to a woman in Anglo-India, Perrin began writing, publishing her first two-volume novel in 1894, entitled Into Temptation.

In 1901 Perrin published her first collection of ghost stories, East of Suez, *and it cemented her reputation as a first-class writer, even drawing comparisons with Rudyard Kipling. In total, Perrin published 17 novels in addition to her short stories, and also took an active role in many London literary societies, including the Women Writers' Club. Perrin was considered a leading figure at the club, alongside Mrs. Baillie Reynolds, who also published supernatural fiction (and was seen earlier in this anthology).*

In Meredith Starr's compilation of interviews with well-known authors, The Future of the Novel, *Perrin predicted the rise of affordable paperbacks and the popularity of mainstream publishing: "If printers and binders and paper-makers continue to obtain the large wages and prices we hear of, it seems to me that the novel must come down in price, since it would be quite possible to produce even cheaper bindings, less good print, and more horrible paper than is being 'put out' at present; more millions of the public would buy, and the incurable novel reader would rejoice."*

The Perrins moved to Switzerland in 1925, where Alice hosted several British writers, including renowned ghost story writer, Algernon Blackwood. Alice Perrin's last novel, Other Sheep, *was published in 1932, two years before her death.*

* * *

When it became known in the village of Hayfield that Adela Roscoe was engaged to be married, every one inquired if the man had money; nobody thought of asking if he were nice till afterwards, because the Major had repeatedly shouted abroad the fact that he intended his daughter to marry a rich man or to be an old maid. Only a few months ago he had sworn himself voiceless and turned the colour of a beetroot for the reason that Chris Mortimer, who was merely the son of a poor clergyman in the next parish, had dared to propose to Adela.

"What! Marry my daughter to a beggarly puppy in the Merchant Service!" he roared at the culprit. "What do you take me for? Let me tell you that the man who marries her must be able to keep a father-in-law in style as well as a wife. Do you hear? The girl's an investment, and one that is going to pay me a thousand per cent too. You clear out of this, you young jackanapes, and if I catch you hanging around, or trying to speak to her, I'll break every bone in your wretched body," &c. &c.

And with such rigid precaution did the unpleasant old gentleman guard his treasure for the next fortnight, that young Mortimer was forced to join his ship and sail away to the South Sea Islands without the opportunity of a word or a look from Adela; and the farewell note he tried to smuggle in, *viâ* the garden boy, was returned to him by post, torn to shreds, in an envelope (unstamped) which bore the Major's crest. The note had contained a passionate assurance of his undying love, an entreaty that she would be true to him, a vow that he would come back with a fortune to claim her—a fortune so large that even her father would be satisfied.

"There is money to be made where I am going," he wrote; "a pal of mine has let me into a secret—it's a dead certainty. Only wait for me and love me, and never think that I shall not return."

But, as we know, Adela did not receive her letter, and the garden boy, who had failed in his best endeavours to deliver it, would have summonsed the Major for knocking out his front teeth, only that Mortimer's bribe had rendered him impervious to suffering.

Then one day, when the ineligible suitor had long been safely on the ocean, a tall, black-haired stranger suddenly appeared in company with the Major and his daughter, and the interested public subsequently discovered that he was a baronet, that he was staying with the Roscoes, and that he had been a friend of the Major's before debt and discredit had driven the latter to a remote and cheap country district.

Adela detested their guest—the first they had entertained since her return from the inexpensive French boarding-school where she had been educated, and where she had spent all her holidays from the time of her mother's death. Sir Bennet Falcon frightened and disgusted her; he would stare into her face with his heavy bloodshot eyes until her cheeks grew crimson, and then he would laugh and say it was so refreshing to see a blush. When he was not playing cards or drinking with her father, he would follow her about, talking to her in a way that she did not understand; or he would tease her as if she were a child—pull her bright hair, pinch her cheeks, and cackle with evil satisfaction when she flew into a rage. He always smelt of whisky; his very clothes seemed to have been steeped in spirit; his face reminded her of a gargoyle; his husky voice rasped her nerves; his odious touch made her shiver. But his presence apparently had a soothing effect upon the Major, who now assumed a fatherly attitude towards his only child, sent for a new hat and parasol for her from London, made a fuss about her health and comfort, and insisted that she should retire to bed early. This she was quite ready to do, for as the evening advanced Sir Bennet's attentions grew increasingly nauseating, and she was thankful to escape to her room, though the loud voices and coarse laughter below invariably kept her awake till long after midnight.

The girl was thoroughly miserable. She had given her love to Chris Mortimer, and her tender heart ached for a sight of the young sailor's frank face and direct grey eyes. The future without him seemed dark and hopeless, and she was also tormented with a fearful suspicion, which was justified one sunny morning, when her father called her into the dining-room and said that Sir Bennet wished to marry her.

"Oh! I couldn't," she cried, with horror in her brown eyes. "I couldn't—I couldn't!" She put out both her hands as though to ward off the revolting suggestion.

"Now, my good girl,"—the Major began to walk up and down the room blowing out his loose red cheeks, and flapping behind him the tail of his rough shooting coat—"I'm not going to have any nonsense. Sir Bennet is waiting for you at the bottom of the garden, and you'll just go straight and tell him you will be his wife, and say 'Thank you,' as well. What the devil can a miserable chit like you want more? You'll be My Lady; he stinks of money; even *he* can't get through his income, and if you let him go on as he's doing now, you'll be a rich widow in no time, and free to marry your fool of a cabin-boy, or whatever he may be."

But Adela only sank into a chair and cried despairingly. She was gentle and timid by nature and utterly incapable of openly defying her father's orders.

"Get up and stop that noise," he continued, halting before her. "What do you suppose I asked the man down here for? Why have I let him drink me out of house and home? Why have I allowed him to clear me out at poker? Because I meant him to marry *you*, of course, and now he's hooked, you've got to keep him. Gad! To think what this marriage means——" the Major slapped his thigh, shut his eyes, and drew a long breath. "It means Life and the World once more! Do you think I'm going to stay and rot in this infernal hole, when there's an easy way out like this? No; I've made a damned good bargain, and you're not going to upset the apple-cart, my lady, I can tell you. Come along——"

He dragged her to her feet, giving her an impatient shake, and with a storm of bad language he drove her before him through the little hall and out of the front door; then he stood in the porch, his legs apart, and menace in his attitude, while with bowed head and faltering footsteps the girl went blindly towards the figure that waited in the distance.

There followed a week of misery for Adela. She felt as though she had committed some horrible crime; she had broken her promise to the man she loved; she was Sir Bennet's promised wife, and there was no chance of escape,—for Chris was hundreds of miles away across the seas and could not help her. What would he think when he came back and found she was Lady Falcon? Would he ever understand and forgive? The wedding day was fixed; Sir Bennet wrote by every post for presents for his fiancée; he was even paying for her trousseau, a proceeding that gratified the father as much as it annoyed the daughter; the two men were boisterous and triumphant, and apparently quite unaffected by the white face, despairing eyes, and spiritless manner of their victim.

Then it became necessary for Sir Bennet to go to London that he might interview lawyers and tailors, arrange about settlements, and the opening of his town and country houses. He was away for three weeks, and Adela felt almost happy by contrast when relieved of his hateful company, though the thought of the future hung like a dark cloud over her mind. The days flew by, and the end of her respite was at hand; this evening Sir Bennet would return with his evil face, his atmosphere of dissipation, and his noxious love-making. She sat at the open window of her little drawing-room, her hands lying limp in her lap, her wistful eyes gazing out at the wealth of summer flowers, the hovering butterflies, the happy birds; she was thinking of Chris as one thinks of a dear, dead friend, with a dumb regret, a finality of sorrow, an absence of hope.

The garden gate clicked and the village postman hurried up the drive. She took the letters from him through the window and nodded pleasantly as the man touched his cap and turned away. There were some bills for the Major, and a curious-looking packet for herself sewn up with red cotton in dirty wax-cloth. The address was blurred and indistinct, but the handwriting brought the colour flooding over her face and neck, and she put it to her lips with a gasp of pleasure. Then she tore it open with shaking fingers and searched desperately for the letter that she felt convinced would be inside, but only a barbaric-looking necklace of faded beads fell on to her lap, and apparently Chris had sent it to her without a word. It was a bitter disappointment, and the tears ran down her cheeks as she examined again and again the wrappings of her strange present. She held the necklace up, and wondered why Chris had wanted her to have it; the beads were common glass, and were strung on to something that looked like stiff brown thread, but they were arranged in squares with curious lines and patterns, and she had certainly never seen anything quite like it before. At any rate it had come from Chris, his dear fingers had held it, his hands had packed it up; she would treasure the wrapper on which he had written her name, and to-night she would wear the necklace, hideous though it might be, as a charm to give her strength for the ordeal of Sir Bennet's return.

She looked enchanting when she came down to the drawing-room that evening before dinner: her cheeks were flushed with emotion; her eyes dreamy with memories of her lost lover; her white gown threw up the brilliance of her hair and added to the shapeliness of her slight figure; the quaint bead necklace lay round her delicate throat. Sir Bennet stood on the hearth-rug: he had asked for a fire, though the summer night was warm to closeness, and he spread his shaking fingers over the flames; his eyes were dull, and his swollen lips twitched as he greeted the girl and kissed her unwilling face. He had evidently been drinking more heavily than usual during his absence.

"What's that ugly thing round your neck?" he asked, and as he peered at the beads a look came into his face as though some unpleasant recollection had been awakened. Adela murmured an incoherent reply. She wished now she had not worn the necklace, and she felt relieved that her father was not in the room to ask further questions. She could hear him in the dining-room drawing corks.

"Come and sit here," said Sir Bennet, flinging himself into a corner of the sofa. She tried to evade his clutch, but he pulled her down into the vacant place by his side.

"See what I've brought for my little white bird." He fumbled in his pocket and produced a long morocco case.

"Open it! I'll bet you've never seen anything to equal what's inside."

She pressed the spring without any feeling of pleasurable curiosity, and beheld a diamond necklace that startled her with its brilliance—it seemed to be made of captive lightning.

"There!" croaked Sir Bennet. "What d'ye think of that? Take that dirty little bead thing off your pretty neck and put this on."

He dragged at the beads as though he would break the fastening, but it held firm.

"Oh! don't," cried Adela; "you'll break it."

"Well, and what then? Who gave it to you?" he asked with sudden fierceness.

Adela, fearful of being pressed on the subject, nervously undid the string and let him take her treasure from her, and again the look of uneasy recollection, almost fear, came into the man's eyes.

"I've seen these things before," he said shortly; "natives wear 'em in the South Sea Islands——"

He put it in his pocket, then clasped the diamonds round her neck and regarded the effect with satisfied complacence. "There!" he added, "that's better."

"May I have my beads back?" she asked timidly; when she had thanked him for his gift with forced gratitude.

"No," he answered, and set his jaw. "I don't want to see a thing like that on your neck again; it's only fit for savages, and it reminds me of a deuced bad time I had once in my life which I prefer to forget. There's the gong."

He rose and offered her his arm. During dinner he was inclined to be sullen and quarrelsome; he ate little, but drank freely of the Major's whisky; and when Adela left the room he got up with difficulty to open the door for her. She passed him swiftly, avoiding his gaze, and fled to her room, where she railed in helpless bitterness against the cruelty of her lot, cried over the loss of her necklace, and kissed the wrapping it had travelled in.

Later, she heard the two men leave the dining-room and come stumbling up the staircase. Her father was laughing foolishly, and Sir Bennet was talking fast in a curious high-pitched tone.

"But didn't you *see* the fellow, Roscoe?" he was saying as they passed her room, and his voice reminded her of a day when she had visited a large hospital and the raving of a delirious patient had reached her ears through a half-closed door. "He looked into the dining-room twice, and then, when we came out, he was hiding behind the curtain in the hall—Lord! He's coming up the stairs now—keep him back, Roscoe, for the love of Heaven—stop him—give me time to lock my door——"

There was a rush of unsteady footsteps down the passage, a loud slam, a helpless giggling laugh from the Major as he blundered into his own room, and then all was quiet. Adela shuddered and turned wearily to the open window; she leaned out and inhaled the fragrance of the flowers beneath, the cool sweetness of the night air; little white moths brushed past her face, and now and then a bird called from the trees at the end of the garden. A faint hint of the rising moon was stealing over the sky, and Adela sat motionless and inert while the weird light slowly increased and clove the darkness into blocks of shadow.

Suddenly the sound of a muffled cry within the house

made her start and draw back her head. Again she heard it, and her heart beat quickly with apprehension. She opened her door and listened; in his room at the end of the passage Sir Bennet seemed to be running violently to and fro and calling hoarsely for help, but before she could dart across to rouse her father, a dishevelled figure with a white terrified face and wild eyes rushed past her and down the stairs. She heard the hall-door bang, and the thud of running feet over the lawn.

In a moment she was at her father's bedside. "Get up—get up!" she shouted, shaking him desperately, "Sir Bennet must have gone mad—he has rushed out of the house half dressed—Father! Father!"

But the Major snored on; she was powerless to rouse him from his heavy stupor, and she ran in bewilderment back to her open window. The moonlight was streaming over the smooth grass; and, in and out among the bushes, as though pursued by a relentless enemy, ran Sir Bennet, stooping, doubling, dodging. His heavy steps and panting breath throbbed on the night air, and once or twice he half fell, recovering himself with a low hunted cry.

It was a sickening sight, but the girl's courage rose unexpectedly, as sometimes happens with timid natures in a sudden crisis. She leant out of the window and called to him. At the sound of her voice he stopped, then hurried towards her and held up his hands. His face, in the moonlight, drawn with terror and delusion, was ghastly.

"Come down!" he called, "come down and help me drive him away—he is waiting there under the trees. If you are with me perhaps he will go, but alone I cannot escape from him, and he will hunt me to my death. After all these years he has come for his revenge—Adela! Adela!"

The fear and supplication in his voice were pitiable; she braced her nerves and prepared to go down. Perhaps her presence would soothe and influence him—even if he should kill her in his delirium it would be better than living to be his wife.

"Wait," she cried softly, "I am coming." And presently her hand was on his trembling arm, and she was firmly reassuring him that he was safe from his imaginary pursuer. She led him to a garden bench under the dining-room window, and he sat down a shaking, huddled heap.

"It was that cursed necklace you were wearing," he stammered; "it made me think of him—the natives on the island used to wear them——" He stopped and drew his hand across his wet forehead. "Of course I didn't really see him—he has been dead for years," he glanced about him fearfully, "and yet he looked into the dining-room, he followed me up the stairs—he was in my room," his voice rose and he gripped her hands, "I am going to tell you all about it—the whole truth—perhaps that will keep him away and satisfy him?"

"Yes," said Adela soothingly, "yes—tell me."

His grasp tightened on her hands, and he began to speak in a harsh, monotonous key, staring intently all the while into the surrounding shadows.

"Years ago I had a friend—a friend who stuck to me when I was under a cloud and people were cutting me; we went away together yachting—he sacrificed a lot to go with me. We cruised about in warm climates and stopped at ports we had never heard of, and at last we got among the South Sea Islands. Then there was a storm —my God, what a storm!—it was like the end of the world—and the yacht went down. All night Horsley and I clung to the same piece of wreckage, and in the morning we were washed ashore, the only survivors. It was a long low island, and the natives were cannibals—we saw them at it one night, watched them through the cocoa-nut palms by the light of the fire they had made, and then we knew what they were keeping us for. We were guarded day and night, though they let us wander within certain limits, and gave us a hut to live in. We saw no ships, we had no chance to build a boat, or escape by swimming, and day by day we waited for our death. Then Horsley ran a poisonous thorn into his foot and had to stay in the hut, and one morning when I went down as usual to the shore in the hope of seeing a sail, there seemed to be no natives on the watch. All night they had been singing and tom-toming, and I suppose the guards had got careless and were asleep, for I saw none of them about. Just as I was thinking of going back through the palm grove to the hut to tell Horsley there might be a chance to take to the sea, a ship came round the corner of the island. She was only a small trading vessel that had got out of her course, but she meant rescue if the natives didn't spot her. I looked all round—there wasn't a soul in sight, the ship was only a few hundred yards off, the water was calm, and I could swim well. I thought if I went back for Horsley, who couldn't walk with his bad foot, the natives would have time to see the ship, and the chances were we should be intercepted and killed. The ship's captain would never send a boat ashore and risk the lives of his crew, I knew that—and I knew if I got away I should be leaving Horsley to a cruel death. I swear I fought the temptation, but all the same I took off my clothes and swam for my life. I reached the ship, I told them about Horsley, but they refused to do more than give me shelter, because the natives of that island were known to be savagely hostile; and we steamed away into safety while Horsley was left there alone——"

He ceased abruptly, his mouth open, his breath coming in quick gasps; he pointed towards the trees:—

"There! Don't you see him? Over by the bushes—he hasn't gone, I've done no good by telling the truth—he is coming out into the moonlight on the lawn—Ah!—I can't bear to see his face. Go back, Horsley!" he shouted; "I never meant to leave you, I meant to get the ship's boat and fetch you—I swear I did!" He pushed past Adela's restraining hand, and ran with superhuman swiftness down the path.

She heard him crash through the old wooden gate, and his rapid footsteps rang clear on the hard road; faster, faster they sped into the distance, until the echo died away on the still night air.

Extract from a local newspaper:—
"An inquest was held yesterday on the body of Sir Bennet Falcon, Baronet, who was found drowned in a pond two miles from the village of Hayfield, where he had been staying on a visit to his friends, Major and Miss Roscoe. The jury returned a verdict of suicide whilst temporarily insane; and much sympathy is felt in the neighbourhood for Miss Roscoe, to whom the deceased gentleman was engaged to be married. We regret to learn that the young lady is at present lying dangerously ill from the effects of the shock, and grave doubts are entertained as to her recovery."

But Adela was called back from the borders of death by news which gave her the promise of a happy future. The secret that had been imparted to Chris Mortimer by his obliging friend had lived up to its character of 'a dead certainty,' and Chris would be arriving home in a few months' time a comparatively rich man. The precious life-giving letter rested day and night beneath Adela's pillow, but in it there was one paragraph which shocked and startled her, and which she never willingly re-read:—

"I wonder if you ever received a rum kind of necklace I sent you? I know you didn't get the letter I wrote at the same time, because the fellow who took it on shore confessed afterwards that he had lost the letter, though he swore he posted the little parcel. I saw an old native wearing the necklace, and it struck me as being rather curious, so I persuaded him to sell the thing, though he made an awful fuss about parting with it, and said it was a most powerful charm against ill-luck; so, being a superstitious sailor, I thought I'd send it to you!—but I'm sorry I did, because I heard later that it had a nasty history. The beads were supposed to be strung on the sinews of a white man who was killed some years ago on one of these islands before the savages were routed out and taught better manners, and though it's probably only a yarn, you'd better throw it away or give it to some one who has a taste for gruesome curiosities. You shall have pearls instead, my darling, and soon I shall be home to fasten them round your neck myself..."

BEHIND THE WALL
by
VIOLET JACOB

Scottish writer Violet Augusta Mary Frederica Kennedy-Erskine (1863-1946) was best known for her poetry and the historical novel Flemington *(1911). The daughter of Henry Kennedy-Erskine and Catherine Jones, an aristocratic family whose seat was the House of Dun, in Angus, she later married Major Arthur Jacob in 1894 and travelled with him to India and Egypt before they settled in England.*

Much of her poetry was written in the Angus dialect, and she was described by Hugh McDiarmid as 'by far the most considerable of contemporary vernacular poets.' Over the course of her career Jacob published several novels, many of which were adventure stories in the vein of H. Rider Haggard, as well as a series of short story collections. Behind the Wall, *a straight-talking ghost story with a distinctly menacing antagonist, is taken from her 1910 collection* The Fortune-Hunters and Other Stories.

* * *

Friday evenings set Arthur Wickham free from the Government office in which his weeks were spent. By nature he was made for an active life, but circumstances had headed him off his natural path and tethered him to London. His friends—and he had a good many—said that golf had spoilt him; that they never saw him nowadays; that it was a great pity to be utterly engrossed, body and soul, in one pursuit, and all sorts of things that friends say when other people's doings do not exactly match their own. But two days' golf compensated him both for their opinions and for the loss of their company on Saturdays and Sundays.

The golf-course at Shorne was a good one, lying on the high ground which sloped up behind the town. The golfers could look down over the roofs of the huddled streets—for Shorne was an ancient little place—to the curving beach, beside which modern hotels and lodgings were disfiguring the seawall. The town seemed to be drawing back in old-fashioned distinction from these second rate attractions to the security of the hill from which the square tower of Shorne Church looked out towards the Romney Marshes.

The golf-course tramped weekly by Wickham had flung its chain of smooth putting-greens out among the humble farmhouses and woods which lie so close to the Kentish shore, and the players could see from their elevation the chalk-scarred downs on one hand, and the sea glittering towards Dungeness on the other. Wickham liked the place better every time he came to it. He had the happy temperament which is attracted by casual sights, and the gift of loitering; so he often strolled among the walled lanes and corners and under the ilex-avenue flanking the massiveness of the church, when the business of golf was over. Shorne was full of Georgian houses, and Wickham, who had a smattering of architectural knowledge, liked Georgian houses.

One evening, when he had sent his clubs back to the inn in the High Street, he whistled to his Aberdeen terrier,

Skittles, and man and dog went strolling up towards the church. They took their way between the high garden-walls which enclose the older houses, and, having no special goal, they turned at random into any byway that happened to appeal to Wickham's fancy. The little dog ran before his master, in the perpetual search for imaginary adventure common to his kind.

The sun of the late June afternoon fell upon just and unjust, upon root and foliage, upon brickwork and stem, and a late season had saved the greens of nature from losing their translucent quality as they sprang towards the blue above them. On either side of Wickham the high walls had a foreign air which translated him, mentally, into the suburbs of some French town. The one on his left was surmounted by a trellis which dripped with a fringe of wistaria; and, above this, he could see the tall head of an acacia-tree which seemed to grow somewhere near the centre of the garden.

To many minds there is no more suggestive sight than that of a door in a dead wall, and the young man stopped before the wooden one which broke the mellow expanse of masonry at his side. It was small and weather-stained and sunk a brick's depth in the surface; and it was old enough to have gained expression, as inanimate things, not in constant use, will gain it with the lapse of time. The secrecy of its look was enhanced by the absence of both handle and key.

Wickham paused before it; he knew that he would like to peer through the empty keyhole, and he also knew that he would not do so. He smiled at himself as he moved away.

Some paces farther on, the wistaria-plant fell over the coping, down to the level of his shoulder, and he paused again to sniff at the trusses of mauve blossom with which it was loaded. As his face came in contact with the leaves, he saw that they covered a square cavity like an unglazed window. Prejudices are strange things; though the particular assortment owned by him had forbidden him the keyhole, they were silent as he peeped between the stems. He pushed them aside with his fingers.

But, if he erred in his act, his punishment was swift. A few inches from his own, a pair of eyes on the inner side of the wall were set on him with an expression which made him start back. There was no movement in them; they looked fixedly out of a pale face as absolutely still as themselves. The presence of the unknown person made no rustle behind the wistaria, and if he or she—for Wickham had no impression of sex—were annoyed by his curiosity, there was neither sound nor sign to indicate the fact. He was not sure whether the eyes were blind, and the thought made him shudder, though there could be nothing to warrant his doing so, were his suspicion correct. He walked on hurriedly. Skittles was at the next corner, waiting to see which way his master would take.

He turned up towards the church, losing the disagreeable feeling produced in him by the little incident as he went along the terrace of ilex and up the steps into the churchyard. The blue sea lay beyond the town, and the crosses and monuments in their ordered rows were beginning to throw long shadows on the grass. The place was empty but for an old man who was clipping a ragged yew-bush within the chain-railing which encompassed an ordinary round-topped tombstone. Wickham's glance fell on the inscription as he passed it: "*Ellen Swaysland, born* 1808, *died* 1865." He had never seen that sirname before.

He entered the great porch of the Norman church, bidding Skittles wait outside, and went to the door leading to the tower, for it had occurred to him that if he climbed it he would be able to see into the garden with the acacia-tree. Soon he was at the top of the stair, and, coming out upon the tower, he looked over the parapet. Skittles was mounting guard by his stick, and the clipping of shears came up to him from Ellen Swaysland's grave. He was above the level of the ilex-trees; there was nothing to obstruct his view of the walled-in houses between himself and the High Street.

He found the one he wanted at once; a narrow-windowed brick house, with a steep roof and stone facings. To his surprise, it had the dead look of an uninhabited building, and the lawn was under high grass. The acacia stood where he had expected to find it, and round its trunk were the remains of a circular seat. A weed-grown path ran the whole length of the lower wall by which he had lately passed, and he could see the hole which looked out on the lane. The wistaria hung round it on the inside also. It seemed to have been trained down purposely in that spot.

While he watched from his isolated height a woman came out of the house, and went quickly, with an odd, shuffling gait, into the alley of bushes running down one side of the garden. It was not only her walk that was strange; and Wickham's lips parted in an astonishment which he could not have explained. He did not know whether it was her dress or her movements which seemed to to him remarkable; but he leaned over the parapet to watch her emerge from the alley and go straight to the hole in the wall. He remained where he was, fascinated, as she stood, a black spot, in the same place, until the striking of the hour from the church reminded him of the futile nature of his occupation. The man below had put away his shears, and Skittles, who had at last discovered his whereabouts, was shivering and whining as he gazed at the silhouette of his master's head and shoulders dark against the sky. Wickham came down the tower-stair.

Perhaps it was his knowledge of what the woman's

eyes were like that made him endow her figure with some sinister quality. He went home to his inn, not sorry to be welcomed back to the commonplace of the company of his dog and the harmless gossip of a waiter to whom he was an established acquaintance.

Next day was Sunday, and again Wickham left the golf-course in the evening to return to the Crown; the early train on the morrow would take him to London in good time for his office-hour. He parted with various men he knew at the golf-house, for most of these stayed at the new hotel on the esplanade, in preference to the old-fashioned inn which had become a familiar haunt to him. He made, as usual, for the church, and thence down to the High Street; and where the lane between the garden-walls crossed his way he turned into it, impelled to pass once more by the half-hidden aperture at which he had seen the strange eyes. But this time he did not wish to look through. He was not anxious to meet those eyes at such close quarters again.

He had almost reached the little wooden door farther on, when it opened and the woman in black stepped out into the road a few paces in front of him. There had been no sound of footsteps in the garden to give warning of her approach. She drew the door to behind her, turning for one moment to face the young man, and her look struck his soul again with the shock of a blow.

She was a middle-aged woman—almost old—the pallor of whose face was accentuated by the uncouth lines of a close bonnet; but all detail was lost on Wickham by reason of her eyes. He was only conscious of them and of the straight eyelids which cut the iris, lying on the upper half, as a band of cloud lies on the disc of the sinking sun. The still, dead malignity, emanating from beneath that level line, made him stop involuntarily and step back a pace from her. Her lips were drawn back, perhaps in a smile; but Wickham could not have told whether she smiled or not. He realised nothing, neither then nor afterwards, but that stream of expression concentrated on him from the unfocussed pupils. He felt that there was nothing in it personal to himself, and that he merely stood, by hazard, in its way, as he might have stood in the way of a bull's-eye lantern; but his horror was not lessened because of that. She turned away, and his wits were brought back by the fury of his dog, who had evidently been unprepared to see the figure emerge from the door.

Skittles's tail was between his legs and his growls and barking filled the lane. Wickham was so much afraid that he would pursue the retreating woman, that he laid hold of his collar and did not let go till she had disappeared round the first corner, which led down to the town. He had reached the Crown before the little terrier had ceased to whine and protest. Skittles stopped, looking behind him at intervals the whole way down the High Street.

Chance brought Wickham back to Shorne the next week sooner than he expected; for some repairs in his particular department of the office liberated the clerks on the following Thursday night. Friday morning found him once more in the train with his golf-clubs, and by luncheon-time he was sitting at his own table in the window of the Crown dining-room, looking into the huddle of old houses and new shops which formed the narrow High Street.

There was more movement going on than he ever remembered seeing in the little place; but those who caused it added nothing to the liveliness of the outlook. Some event had produced an outbreak of black-coated and tall-hatted men, as a spell of summer after cold weather will produce flies from hidden corners. All moved in one direction, and all had the air of rising consciously to an occasion. The explanation could only be a funeral.

"Who's being buried?" inquired Wickham of his friend the waiter.

"Mr. Swaysland, sir; solicitor, sir," replied the man, whipping his napkin under his arm, and going to the window as though he expected to see the deceased in the street.

Wickham stared.

"Swaysland—Swaysland," he repeated, looking through the waiter's head. Then he remembered Ellen Swaysland's tombstone, and the man with the shears clipping the yew-bush on her grave as he entered the church last week.

"Acquainted with the family, sir?" hazarded his companion.

"No—no," said Wickham. "I only noticed the name in the churchyard. I suppose they're well-known people here?"

"Lor', yes, sir; they've been here for more than a hundred years. Two houses here Mr. Swaysland had. One at the bottom of this street, and one between this and the church. But he lived in the small one down here, sir. He couldn't abide to be in the other. He hadn't gone inside the walls since Miss Ellen's death—his half-sister, sir. Fine garden it has too."

Wickham pricked up his ears.

"You can't see the house from the road, the walls is that high. Old Mr. Swaysland——"

"Is it the one with the acacia-tree in the middle?"

"I'm sure I couldn't say, sir," replied the waiter, looking puzzled. Like most indoor servants, he did not know one tree from another.

"But there's a door at the bottom of the garden—a

little wooden door?" continued Wickham. "When you turn the corner of the wall, coming this way, you go straight up to the church?"

"That's it, sir." The interest on Wickham's face appeared to please his companion. He came close to the table, and laid his hand on the empty chair opposite to the young man.

"I expect you've heard something about it," said he. "Well, I was born in this town, and I've seen Miss Ellen myself when I was a little brat of a boy. I'm a good bit older than you, sir, if I may take the liberty to say so."

"Miss Ellen?" said Wickham. "I know nothing about Miss Ellen. I've never even heard the name Swaysland before."

The waiter dropped his voice confidentially.

"Twenty years, sir, she lived there. She was thirty-seven when they put her in that house, and she was fifty-seven when they took her out of it to lay her in the churchyard."

"How do you mean 'put her in'?" asked Wickham, quickly. "Was she mad?"

"Ah! that's what nobody knows. But old Swaysland said so, and that was good enough for the doctors and lawyers. Her being mad meant a fine bit of money to her half-brother, you see—Mr. Swaysland, that is."

"And so you mean that they shut her up there?"

"They did—between them," said the waiter. "She never came out of them walls again. There used to be a little square hole, a little place where she could see into the road, and she used to sit there looking out, day after day. That's when I saw her, sir, when I was a boy."

Wickham had laid down his knife and fork; he leaned across the table, drinking in every word.

"He never went into that house again after Miss Ellen's death, Mr. Swaysland didn't," continued the man.

"I was too young to understand anything about it when it happened, but I heard enough about it when I grew older. My father's sister was a kind of a nurse hereabouts, before them ladies in the white caps was invented (she's gone, now, poor soul, too), and she was sent for to Miss Ellen. Many's the time I've heard her telling mother about it. Mr. Swaysland come into the room the night the lady died, but he kept out of sight of the bed till the doctor thought she was going and beckoned to him. When he come close, Miss Ellen opened her eyes, and aunt used to say they were like the eyes of a serpent. 'Richard,' says she, looking at him (Mr. Swaysland's name was Richard), 'you can't keep me here any longer, for I'm going. Some day,' says she, 'your turn'll come, as mine's coming now, and when it does, I'll fetch you. You've kept me here for twenty years,' she says, 'but you won't be able to keep me back—not then. I'll come for you.' And she died, with her face turned to Mr. Swaysland. Here they are now, sir," he added, looking down the street; "they're obliged to go the longest way. The 'osses can't get up the asphalted lanes to the church."

But Wickham did not look out. He saw in his mind a stranger sight than that which occupied his companion; for he was standing again, in recollection, by the door in the wall.

"Can you tell me exactly when Mr. Swaysland died?" he said, at last.

"It was very sudden," replied the waiter, who was now absorbed in the passing procession; "it was last Sunday evening about this time—a little earlier, perhaps."

When the last carriage had gone by, he turned again to the young man.

"People think of queer things sometimes," he observed apologetically. "D'you know, sir, I've wondered two or three times since last Sunday whether the poor lady kept her word."

Wickham looked at him for a moment in silence. "I think she did," said he, with a curious smile; "and, what's more, my dog thinks so too."

AFTERWORD
by
JOHNNY MAINS

The longest phone call I've ever had in my life was with Hugh Lamb. It happened in 2013, lasted for about three and a half hours, and at the end of it I was knackered, but was instantly a much richer and wiser person for it.

In that call Hugh had finally given up the secrets to good, dedicated research; how to find stories by popular authors that have never been reprinted and have stayed hidden for decades. He had drip-fed me little bits along the way. But in this marathon session he brought out the big guns. How inter-library loans worked. How to access archives. How to get in touch with strangers and ask them about deceased family members who had written stories.

The knowledge and expertise he passed on has meant that I've since found unreprinted ('lost') works by known authors such as Algernon Blackwood, E. Nesbit (oh how I wish Hugh had been around for that discovery), Charles Birkin, Daphne Du Maurier, E.F. Benson, Arthur Machen and H.D. Everett.

He also opened up the door to what I do now, finding unknown genre tales by unknown writers. He uttered one fateful line that fired up my imagination.

"Johnny, there are thousands of stories out there yet to be discovered."

I, the untrained foolish twerp, scoffed, saying that all

the good stories had surely been found, that there was nothing left to mine - all of the anthologists who had come before, Richard Dalby, Peter Haining, Jessica Amanda Salmanson and even Hugh's mortal enemy Jack Adrian had surely squeezed every drop of ink from forgotten magazines, anthologies and collections?

"Don't be an idiot, Johnny," Hugh said. "Do your homework, start looking and you'll be an important anthologist. At the moment you're a directionless prat."

I'm pleased to announce that I haven't been an idiot, I have heeded his words. Hugh's encouragement and faith in me has meant that I'm now the editor of five works of 'lost' supernatural literature and I've also discovered a new author called Catherine Lord who wrote under the name of 'Lucy Hardy'. I hope that one day I can pass on the knowledge I've gained from one of the greatest anthologists Britain has ever seen.

With this anthology *And Midnight Never Come*, (which you have now finished and I'm sure you've enjoyed heartily) it's comforting to see stories by Frederick Cowles and Bernard Capes, authors he championed so much - to Alice Perrin's 'The Bead Necklace' a work that was also respected and used by Hugh's friend, the late Richard Dalby. The highlight for me is the Scottish writer Violet Jacob's straight to the point 'Behind the Wall' - and shows that Hugh never lost his touch when putting together anthologies that both made you feel uneasy and may have even made you raise an eyebrow with delight.

I miss Hugh and I miss our funny, acerbic, insightful chats. But his massive body of work remains and his anthologies are testament to a dogged and determined anthologist who wanted to bring the very best of lost works back into the public consciousness. When I ever find a Lamb anthology out in the wild, I'll always buy it, even if I have a copy - because there are people who love horror who might not know about the good work Hugh did and they have to be made aware that he found the stories first before other fly by night publishers reprint the stories and take all the glory. Hugh got there first and don't you ever forget it.

I'd like to thank Richard, Hugh's son, for keeping his father's legacy and work alive. Editing and publishing can be a thankless task, and one that can sometimes seem impossible when there's such an emotional stake attached to it. The weight of your responsibility is acknowledged, Richard. You're doing a brilliant job and I know that Hugh would be very, very proud of you.

JOHNNY MAINS
PLYMOUTH
8/9/21

ACKNOWLEDGEMENTS

Re-publishing an existing anthology is one thing, but deciding to attach your father's name to a brand new one comes with its own unique pressures. So, once again, I am going to shower gratitude upon the great Mike Ashley. He offered not just excellent advice but some much needed reassurance as I embarked on this rather nerve-wracking venture. Thank you, Mike.

I am also indebted to the brilliant Johnny Mains for his insight and for his wonderful contribution to this volume. It's nice to have someone out there who understands when I say 'VSM'.

A big thank you to the owners, moderators and members of the *Vault of Evil* forum at vaultofevil.proboards.com and the *Internet Speculative Fiction Database* at isfdb.org for their continued diligence and enthusiasm for both my father's work and the genre in general. You are both wonderful resources.

Thank you to the various parties who helped me try to uncover the identity of the author of *In the Interests of Science*. Just because we failed does not make the efforts to succeed any less laudable.

This book was researched, edited and published during the COVID-19 pandemic. If you have reached the end of this book it is because you enjoy the thrill of fictional horror. The last year and a half we have all seen far too many real horrors, and they are not so thrilling. As a New Yorker I witnessed my local hospital using freezer trucks to store bodies as capacity became an issue.

So I would like to thank all the medical professionals, researchers, scientists and front-line care workers who have fought relentlessly to keep the real-life horrors from our doors. The world owes you a debt.

RICHARD LAMB
New York
2021

ABOUT THE EDITORS

HUGH LAMB

The seventies were something of a renaissance for horror and supernatural fiction in Britain, including a new lease of life for the horror anthology. One of the foremost among the anthologists enjoying this output was Hugh Lamb, responsible for bringing more long-forgotten authors back into the light than any other editor of the time.

Weary of the constant reprinting of such well known stories as *The Monkey's Paw* and *The Signalman* to satisfy the new desire for supernatural short stories, Hugh decided to gather the lesser-known stories and authors he had unearthed in his own quest for fresh reading material. Using the inter-library loan service and the Joint-Fiction Reserve of London libraries, Hugh had accumulated an impressive collection of tales. In fact, this turned out to be an inspired method for searching old editions and unearthing rare treasures ripe for republishing. He estimates that around 5,000 books crossed his path this way.

While Hugh had peers, such as Mary Danby, Michel Parry, Richard Dalby and Mike Ashley, already at work in the field, it was to Peter Haining he began corresponding, with suggestions of stories he might include in his anthologies. Haining suggested Hugh acquire reprint rights and approach publishers with his own anthology.

In 1971, W. H. Allen agreed to publish *A Tide of Terror*, which hit the market to no small acclaim. It was the first book to include stories from all three Benson brothers, rather than just the well known E. F. Benson. As with many of Hugh's anthologies, the majority of stories had not been reprinted in decades and some had never been reprinted since their publication in the late 1800s.

W. H. Allen would go on to publish another ten Hugh Lamb anthologies through the seventies, as well as two for the publisher's Star paperback imprint. Hugh introduced new stories into the mix, including some from Ramsey Campbell, John Blackburn, L. T. C. Rolt, and Peter Haining's brother, Robert.

Tales from a *Gas-Lit Graveyard* (1979) was the final anthology from W. H. Allen. The eighties represented a drier spell, as Hugh tried to find another publisher. He produced several anthologies with publishers such as Futura and Equation. *The Best Tales of Terror of Erckmann-Chatrian* was notable for its limited life after the publisher, Millington, went through a financial crisis and out of business just after the book's release.

The Futura publications, *Gaslit Nightmares* and the subsequent *Gaslit Nightmares 2*, were the last of Hugh's new anthologies. Ash-Tree Press published a series of six hardcover collections, reprinted from previous anthologies, between 1996 and 2002, and the 2000's also saw a few American reprints from Dover in New York.

HarperCollins published three revised anthologies from Hugh Lamb in 2017 and a further three in 2018. These were to be the last anthologies produced by Hugh Lamb.

Hugh passed away on the 2nd March 2019, peacefully and with his two sons at his bedside. He was 73.

Find out more at hughlamb.com.

RICHARD LAMB

With the inevitable influences that are present when Hugh Lamb is your father, it is perhaps no surprise that Richard developed a love for all things horror. Growing up with a passion for ghost stories, real or fictional, Richard was an avid fan of his father's collections and even attended a few World Fantasy Conventions with him.

He studied Art and Design at both Croydon and Portsmouth universities, eventually settling into a career as a web designer. Richard also followed in his father's literary footsteps, writing several screenplays (mostly ghosts stories), one of which won the BAFTA/Rocliffe New Writers Award in 2008.

When Hugh Lamb passed away in 2019, Richard decided to republish some of his father's older anthologies. He found the experience so rewarding that he took the next step of curating, editing and publishing *And Midnight Never Come*, the first brand new Hugh Lamb anthology since 1991.

Richard lives in the United States with his wife and cat.

Also available!

Terror By Gaslight
Memorial Edition

Hugh Lamb's groundbreaking anthology of vintage horrors, first published in 1975, and now republished with additional stories.

Get it here:
https://www.amazon.com/dp/B08SKB8WYM

Victorian Tales of Terror

First published in 1974, this definitive collection of Victorian spooky tales is available once again. A must-have for ghost story lovers.

Get it here:
https://www.amazon.com/dp/1699033072

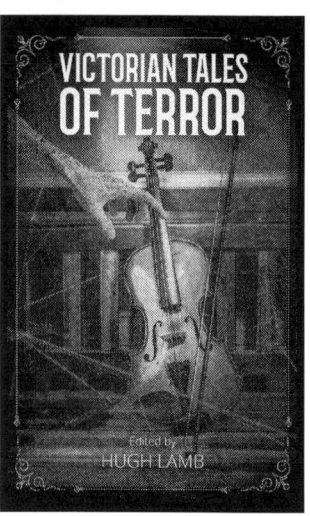